FORGIVE OUR FIGHT

THE FORGIVE ME FATHER SERIES

BOOK FOUR

CAITLIN MAZUR

WPC PRESS

For all the girls who have ever had to make themselves small, this one's for you.

AUTHOR'S NOTE

This story takes place across New Hampshire, upstate New York, and Vermont, with the Coutts commune established in what was once White Mountain National Forest and Coutts Peak established on what was once Mount Washington. For the sake of storytelling, some details of the landscape may have been altered.

A NOTE ABOUT AI

**No Artificial Intelligence was used to create this novel
or its cover.**

Please note that thousands of authors have had their works
illegally downloaded and used to train artificial
intelligence systems without permission or compensation.
Authors have been using em dashes, Oxford commas,
clichés, and other 'signs' of AI long before people decided
to use it to write books. Please consider this before
accusing any author of utilizing AI to craft their work.
Thank you!

1

———

MAURA

THE SLEEPING PILLS crumbled under the weight of the water glass I rolled back and forth across the marble countertop. I had captured the tablets between a small bit of paper; a ritual I'd performed the last few nights. Last week, before my ovulating window started, Morgan told me she'd hidden the pills behind a false wall beneath the bathroom sink. She'd reassured me our husband, Andrew, wouldn't notice they were missing.

She was right.

The glass hit a clump. I pushed against it and felt it crack under the weight. Something shifted outside the closed bathroom door. Eyes wide, heart pounding, I left the half-crushed pills on the counter and flushed the toilet. The water swirled around the bowl as I waited for Andrew to burst drunkenly through the door and demand to know what I was doing.

But the door remained in place. The toilet quieted. I returned to the counter, turned the sink on, and finished crushing the pills into fine powder as the water ran.

I hated this part. Curling up the paper so it sat in my

pocket just right. The fear of getting the precious contents into the glass and into Andrew's stomach before he decided he wanted to begin the evening's ritual. Every time I worried. And every time since I'd returned, I'd succeeded.

Surely my luck would run out soon.

I sealed the paper's edges, securing the powder into a little pouch before I slipped it in my pocket, turned off the sink, and opened the door.

Night filled the bedroom windows, offering a breathtaking view across the mountain's crest. The past few days had brought snow, winter taking one last stand on Coutts Peak. Moonlight shone over the white landscape, reflecting off its icy surface, as if glass covered the ground. The bedroom itself was dark. Light spilled from Andrew's small sitting area at the entrance to the room.

He waited for me in his velvet green chair, hand curled around his half-drunk whiskey, head tilted backward. He was shirtless, his dark chest hair glimmering in the low light that came from the fire crackling beside him. It shadowed his full face and the whiskers on his chin. Deep wrinkles creased the corners of his eyes, his forehead, and the sides of his lips, even as his features rested. Be it the new alcohol habits or the hate-fueled murder sprees, he looked decades older now than he had even a year ago.

I watched from the shadows as he lifted his droopy eyelids, swirled the amber liquid in his glass, and drank deeply. With one good tilt of the glass, he emptied it. Lip imprints fogged the rim.

Perfect timing.

"Another?" I asked, working hard to keep my voice level.

Andrew's blue eyes slid to meet mine, lips curving into a coy smile. He batted his eyelashes, and I squashed the sneer that rose on my lip. He was trying to flirt with me, like he did every night. Like he didn't get so drunk that he could barely stand. Like he didn't fall asleep with one leg still in his pants. Like he hadn't married my younger sister, or turned the other cheek when Luke murdered my mother.

"Please." He carried out the end of the word like a hissing snake. *The Devil is in him*, I thought, illogically. The fear was unwarranted, but hard to shake. Still, I plastered on a grin; one I'd been perfecting in the mirror since my return. I wasn't sure it mattered. I had a deepening suspicion Andrew saw two of me now.

I took the glass from his limp grip and brought it to the built-in bar. Crystal glasses filled with different liquids lined a neat shelf. I retrieved the one I knew to be whiskey and poured it in. Then, with careful precision, I knocked the stopper off the bar's edge.

"Whoops," I said, the line rehearsed. I supposed if he were sober, he might recognize this same trick night after night. But when I looked over my shoulder at Andrew, his eyes were closed and his hands were still. He might've been sleeping already.

I pulled out my wrapped package, folding it with steady hands. In one swift movement, I scooped up the stopper, poured the powder into the liquid, and secured the whiskey bottle closed. The crumpled paper went back in my pocket as I used my finger to dissolve the sleeping pills, then sucked it dry. Another rule broken. I relished the burn, conflicted at the pleasure I felt from the sharp sting of alcohol against my gums.

With the now full glass gripped tightly in my hand, I brought it to Andrew. He slumped over the side of the chair, seemingly unable to sit up straight.

"Whythankya," he said, one big jumbled word. I might not have even needed the sleeping pills tonight, the way he'd been throwing back his liquor. Whatever was going on with Father's Hunters was getting worse.

Sweat broke out on the back of my neck as he took a sip from the fresh glass. In the firelight, the powder swirled; a blemish in the amber liquid. I held my breath, waiting for him to realize, for him to taste the pills, to comment that something wasn't quite right.

But he did none of those things.

Instead, he tipped the drink back, swallowing the liquid in two long gulps. Pill remnants clung to the bottom of the glass, like sediment clinging to shore. But Andrew's unfocused eyes saw nothing.

"Bed," he said, shoving the glass toward me.

I took it gladly, putting it on the bar, knowing I'd need to wash it out before I went to sleep. No evidence could remain. He needed to believe the lies we were going to spoon-feed him over the next few days. There could be no doubt.

I offered an arm to Andrew as he stood from his chair. His unsteady feet moved forward, body teeter-tottering from side to side, like an overgrown toddler being guided to their crib. I carried most of his weight on my shoulder, pushing him toward his side of the bed, where he collapsed into a heap, chuckling and muttering to himself.

"Morrrgan," he sang.

Now, I did sneer. Mixing up our names was a consequence of his state of mind, but that didn't make it any better. Once, I had thought this situation normal. I'd grown up with a father who had many wives. But to have the same husband as my sister was a sick cruelty I'd never grow used to. Coutts men viewed women only as objects. There was no distinction between us. We were servants and breeders to serve their greater good.

"I'm coming," I said, walking back toward the sitting area. "I'll be right there."

He lifted his head briefly, eyeing me, and I froze. Was it suspicion that flashed across his features? Did he know what I'd done? That I'd been deceitful?

I inhaled. Exhaled. Focused on picking up the empty glass, waiting for his outburst.

But it didn't come. It wouldn't. Morgan had told me he'd been drinking almost an entire bottle of whiskey a night.

You could put the pills straight into his mouth and he'd thank you.

Well, I wasn't as ambitious as Morgan. I remained in Father's clutches, and I needed to be careful if I wanted a chance of getting out of here alive. I glanced down, the tracking monitor brushing against my ankle bone, reminding me of my place. Of where I belonged. Of whom I was still indebted to.

I went back into the bathroom with the dirty cup. White particles stuck to the side of the glass, soaked in the shallow pool of remaining whiskey, but it didn't matter. One pill was plenty to knock him out, and with all the liquor in his system, I had no doubt he'd fall asleep within the next few minutes.

All I needed to do was linger a little longer and climb into bed beside him. The rest of it was all pretend. And that, I did well.

Water washed the evidence inside the glass away. I watched the drain swallow the last remnants, wiping the sides of the sink clean with my fingers.

A heavy snore came from the partially opened door. I lifted my head and caught a glimpse of myself in the mirror. My curly hair hung long, face flushed from anxiety with pink circles high on my cheekbones. My eyes, normally dull brown, were darker. More intense.

Determined.

By this time tomorrow, our plan would be in action. We would convene as a family for dinner, and I would sell the most important lie of my life. We needed Andrew to believe the lie so deeply that he would choose it over his loyalty to Father. It was the key to my safety. To Morgan's safety.

The key to keeping our rebellion alive.

2

MAURA

Abigail never came downstairs. It was a clear power move; the distinction between me and her. She deserved her spacious, comfortable bedroom with an ensuite bath, while I deserved the cold, cavernous basement. The commune thrived on this hierarchical foundation, and no one loved upholding it more than Abigail.

She would be dismayed to know I found the basement oddly comforting. Here, I had solitude. A routine. And in a way, the concrete walls, the minimal sunlight, even the cold spots, reminded me of The Centre. Of what I was still fighting for. Even though some mornings, it didn't feel like I was fighting at all.

I eased from my pile of blankets to stand, waking up my aching shoulders and tight muscles. Sunlight filtered through the small, barred window at the far end of the room. I stretched my hamstrings and arms, rotated my ankles and wrists, and tilted my head from ear to shoulder on both sides. My neck gave an almighty pop. I winced. Yeah. As much as I might try to tell myself otherwise, there *were* drawbacks to sleeping on a cold, concrete floor.

This morning, squats and lunges came first. Slow and measured, but enough to build up a sweat. Exercise was encouraged at the Centre, but never a requirement. We did enough walking and working to keep our bodies busy. But for the past few weeks in the commune, while I wasn't locked away in the basement or forced to perform at Andrew's, a truck or bus had carted me around so someone could monitor me. Within the first week, I'd felt my body getting sedentary. And given what I knew was coming, I needed as much agility through my muscles as I could get.

Sit-ups were next. I lifted my body from the floor, knees bent, hands tucked behind my head as I breathed in and out in short bursts. My core burned as I powered through a dozen sets. It was amazing how well rage fueled a good workout. Once finished, I laid down on the cold concrete floor, pleasant against my sweaty back.

Above, footsteps came and went as I began my jog around the room. Lighter steps suggested the children were awake. Abigail's heavier footfalls came moments later, hurried and urgent. I could visualize her, eyes narrowed as she shouted at them to finish their breakfast and begin their prayers.

We'll be late! Hurry up!

I still had twenty minutes or so before she ushered them out the door for their schooling.

Focus.

Inhale. Exhale.

Steady.

Sweat formed on my upper lip as I skirted the poles supporting the house's foundation, around the boxes that held the remains of Joanna's home, and behind my makeshift bed. I would shower later, after work, at Andrew's. I'd requested the pregnancy test yesterday, so it would be there today. Andrew's eyes had teared at my request, his joy so evident that he'd drawn me into his chest and cradled me. He had smelled sour, like milk gone bad.

The thought pushed me harder. I used my fingertips to push myself off the walls, gaining speed as I traveled the room again. Warmth spread in my muscles. My heart pounded in my ears.

Once the test came back positive, we needed to move quickly. Andrew would set a doctor's appointment in the coming days. Silas had promised to get this tracker off my ankle and get me out of Andrew's house before then. Because in Andrew's eyes, there would be no worse sin than lying about a pregnancy.

A door slammed upstairs.

I reduced my jog to a walk around the foot of the stairs. After two more laps, I paused, leaning up against the basement's exposed brick wall beneath the window. Sunlight splashed across the floor, revealing dust I'd kicked up. It settled in corners, on top of boxes, and on the work clothes I'd laid out beside my pitiful bed.

Even though I knew Abigail intended to make this place my prison, I felt a little grief at the loss. Because after today, I didn't plan on coming back here.

I traded my sweaty pajamas for my old jeans, boots, and long-sleeved shirt. Carefully, I tucked the Polaroid of me and Eli in my bra, finally pulling on my winter flannel coat as footsteps cut through the silence upstairs.

Abigail's boots grew louder until the basement door's lock pulled back with a clink. Light spilled down the stairs. I approached, peering up at her looming figure.

"Get up here," she barked.

Abigail had once been my teacher when I was a child. She had stood at the front of the church's classroom, discussing the importance of social niceties. *A non-negotiable for upstanding Coutts women.* Well, I guess those rules didn't apply when you were dealing with a rebel.

She waited impatiently, her back against the basement door. As I reached the top, I squinted against the bright white kitchen, wiping the remaining sweat from my upper lip. Abigail looked at me in disgust, like I was a disobedient dog, before she slammed the door behind me.

"Hurry up and get out of here before you stink my entire house up," she spat, leading me through the kitchen. My stomach growled at the lingering smell of syrup. We passed a full fruit bowl, a box of granola bars, and a pantry I knew was filled with the children's snacks. But I would not ask, and she would not offer. I was to eat at the stables, like an animal.

Outside, winter still clutched the Peak in her icy grip. Even though it was technically spring, the wind howled against the houses, disturbing the fresh layer of snow we'd gotten overnight. The chill seeped through my clothes, directly into my bones.

Brr.

I gripped my elbows as I hurried down the porch steps toward Jeremiah's large pickup, which idled at the end of the snow-covered path at the entrance to Andrew's estate. Ice clung to the roof and corners of the windshield.

It was a brand-new pickup. Jeremiah had told me as much when he had first been assigned as my chauffeur. I thought my presence would annoy the man who oversaw the JC Family Ranch. Surely, he would consider himself important enough to have better things to do. But I soon learned he was just happy to have someone to talk at.

I opened the passenger-side door and hopped into the seat.

"Good morning," I said.

Jeremiah held up a finger to silence me, using his other hand to hold a radio to his lips. I curled my shoulders, closing the door quietly.

"*—farrier in two hours,*" the voice on the other end said. "*Oh, and the driver called. You're two short today.*"

"Two more?" Jeremiah scowled, pulling the gear into drive. The truck jumped forward, settling into a smooth glide. Muddy snow piled up on either side of the road, water trickling down the incline we followed.

"*Yeah, boss—*"

"You alerted Luke's team?"

"*Yep, they're sending 'em out.*"

"Fine." Jeremiah sighed, running a hand through his thinning blonde hair. "Thanks for the update."

"*God bless, over and out.*"

Jeremiah stuffed the radio into his belt. "We're six short," he grumbled. "Outrageous." An angry pink flush crept up his neck and into his cheeks. I pressed my mouth against the inside of my hand, gaze focused outside the window.

Six gone now. That meant two more people working at the ranch had been on last night's convoy back to the Centre. Whether they'd made it safely was a question I couldn't answer. But it did mean one thing. Disruption was spreading. Just like we'd planned.

"The farrier's coming today," Jeremiah said. He'd turned off whatever frustration had lingered after his conversation. Buttoned himself up. Gotten himself together. Just like a good Coutts boy should. "So, hoof cleaning is the priority before he comes in two hours. Then you can muck."

It'd make more sense to muck before hoof cleaning, but I didn't care to argue.

"Okay," I said.

I felt his eyes on me; a steady, narrowed stare. Jeremiah did this often, as if he were looking for me to break. I knew he wanted to find a crack in my facade. He probably lay awake at night, imagining how highly Father would reward him if I'd revealed my deepest secrets to him.

He clearly didn't understand how deep my loyalties lay, or how much anger I harbored beneath my calm demeanor. A bit of mucking didn't bother me. Taking orders had been part of my entire life. I would no sooner crack than he would give up his precious truck.

Outside, I studied the houses we passed down the back of the Peak. I had taken this journey for over a year as a scavenger. It was the only thing that had kept me going. Hours of alone time away from my unsatisfied family, deep in nature with my horse, Sweetheart. It had been my first taste of freedom. But that girl felt so far from the woman I was now.

For now, my freedom was limited. But it would all be worth it. I had to believe it would be. There was a rebellion brewing right under the noses of Father and his most powerful men.

We rode in silence except for the occasional radio update. Jeremiah's irritation grew as we approached our destination. Good. We needed these men in charge to feel the strain. Maybe even get a little fearful.

The barn came into view at the bottom of the next hill. We pulled in past the white, C-shaped structure to a back road that led to the rear of the stables. Ushering me in through the back door was intentional. My father had done everything he could to keep me hidden away since the one evening in the church when people had begged me for answers. I was to stay busy. Subservient. Give people just enough glimpses to know I was still alive and dedicated to the Coutts cause. He'd told followers that this was what I'd chosen. To serve a penance. I was living to serve God and my family. But otherwise, he told them, I'd wanted solitude.

It was, he'd said, *my destiny.*

Wrong again, Father.

But I still needed to be careful. Now that our plans were picking up speed, things were bound to get worse. That was why a pregnancy was the only way out. There was nothing so valuable to my father and his men as an unborn child.

Jeremiah parked the truck at the back of the stables, and together, we walked into the high-ceilinged barn. Manure, hay, and leather lingered in the air. Horses whinnied, sighed, and kicked their stall doors, creating a pleasant, familiar symphony of senses.

"Get to work," Jeremiah ordered, brushing past me on his way into the main area, where he'd meet the scavengers. "I'll send Zeke in when he gets here."

I nodded, watching as he went, a smile spreading across my face. I would get to work. But today would be the last day I'd be allowed to do hard labor.

And in a week, I wouldn't be here at all.

ALTHOUGH I HAD BEEN ALLOWED to work outside of Abigail and Andrew's homes, I still could not be left alone. Zeke was a low-level Hunter who'd been assigned guard duty. It seemed like such a waste of resources, but again, necessary to make a point. I was off-limits. His presence existed under the guise of protecting my solitude.

But Zeke, God love him, was also a rebel.

I lingered in the feed and tackle room, gathering my supplies. As I tucked a hoof pick and a curry comb into my bag, Zeke appeared in the doorway. He was a large man, with wide shoulders and a thick chest that barely squeezed into his Hunter uniform. Like me, he was dark-skinned and dark-featured. He did not fit the typical Hunter image, but Father had long been desperate to increase his ranks.

"Good morning," I said, keeping my tone even.

Zeke lifted his chin, looking over his shoulder momentarily, before he approached me.

"Morning," he grunted. "There's a horse in need of attention in Stall 8." He stepped in front of me, blocking the door's exit. "Make sure you take care of it."

His hand brushed mine, sliding something small and flat against my palm. I grasped it, making sense of the folded paper, which I tucked into my bag beside the comb and pick.

"Yes, sir." I moved past him and back out into the stables.

Zeke followed at a distance as I grabbed the rake and made my way into Stall 8. A Thoroughbred named Fran chewed lazily at her hay in the corner.

"Hey girl," I greeted her. She lifted her head and nuzzled into my hand before going back to her snack. Careful to lean the rake against the door in case someone came barging in, I squatted in the corner, pulling the note from my bag.

C Zone is prepared to receive 50+ early AM tmw. Note S Priority 1 will exit AC's at 200 hours tm. Confirm with Z plan is a go on your end.

My heart leapt as I recognized Silas's scrawl. So many things could've gone wrong between the last time I spoke to him and now. He could've been found out. Captured.

Killed. Our messages could've been intercepted. Hunters could have betrayed us. Father could've sniffed us out.

But everything was moving as smoothly as we'd intended.

I shredded the message and scattered it in Fran's mess. I'd muck it out later, once the horses were taken out and no one would be the wiser. Shouldering the rake, I exited the stall just as Scavengers poured in through the door Jeremiah had disappeared through. Zeke stepped away from the stable door, leading us back toward the feed and tackle room. As we passed the incoming Scavengers, I met a few eyes, but nobody dared to utter a word to me.

Zeke paused at the door and turned to face me. "Is it done?" he asked, keeping his voice low.

I nodded. "Yes," I said.

He matched my nod as confirmation.

Silas's message was the reassurance I needed to get through the rest of the day. It was a weight lifted off my shoulders. After work, I'd go back to Andrew's to get Morgan ready. He would send a team to take her from there to the Safe House. She'd be at the Centre by morning, as long as everything went according to plan.

And it would. I had faith in that.

I had to.

3

MAURA

Morgan ran a serrated knife through a still-hot loaf of bread, releasing the warm scent of yeast into the air. I inhaled, eager to eat, but my sister kept her lips tight, a grimace brimming beneath her stoic features. Sweat gleamed on her forehead. I knew she was nauseated and working hard to conceal it. I couldn't take away her queasiness, but I knew Holli would whip up a tincture as soon as she got to the Centre. Just a few more hours.

I stirred the large pot of soup on the stove, pushing my curls out of my face as I peered beneath the lid. Rabbit, garlic, rosemary, carrots, and potatoes. Hearty, sharp, and earthy. One of Andrew's favorites.

"God help me," Morgan hissed under her breath. Her left hand trembled. She gripped the side of the counter and squeezed her eyes shut. Another wave of nausea. I closed the pot and waved my hand to dissolve the smell.

"Sorry," I said. "Have some bread." I eyed the door where Abigail, Andrew, and the children would soon appear. "Maybe it'll settle your stomach before dinner?"

My sister shook her head.

"Holli will make you something to ease your nausea," I reassured her.

"It's not that," Morgan whispered, meeting my gaze with wide eyes. "I'm so nervous." Worry swam in her brown irises, and it made my breath catch in my throat. Her fear was so obvious. Like a deer in headlights. Andrew might not notice, but Abigail would.

"It's going to be fine," I soothed, coming around the island to place a reassuring hand on her back. "Silas isn't going to let anything happen to you. You know him. He'll send the best, most experienced team to get you. Plus, plenty of groups have already done this successfully. They never take the same route out. The Hunters have no idea where you'll be, and by the time they realize you're missing, you'll be long gone. Okay?"

"And what then?" she asked. Her voice rose in pitch. She'd stopped cutting the bread entirely. "You'll be here with him, fighting a war I won't be able to help with. What if…what if…" She bit her lip, blinking away tears. "What if something bad happens?"

"Nothing bad is going to happen."

"Maybe I should stay."

"Morgan." I sighed. "You can't stay."

"I *can*. I can help. I want to."

I shook my head. "No. You need to go to the Centre. They'll protect you there."

"I'll be careful," she promised.

I turned her, gripping her shoulders, keeping my eyes steady on hers.

"You can't. You have to go. The plan doesn't work unless you're gone, remember? They *cannot* find out you're pregnant." I sighed. "You left what we discussed in the bathroom?"

She nodded.

"Good."

"Maura," she moaned, squeezing her eyes closed. Two tears plopped down her flushed cheeks. "What if something happens to you? Or to Silas? What if I'm stuck there without anyone?" Her lip quivered. "What if I have to have this baby alone?" It came out as a whisper — a declaration of her worst fear.

My chest tightened. There was nothing I could do to ease her worry, and, the truth was, she might be right. Silas and I would be top targets once everything was set in motion. But I inhaled, squared my shoulders, and pulled her close. I squeezed her, like I had when we were girls and she'd had a nightmare and needed comfort. Like I had after I'd been married off to Andrew, and she worried we'd never see each other again.

Like I had when I'd told her our mother died.

"You *won't* be alone. There're good people at the Centre, and they'll take care of you," I said, knowing I was glazing over her fear, as if not touching it might make it disappear. "Holli is the smartest person I know. She's a skilled healer. And Shelly and Doctor Mick are both just as good as any doctor here. Whatever you need, they'll help you. I promise." I pulled back, keeping her at arm's length. Her shoulders trembled as she cried, tears gathering at her chin. I wiped them away and pressed my palm to her cheek.

"I just can't bear to think—"

"Then don't," I said, shaking my head. "Don't go there. There's no reason to." I focused my gaze and gave her a stern look. "One step at a time. You can do this," I said.

"I'm not as strong as you."

"Morgan," I said, warningly. "You're the one who escaped first! You're the one who came back and had the courage to tell us all what you saw out there, even though you *knew* we wouldn't believe you. You wanted more for yourself. For us." I tilted my head at her, desperate for her to see what I saw in her: strength, resilience, and bravery. "There *is* no me without you."

"*Stop*," she whined, crying harder. She pressed her fists into her eyes.

"You stop," I told her. "Everything is going to be fine."

We embraced once more, and I held my sister until her breathing slowed. She pulled back and dabbed at her eyes with a dishtowel as the mudroom door creaked open. A howl of wind came from beyond the walls. The house filled with shuffling feet and sniffling noses.

Showtime.

I squeezed Morgan's shoulders and returned to my soup, keeping her in my peripheral vision as she finished cutting the bread.

We just had to get through dinner. It was a ritual we both performed well. This was the last time we needed to be subjected to this. Come tomorrow, our lives as we once knew them would change forever.

DINNER WENT OFF WITHOUT A HITCH. I avoided Morgan's gaze and purposefully sat on the other end of the table so we had no excuse to interact. It was too risky. Too emotional. Abigail was a hawk when it came to noticing things out of place.

Once we were finished and the older children began cleaning up our dishes, Andrew cleared his throat and wiped his face clean with his napkin.

"Maura? Come with me, please?"

He slid his chair back against the wooden floor and stood, offering his hand to me. Abigail stiffened. Morgan looked at the ceiling. I slipped my hand into his and got up from the table.

He linked his arm with mine and led me from the kitchen, down through the foyer, and into his room. I had developed this plan. I had carefully crafted and planted these lies, and still, my pulse pounded in my ears. Morgan had confirmed she'd left her urine in the bathroom, but what if something had gone wrong? What if it had spilled? What if it didn't work? What if she wasn't actually pregnant? No positive pregnancy test would ruin our plans, and then what would we do?

Dizziness took hold of me, and I gripped Andrew tighter as we walked toward the bathroom. He looked down and smiled at me, as if this were a show of affection. I forced a smile up at him, knowing how necessary it was to play into the role of excited wife. I squeezed his hand in mine.

"God will bless us today," he said as we reached the bathroom. "I can feel it."

"Me too."

His gaze moved past me, and I followed his eyes to the small pink package that sat on top of the pristine white counter. It was meant to be a welcoming, exciting sign. I had dreamt of the day I asked for the pregnancy test and it turned positive. I had prayed day after day for it to be my turn. And as months went by with negative results, it became associated with crushing, debilitating disappointment.

I had never wanted to see that package again.

But now, I welcomed its sight. It wasn't a beacon of hope in the way it was intended. At least not for me. This was a pawn in my game, a crucial part of our plan to get Morgan to safety. It was a manipulation tactic to free me from Abigail's chains so I could help build the wrecking ball that would bring Father down.

"I'll be right out," I promised, patting Andrew's hand. Momentarily, I worried he would insist on following me into the bathroom, but he stayed rooted to the spot, stuffing his hands in his pockets.

"I'll be right here."

I was too aware of myself as I turned and walked into the bathroom. Every movement felt unnatural. Surely Andrew would grab me by the shoulders and stop me in my tracks, asking what I thought I was doing, who I thought I was fooling. But I made it over the threshold, flashed him one last smile, and closed the door.

For a moment, I stared at the package. Outside, I heard Andrew pace across the carpet.

Get moving.

I unwrapped the test clumsily, carelessly stuffing the wrapping into the garbage can. It was weightless in my hand. As silently as possible, I opened the cabinets beneath the sink and moved aside the false wall, revealing the small paper cup. I felt every beat of my heart. My throat was so dry I couldn't swallow. Carefully, I lifted the cup, steadying my arm by holding my elbow.

Careful.

At the toilet, I dunked the test into the urine, letting it soak for a few moments as I watched the pink control line appear. Then, I took it out, covered the end, and put it back on the counter. I dumped the urine, flushed, and washed my hands and the cup. After crumpling it into a ball, I tucked it behind the false wall. I'd dispose of it later.

There.

I straightened. Stared at myself in the mirror. Tried to calm my features. My breaths came short and shallow. In the mirror, I saw Andrew's shadow pace back and forth in the gap between the door.

Breathe.

I crossed the bathroom. Steadied my hand on the door-knob. I opened the door.

Andrew burst into the room toward the counter like a wild animal. He stared at the pregnancy test, then at me, before he looked at his wrist.

"Three minutes," he said, tapping his watch.

I nodded, hands clasped behind my back, trying to put on a show of eagerness. It was hard. Every time I looked at Andrew, I felt more and more disgusted. I wasn't sure I could be more revolted. So confident was a man who had done nothing but fall into a drunken, drug-induced slumber. He thought he'd gotten me pregnant.

This kind of unjustified view of a man's greatness was exactly why the rebellion would succeed. Men like Andrew considered themselves undeservedly competent in matters they hadn't even participated in. When we had talked through this plan with Silas, we'd all agreed that Andrew would feel confident in the idea that he'd gotten me pregnant. When he actually hadn't put his hands on me in months.

"Two minutes," he said, looking up at me through the mirror.

I raised my brows and forced a smile. He looked down at the counter again, hovering over the test like a boy eager for his ice cream.

We had done this many times before, stood in this very bathroom, waiting for my results. So often I'd lost myself in fantasies of what life would become once I had children, how desperate I was to be a mother, how I'd finally be worth something in Abigail, Joanna, and Andrew's eyes.

"Maura!" Andrew's voice rose an octave. He pressed his

hands down on the counter and jumped before turning to me. Effortlessly, he swept me up in his arms and swung me around the bathroom before placing me down, his hands gripping my cheeks. He kissed me, tasting of dinner and stomach acid.

"It's *positive!*"

I knew it would be, but a gasp escaped me, nonetheless. The test rested on the counter, the two pink lines clearly visible. A spark of joy flitted through me, and for a moment I let myself pretend it was real. Andrew looked at me in wonder, lips curving into a smile as he pulled me into his chest.

At his touch, my stomach rolled over. This was not real, for God's sake. I had *planned* this outcome, and yet I couldn't help my instinctive reaction. I had been so conditioned to want this for so long that I'd actually let myself believe it, if only for a moment.

"Maura," he said, rocking me back and forth. "Finally! We're going to have a baby! Oh, praise God! Praise the Prophet! We have truly been blessed."

My body tensed. I turned my head, tightening my jaw. Andrew had minimized my worth to a pregnancy. I had been ridiculed for something completely out of my control for nearly a year. But Andrew was so blinded by his own ego and obsession with procreation that he wouldn't understand, even if I told him, that I now had the upper hand.

"Praise God," I mumbled into his chest, making a dramatic show of my disappointment.

He released me, studying my features. "Are you not pleased?"

"Oh, I am," I said, showing him a small, sad smile. "You know how hard I've prayed for this day."

"Then what is it?"

"It's just…" I looked at my feet.

"Tell me, Maura," Andrew murmured. "You can tell me anything."

I looked up, meeting his eyes, careful to keep my chin tilted down. *Blessed be the meek.* "I don't think I can have a healthy pregnancy, Andrew. Not while I'm at Abigail's."

He stiffened, his pupils growing small as he rolled over my words.

"Abigail loves children—"

"Yes," I said, nodding. "But…you've heard how she speaks to me. She doesn't believe I'm devout or worthy of even being a Coutts anymore. The things she's said to me…"

"I'll speak with her. I'll tell her to be kinder." His tone was stern. I was losing him.

"Andrew. I'm sleeping in a basement. Am I to expect to grow a healthy baby in a *basement*?" His brows furrowed in confusion. Had he not known? Had Abigail concealed this truth from him?

"A basement? Well…" He shook his head, trying to find an excuse.

"Even if she promised a better living arrangement, how could I trust her not to get angry at me and lock me down there?" I asked, leaning into the doubt I saw crossing his face. "Plus, with so many children running around, I barely get enough sleep as it is. Oh, Andrew…" I launched myself into his arms and began to cry.

He stroked my curls, softly shushing me. "It's alright, Maura. It's alright. Maybe you can stay here."

"Oh, Andrew!" I sobbed harder.

"Shhh," he said. "You can stay here, sweetheart. You'll stay here. It'll all be okay."

I nodded into his chest, holding back a smile.

4

MAURA

Andrew and Abigail stood outside the mudroom door, arguing on my behalf. Once again, I was a child to be dealt with. It didn't matter that I was supposedly pregnant or that half the commune viewed me as a holy martyr. What mattered to Abigail was control. What mattered to my husband was the unborn baby.

Andrew would win this fight. Tonight, he argued for me in a way he never would have if he hadn't thought I was pregnant. I eavesdropped in the doorway to the kitchen, banking on his predictability.

"She's afraid the home is too stressful for the baby," Andrew said.

"Then I'll move her upstairs," Abigail countered.

Silence. "I think it's better if she stays here, Abigail. I know how you…view her."

"I would never do anything to harm a child."

"Of course not. I just think—"

"She's dishonest. She lies constantly! You can see it on her face every time she opens her mouth," Abigail spat.

Even behind a closed door, I could tell she was holding back her true feelings. "You'll have her stay under the same roof as her sister? Free to do as she pleases?"

"She's no longer a child," Andrew argued. "She'll be a mother in nine months. She'll have a home of her own."

Abigail scoffed. Even though I couldn't see her, I imagined her crossing her arms.

"I assure you, I will have all the necessary security in place. She will be monitored constantly. We will post Hunters at all doors. What else would you have me do?"

"She has escaped before. How do you know she won't do it again?"

"You have no faith in me," Andrew answered. This time, his voice was firm. Authoritative. "You do not trust me."

It wasn't so much a question as it was a statement.

"You know I do." Abigail's tone was softer this time.

It was Andrew's turn to scoff. I pulled away from the door, tiptoeing back into the kitchen. The children's chatter drifted down the hall from the living room. Morgan stood at the sink, drying off the last of the dishes. She looked up and over her tensed shoulder at me, brows raised. I walked over, placed my arm around her, and squeezed.

"I think it's working," I whispered.

"Maura," she said softly. I turned, put my forehead against hers, and closed my eyes. "I don't know if I can do this."

"Yes, you can."

She shook her head, rolling her forehead against mine.

"I'll be there soon," I promised. "All you need to do is follow. Stay hidden. Listen to every instruction they give you. Once you get to the Safe House, you'll be home free. Okay?"

I felt her nod.

"You make sure you're at the back door at 1:55. I'll meet you there."

"Okay. But—"

The door opened, silencing her. We pulled away. I tried to memorize her before Andrew came back into the kitchen. The way her hair fell over her shoulders, down her back. The freckles across her nose, the color of her skin, her eyes. The scar on her cheek from the chicken pox, the shape of her shoulders, her hips. I had been so startled before when I tried to remember my family. I had taken their appearances for granted and never really lingered on them, always so certain I'd see them again.

But when they weren't in front of me anymore, I found their details faded. Faces became fuzzy and muddled in my memories and dreams. I didn't want to lose that. Especially not with Morgan. Especially when I didn't know how long it would be until we saw each other again.

Andrew's large figure appeared in the kitchen's archway, peering in at the two of us. Theatrically, I put down a dish towel. Andrew smiled.

"Maura," he said. "You'll stay here." He sounded satisfied, like he'd just won a hard-fought battle. I gave him the first genuine smile in a long time.

ACCORDING to Coutts rule and tradition, because I was now pregnant, there was no reason for me to lie with Andrew until after the baby was born. I was certain it was a rule rarely followed, but because Andrew still viewed himself as a holy man of God, he sent me to one of the guest bedrooms on the second floor. It would be Morgan who he'd close himself in with and Morgan who would feed him the sleeping pills tonight.

I sat on the edge of the bed in the dark. The sky beyond the sheer curtain was cloudless, and the silver half-moon hung in the distance. There would be plenty of light for their journey through the forest this evening.

The digital clock on the empty bedside table switched to 1:50. I edged forward, sliding my feet into a pair of slippers. From the chair in the corner, I wrapped myself in a warm robe, tying it around my waist before I looked out the window again, down Andrew's long driveway that connected to the Peak's dirt road. Whoever they were sending would likely come in a Hunter's truck, but we would wait for them to retrieve Morgan, just in case of infiltration. Anxiety hovered over me. Like yesterday, there were so many things that could go wrong tonight.

Carefully, I made my way to the door and opened it. Nightlights lined the long hallway, illuminating the oak floors that covered most of Andrew's home. I crept out and down the stairs. The slippers muffled my footsteps as I reached the bottom. I paused, looking in both directions at the rear of the house. On the left was an entrance to the living room. To the right, Andrew's study.

I went straight, pausing at the laundry room to grab Morgan's winter jacket, and then waited at the end of the hall where the back door led to a large, covered porch. Cold air snuck under the door, chilling my bare legs. I hoped the jacket would be enough for her journey.

The house was so silent that the creaking door made me jump. I swallowed. Curled my fingers around the fabric in my hands. I turned toward the noise, searching for an excuse to give Andrew in case it was him who came around the corner.

I just needed some air.

The door closed, the latch settling into place. I studied the footsteps that came next. Light. Cautious.

I exhaled.

Morgan tiptoed around the corner, her eyes wide until they found me. She breathed a sigh of relief. Careful not to rustle, we hugged. I helped her into her jacket, she retrieved her boots from the closet, and then we exited through the back door.

Outside, our breath plumed in the cold, dark air. The porch circled the entire rear of Andrew's lodge, filled with high-quality wooden furniture, thick outdoor rugs, and brick decor. A few lights dotted the dark mountain beyond, twinkling like stars.

"He's asleep?" I confirmed in a whisper.

Morgan nodded, squeezing her arms to her chest. "No trouble. He was so excited about your *announcement* that he chugged three glasses of whiskey in half an hour." She rolled her eyes, then sucked air through her teeth. "Gosh. It's so cold."

"I know. You'll warm up once you start moving."

An engine rumbled somewhere in the distance. We both tensed. I was relieved the porch had so many shadows to hide within, but it made it hard to see beyond the house.

"You think that's them?" Morgan asked, her voice wobbling in fear.

"Yes," I said, trying to sound confident. "Remember what I told you?"

She nodded.

Every ounce of love I had for Morgan rose in my throat. Tears formed, and I tried desperately to blink them away as I put both hands on her shoulders. "They will protect you," I said. "They're good people. Just get to the Safe House. Everything will be easy from there."

I let my hands trail down her arms, then pulled her jacket tight, carefully doing up each button. Hot tears stung my cheeks, but there was nothing I could do to quell them. I focused on getting each button through its hole.

"Maura..."

I looked up at my sister. She was crying too.

"Stop that," I said, knowing it would do nothing.

"Please be careful," she whispered. "Please come back to me."

I did up the last button and patted her chest gently. "I'll do my best, Morgan. You know I will." It was all I could offer.

She burst into tears, launching herself at me, and we stood in the shadows silently crying in each other's arms. It was fitting that we couldn't cry as loud as we wanted. That we couldn't express our grief and our fear openly. But it was something I vowed to change.

In the distance, shuffling footsteps approached, growing louder around the side of the house. I froze, gripping Morgan's shoulders as I pushed her away from me.

"Wait."

I wiped my tears as I hurried down the back porch stairs into the trimmed grass. A figure moved quickly in the shadows against the side of Andrew's house, his face coming into view in the sparse moonlight allowed in the backyard. White-blonde hair and a sharp chin. Silas smiled when he saw me.

I shook my head at him. He shouldn't be here. My heart kicked up its pace.

"*What* are you doing here?" I asked.

He approached, giving me a quick hug. But he only had eyes for my sister, who he found on the porch. His face broke into a wide, wild grin.

"You think I was going to let my best girl go off without seeing to her myself?"

"Silas," I said sternly, following him as he scooped my

shocked sister up into his arms. "You can't go to the Safe House."

He dipped his head and found Morgan's lips, hands threading into her hair. She melted in his arms as he kissed her deeply.

"Silas!" I hissed.

He broke their kiss, nudged my sister with his nose, then looked back at me. "I *know*. I'll take her as far as the border. We've got two others scheduled to take her and the others the rest of the way."

I released the tension in my shoulders and looked at my feet. There was no one, maybe except Sid or Eli, I'd trust more to take Morgan where she needed to go. Silas loved her. He would let no harm come to her. And he'd put her worried mind at ease.

"You could've told me you were coming," Morgan said.

Silas led my sister by the hand down the stairs and into the grass. "What? And ruin the surprise?" He grinned at Morgan, who looked up at him like he hung the moon.

"You keep her safe," I said.

"You know I will."

"And you," I said, turning toward my sister.

"And you."

I swept her into one last hug, inhaling her, trying to hold on to her smell so I wouldn't forget. "I love you," I said.

"Love you back."

"I'll be back for you tomorrow," Silas said, eyeing my ankle.

"Really?" I asked.

He nodded. "After the guard change. I'll meet you out here."

I drew a breath through my nose and smiled.

Finally.

That was that. There was nothing left to say. The less time they spent here, the better.

"Get going," I ordered. "You tell me when she's safe."

Silas nodded.

They waved, and before I knew it, I was alone, watching him steal my sister off into the dark.

5

ELI

WIND BATTERED the side of the old Auto Shop building, rattling the flimsy wooden boards we'd nailed into the siding to block the cold from coming in. A lot of good it did. It was fucking freezing.

I rubbed my hands together and blew into my gloves, wishing I could ignore the bone-chilling cold. My partner Francis and I had slept a few hours in the truck since it was warmer, but as night approached, it was better to be inside the shop. The bathroom window gave a clear view into the woods, where the refugees would arrive from. We hung a green shirt out from the bottom, signaling safety on our end. If all went well, we'd get nearly fifty newcomers today.

New arrivals made me nervous, even though I had done this over a dozen times. There was always a chance a loyalist was among them, someone who would figure out a way to get information back to Peter and the Hunters about our plans. But every time I met the Coutts members, they were as terrified as Maura had been the first day I'd met her.

But that wasn't why I was nervous tonight. This arrival was different because we were transporting Maura's sister, Morgan.

We'd gotten word from Silas a week ago that Morgan would be coming to the Centre. It was no different than any of the other refugees, I'd reminded myself. But this *was* different. This was Maura's family. The person who knew her best in the world. And since we'd ceased all non-essential messages about a month ago, it would be the first time I'd be able to hear how Maura was doing.

All Silas had relayed was that she was alive and working in the stables. I imagined that made her happy, working with the horses. But not knowing much else made me feel crazy. She was so isolated. What the men in that commune might've subjected her to kept me up at night. I hated being so helpless. She'd assured me she'd been through much worse, but knowing that didn't help.

I knew she was strong and could handle her own, but it didn't matter. The way I felt about Maura was…complicated, to say the least. Complicated in its own right — we were two different people from two very different worlds. But also complicated by circumstance. The world we existed in. The fight we fought.

But my mother used to say that love knows no bounds.

Was that what this was, though? Love? I still wasn't sure. The word felt too heavy and frightening to bring into existence and attach to someone I could no longer protect. Love like that only meant constant fear and eventual grief.

"Eli," Francis called. He emerged from the doorway, rifle slung over his shoulder, a flickering lantern in his hand. He was a short, dark-skinned man with a square jaw and a long, thin beard. "C'mon. They're here."

Go time. I eased my stiff back with a series of stretches before grabbing my gun. Francis left the lantern by the door, and together, we headed out into the cold. Towers of hollow cars, flat tires, and spare parts littered the area. We'd reinforced the chain-link fence around the perimeter with wooden pallets, offering better hiding spots. Francis ducked behind one of them, and I did the same, a few feet away.

I peered through the wide slats. The forest had lost its greenery months ago; a desolate cluster of bark, with pines spotted between. In the dark, they looked like spindly creatures rising from the frost-covered floor.

In the distance, a sound like static permeated the staggering silence. Quiet at first, then louder. An eerie noise rose from the dead forest. Shuffling feet. Fabric rubbing against fabric. Labored breath. Without seeing the crowd, it might've been a creature erupting from the darkness.

I shivered.

Figures emerged between the trees, stopping short of the fence. In the front, the familiar green shade of a Hunter suit came into view. My shoulders tensed. Those suits had been a source of such visceral fear for so long that it was hard to break the habit. I tightened my grip around my gun.

Beside me, Francis stood first. I straightened to full height and followed him around the fence. The Hunters who led the refugees to our Safe House were always different. Too much risk went into the same Hunters constantly disappearing from base. I supposed it was a good thing that there were so many men willing to risk themselves for rebellion, but I still felt uneasy about the process. More people meant more chances for someone to turn on us.

"Evening, gentlemen," the Hunter said, holding his hooked fingers up in an "M" shape — the familiar signal of a friendly. He clicked on a flashlight and, without warning, shone it in both our faces. I squeezed my eyes closed and then squinted through the light.

"Jesus," Francis said, waving his hand.

Murmurs spread through the crowd.

"Turn that thing off!" I hissed. "No lights in the open."

The Hunter lowered his flashlight and clicked it off. I blinked away the white spots in my vision and focused on the newcomer. He was older, if I had to guess, in his 50s. He wore a green beanie and a grim smile, his face bright red from the cold.

"Did you have that thing on the whole way?" Francis asked.

"How else were we supposed to see?"

I glanced upward. "Plenty of moonlight tonight," I said. "Lights are a risk. Silas should've told—"

"Silas is a boy," the man answered. "I have fifty-two people following me through the dark. We needed a light."

Francis shook his head. "The precautions are in place for a reason."

The Hunter bristled. "Silas sent me with an urgent message," he said flippantly. "Do you want it, or not?"

This guy. I cocked my head.

"Yeah?" Francis said.

"He said 686. And would not elaborate."

Francis nodded curtly. "Noted. Thanks."

The Hunter crossed his arms, as though he expected us a detailed rundown of what the code word meant. Silence hovered between the three of us. Someone in the crowd coughed.

"I should go."

You don't say.

"Thank you." Francis stuck out his hand. The Hunter stared at it for a minute, then reluctantly shook it.

"Keep them safe." The Hunter's voice was forced. Slightly fearful.

Oh.

Someone in this crowd meant something to him.

"We will," I promised.

There was no need for additional conversation. The Hunter saluted us and turned on his heel, squeezing a few shoulders on his way back into the forest, until he disappeared into the dark. The crowd he'd brought with him was definitely fifty large, wrapped in different shades of jackets, coats, scarves, and hats. The dark shadowed their faces, but I knew they must be exhausted by the journey. It wasn't a short one from the commune.

"Come on," Francis said, holding his hand high in the air as he waved the group after him. He walked back around the fence, disappearing into the maze of junk. This was the part I hated most, even though it was necessary. These people needed to be searched for anything dangerous. Weapons and wires, especially.

The crowd followed Francis, and I waited to bring up the rear, inspecting each person as they passed. A mother with six children. Twin girls, no older than eight. An older couple. More kids — boys, girls, babies. A man with a nose that had healed badly from a break. A woman wearing her baby on her chest and a sleeping toddler on her hip.

So many children. So few parents. I could only imagine the people who had sent their kids off without them, how desperate and vulnerable they must have felt. They had done the unthinkable. All in the hopes of a better life for their children.

The crowd shuffled forward, taking in their new surroundings with wide eyes. I grazed over the heads of more people, scanning, until…

A curly-haired woman brought up the back of the line.

A scarf covered her mouth, but as she raised her eyes to mine in the darkness, my heart slowed. It was Maura's face. Her warm brown eyes. The woman nudged the scarf away, and I saw the differences instantly; her edges were a bit sharper, her jaw more pointed. My lips lifted into a smile, matching hers.

"Morgan?"

"Hi," she said, her breath fogging in the air.

"Eli," I said, pointing at myself.

"Eli." She reached for me, squeezing my arm knowingly, before following the others.

I squinted into the forest. It was dark and empty. Just the way we liked it. I only hoped the Hunter didn't use his flashlight on his way back. 686 was the go-code; a reference to Psalm 68:6, Silas had said. Something to do with rebellion. This would be our last caravan out of the commune.

Relief spread through me as I followed the group past the fence. The auto body shop was too small to fit everyone, so Francis had started a line outside of the truck and trailer we'd use to get everyone back to the Centre. I rubbed my arms to stave off the cold and reminded myself we'd be back at safe, warmer grounds in just a few hours.

I moved to open the door of the trailer we had hitched to the truck, checking for the box of rations inside. I tore open the top, placing it beside the blankets we had available for anyone who needed them.

A gunshot cut through the cold air.

I froze, toes curling in my boots. Outside the trailer, I found Francis's eyes, wide and dark in the shadows.

Another shot.

The blast echoed in the forest surrounding us, making it hard to distinguish its origin. North? South? Someone cried out from the crowd. I craned my head toward the fence, then around toward the front of the truck.

The Hunter had just left. Had he used his flashlight? Did his own men find him? Someone else? Had they shot and killed him? Wounded him? He must've had a gun on him. Maybe he was fighting back?

I knew the likelihood of that was slim.

Voices rose, chatter increasing to panic. Francis approached me with wide strides.

"Where'd it come from?" He looked out toward the fence.

I shook my head. "Hard to tell."

"It has to be the Hunter." His neck was tense, hands clenched at his sides.

"Yeah," I agreed.

"That God-damned flashlight."

I grimaced. No use in dwelling on that now.

"We need to move."

"Let's get them inside, then."

Time slowed. The search was off. We needed to get these people into the trailer and move.

Now.

"Alright," Francis said. "Into the trailer, please. I can take four in the truck. Children? Moms with babies?" The crowd shuffled. I focused on holding the trailer's door open, waving people in. The motor home wobbled with weight as people shifted inside.

The forest beyond the gate was so dark. Anyone could be out there. If they *were* out there and chasing us, then they had the tools they needed to see us easily. Hiding only worked out here if your enemy didn't know where you were. If they had a location, if they caught the Hunter so soon after leaving the Safe House, they would catch us in minutes.

We were moving too slowly.

My hand kept drifting to the gun at my hip, a reassuring presence. But what good would it do if we were ambushed? Suddenly, it felt foolish to have only two of us out here with so many people. The crowd grew smaller. The rear wheels of the trailer sagged with weight. I searched for Morgan, so reminded of Maura that first day I'd met her. She held the hands of two children, and they eagerly scurried inside.

"Come on, come on," Francis said, closing the back doors of the truck. "Come on!"

I turned, hooking my hands on the doorway to the trailer, ready to hop up and inside. Francis skirted the front of the truck, and I heard the truck's door open.

All I saw was a flash of green before someone yanked me away from the trailer. My fingers searched for purchase on the side of the door, nails scratching painfully against the wooden interior. But nothing remained in my grasp. I fell sideways, landing on my shoulder. The full weight of something — *someone* — else on top of me forced me flat on my stomach.

I reached for the gun, fingers itching for it. An impossible weight crushed my elbow, and I felt something snap. Excruciating pain fired up my arm, into my shoulder. I screamed. Someone gripped at my side. The gun loosened from my holster.

The person on my back secured my hands with theirs. I thrashed in their grip, scraping my cheek, ear, and jaw against the rocky ground. But the hands remained firm with a strength I couldn't match. Not with the rations I had in my stomach and certainly not with my injured shoulder.

"GO!" I screamed at the door I'd left open.

Francis didn't hesitate. He couldn't. And I couldn't

blame him. There were too many people in that trailer, and those were the commands given by Avi. We knew what we'd signed up for. If we were in trouble and someone needed to be left behind, they would be. There was no shame in it.

The truck pulled away in slow motion, tires rolling over the dead grass as it gained speed. Gunshots echoed into the night. The trailer tilted precariously, and I heard shrieks of fear from inside. The side door hung open like a lolling tongue, the inside dark and looming. I watched an arm reach out and pull the door closed with a slam, like a slap in the face. The finality of it made me cry out. Brake lights illuminated before the truck disappeared between the towers of trash in the distance.

My mind went blank, ears ringing from the gunshots.

"Y'alright?" A distant voice.

I couldn't move. Weight pinned my body. I breathed dirt in through my nose. A knee found the small of my back, securing my wrists at a painful angle.

"Yep." My captor's voice was young.

"Here," the new voice offered.

"Thanks."

I thrashed again, but felt cool metal slip around my wrists. Handcuffs. They'd certainly upped their game since they'd kidnapped Mom and me with zip ties. The cuffs wrapped around my bone with a neat click, and the knee and weight disappeared.

I coughed. Sucked in a breath. Shifted my shoulder to try to get a glimpse of my attacker. My vision was warped, a little blurry. The bare trees blended together, dark against the gray sky.

Hands crept up my back, beneath my jacket collar, grasping my neck with long fingernails. They forced my head down, nose to the dirt. I struggled against the grip, but with the cuffs around my arms, I couldn't get enough momentum to roll.

"Hold still, you heathen," the too-young voice said.

A rustle of fabric. The forest disappeared, and I saw spots of brightness before everything went dark. Something textured covered my face. Two strong hands hooked beneath my arms, forcing me to stand, and I stumbled on my footing, uncertain where to put my feet.

A radio crackled nearby. The person on my left shifted.

"Did you find it?" he asked.

Another crackle. "We have it," a voice on the other side answered. "We have the truck."

6

MAURA

THE BLANK PIECE of paper spread over Andrew's broad, oak desk taunted me with its whiteness. I held a pen in my right hand, letting my left hand's fingers run over the smooth exterior as if it might give me an idea.

I had dreamt of this moment for nearly a year. When I finally got pregnant, Andrew would give me the task: draft thoughts for a house of my own. Anything I wanted. No expense spared. I'd stared at Abigail and Joanna's houses with such envy for so long and dreamt of the day I'd have my own. A quaint cottage with lots of flowers. A large kitchen for homemade meals. Wood-lined walls, ricocheting with children's laughter.

Now, the idea of a house made me sick to my stomach. The act of sitting on the edge of the biggest lie I'd ever told, trying to dream up something I knew would never exist — shouldn't exist — froze me.

Outside, clouds covered the moon. Today had been a long day. A very bad day for Andrew. Morgan was officially missing. Abigail had stomped around his house all day, berating me about my mother and the poor job she did raising us. If she weren't already dead, she might've gone out and killed her herself.

"Such shame on this family!" she kept yelling. "Such shame!"

Andrew was called out to meet with Hunters, with Father, with Morgan's work crew, to figure out where she might've disappeared to. At least that's what he told us. With fifty gone, the crisis management must have been much bigger than that.

When he'd come home after dinner, he acted like Morgan had never existed. There was no mention of her as he scarfed down his roast. He sent Abigail and the children home. He demanded that I work on my house in his office. And then he disappeared into the bedroom.

I knew Andrew would only give us news if they had caught the refugees, so it was a good sign he had no information. But I still felt uneasy. There was no doubt in my mind they'd question me tomorrow. But if everything went to plan like Silas said, he'd have me out of this house tonight, and I wouldn't need to worry about tomorrow.

A door slammed. Through the open study door, I heard the distinct clink of ice against glass. I curled my toes and put down my pencil. He would be drunk. And that was fine. It made lying much easier.

I smoothed my pants and curls and stood from the desk. Andrew appeared in the doorframe, dressed in his pajamas, his hair dripping wet from a shower. His eyes were so bloodshot they looked completely red. It gave me pause, a moment to look at him. He'd lost weight in the last few weeks, enough so that his jowls sagged beneath his chin. He'd aged, with new fine lines and wrinkles creasing areas of his face they hadn't before. His skin was blotchy, his under eyes bruised purple. Whatever was going on within the Hunters' ranks was really getting to him.

"Have you started?" he asked, tipping his chin forward to indicate the paper in front of me.

"No," I said honestly. "I have some ideas, but…"

"You want them to be perfect."

I hummed my agreement.

Andrew crossed the room and sat in a leather-backed chair opposite me. He swirled the liquid in his glass and took a small sip. When he looked up, his eyes were heavy-lidded.

I decided to test my luck.

"Has there been any sign of her?" I asked, my voice quiet and stilted. I wrung my hands together, genuinely nervous about his answer.

He looked down and sniffled.

"Is it so terrible?" he asked, not answering me.

"What?"

"Is it?"

"Is *what* so terrible?"

"Is being here so terrible?" He lifted his eyes, and for the first time, I saw genuine sadness behind them.

"Of course not—"

"I have done what is within my power to provide you all with a blessed life. And yet? She runs?" He shook his head. Took another drink.

I pressed my lips together, unsure of what to say.

"I gave her everything she'd asked for," he continued. "And she promised to serve me. To love me." He sighed. "But you returned to me, didn't you?" He leaned forward as though he'd just realized I was there.

"Yes," I said, settling back into the desk chair. "I did."

"I never thought we'd have a baby, Maura. But…I must be doing something right if we conceived such a miracle. God has seen my suffering. He blessed us with a new life. Your sister be damned." He paused. I squeezed my thumb with my fingers to curb my temptation to defend Morgan. "We were so sure you couldn't get pregnant."

I took a moment to digest his words. *We?* I searched his face as he lifted the glass to his lips again. *We?* I swallowed. Braced my hands on the bottom of the chair.

"What do you mean?" My voice was distant. Shaky. Anger bubbled in my stomach, a terrible, raging beast. I felt it, warm against my empty womb, rising to the middle of my chest. "What do you mean, *we?*"

"Oh." He waved me away, his eyes closed as he leaned back in his seat. "When you were sick, remember? With the flu? We had you checked," he said, as if this were information I should've known.

"You had me...checked?"

Surely that was something I would have remembered. My brain worked. Something clicked; a memory slid into place. Yes, right after we had gotten married, I'd been sick. So sick I'd been laid up in bed at the back of the house, vomiting and sleeping, only waking for water and the bathroom. The doctor had made multiple house calls. Taken my blood. Given me pills. A series of shots. It had been two weeks before I felt back to normal.

"Yes, yes," he said, exasperated. "They tested your blood. The doctor came back after all those tests they do, said your hormones were low. You'd be unlikely to conceive. But we knew if we prayed enough—"

"*What do you mean by* we?" Anger broke free from my chest and spilled out of my mouth. My nails dug so deeply into the chair I sat on, I felt the leather begin to crack beneath my grip.

"Why, me and Abigail, of course."

Air filled my lungs. I stared at Andrew. Watched him as he drunkenly finished off the rest of his liquor, some of it slopping down the side of his mouth, completely oblivious to the truth he had just divulged to me. He wiped his mouth. Swallowed. Sucked air through his teeth. The corners of my vision blackened. I watched him struggle to stand without stumbling. He steadied himself on the back of the chair with a laugh.

"It's a miracle," he said, moving toward the door with his hands in the air, "a miracle, a miracle!" He swayed as he exited the room.

Acid rose in my throat, making my eyes and nose water. My mouth had dropped open, and I couldn't bring myself to close it. I focused on my belly, letting my fingers drop to the bottom of my shirt as I lifted it slowly, revealing my dark skin beneath, and pressed my hands against my warm flesh.

They had known. All along, they had known. Abigail, Andrew, and probably Joanna.

I couldn't breathe. It was as if someone had put their hands around my throat and squeezed. My chest tightened. Air left my lungs, and I gasped for more, hands tightening around the edge of the chair's seat. My anger was red-hot now, a searing, scorching thing that bled from my veins and into my tendons. The room warped into a dizzying kaleidoscope of things, like the fabric of my world was splitting at the seams.

All this time. All this time, they'd let me believe I was the problem. I had been ridiculed and shamed, told I wasn't trying hard enough. That I wasn't a woman of God. That if only I could *pray* harder, if only I could become more devout, even though I had sacrificed everything and anyone I'd ever loved just to be considered. Even though I had worked my entire life towards this very thing. Even though I had let myself be defiled month after month. These people who called themselves my *family* — they watched me suffer and let me believe *I* hadn't done *enough*.

A scream worked its way up my throat, hovering at the back of my tongue, choking me. I clenched my teeth, working to keep it inside. I felt so horribly enraged that I could vomit. Adrenaline promised I could throw the chair through the window, drive the pencil through Andrew's throat, and kick Abigail down her basement stairs.

But I would do none of those things.

Instead, I let my tears roll, cooling the flush of anger on my cheeks. I just had to hold on a little longer. Silas promised he'd get me out tonight. The fight would begin, and I could put all of this behind me. I could find solace in the conflict. Everything would be okay as long as I got out of here tonight.

Clarity found me, and the room came back into focus. Down the hall, I heard a glass shatter against something hard, and I jolted in my seat. Hastily, I wiped my tears with the back of my hand and my nose on the inside of my shirt. Teardrops stained the blank white paper on the desk. How fitting.

I checked the clock on the wall to the left of the door. 8:53 p.m. The guards changed at midnight. That was when Silas would be back. I needed to focus on that. I couldn't change my circumstances now. I needed to swallow my anger and force it down. Use it as fuel to fight in the war that was coming. I needed to stay the course, no matter how hard it was.

I glanced beneath the desk, twisting my ankle so I could see the gleaming metal hidden beneath my loose black pants. The monitor was the last hold they had on me. Once I had this off, I would be unstoppable. A fierce woman filled with rage. I could go back to the group that loved me without conditions.

I could fight to make sure nobody ever had to feel the way I did right now.

7

MAURA

AFTER CLEANING Andrew's mess and guiding him to bed, I worked on tidying up to keep myself busy. Even though Morgan and I had rarely had time together in Andrew's house since I'd been back, it still felt empty without her presence.

Ten minutes before the guard shift changed, I went into my bedroom and gathered the few belongings I still had: the Polaroid of me and Eli, my work boots, and a winter jacket. From the kitchen, I stuffed a few snacks in my pockets and went out to the porch to wait for Silas.

The clouds had thinned, allowing a view of the rest of the commune. Lights from the Sciences and Innovations area illuminated the two nuclear cooling towers. Beyond the large buildings, a sea of black trees disappeared into the night.

It was a comfort to look at the world this way. Familiar. There had been times during my return to the commune where I'd felt a deep sense of nostalgia. I knew it was longing for something that had never existed in the first place. Now, it was brief, muddled by the reminder that everything had been a lie.

No, not everything. Not Morgan. Not Mother. Not the rest of my siblings. Our love had been real. Our relationship had been strong — as strong as it could've been in a community that insisted on loyalty to one man. We'd had deep familial ties until we were forced to pretend they never existed. Everything had changed when I'd come to Andrew's estate. I'd been so excited, so sure God himself had coordinated the rest of my life.

My limbs tingled. I was anxious now to be away from this place so I could stop playing pretend. I wanted to fight. And after what Andrew told me tonight, I was *ready* to fight.

A rustle came from the side of the house. Andrew? An animal? Or the man I'd been waiting for? I put a hand on my chest. Inhaled. Exhaled. Carefully, I moved toward the stairs, my heart pounding in my ears. I'd run the gamut of emotions in the last few hours, and the realization made me suddenly tired.

From the shadows, Silas's silhouette appeared and came around to where I stood. His hair stuck to his sweaty forehead, brow furrowed in concern. My stomach rolled. He wouldn't meet my eyes.

"Hi," I said cautiously.

"Maura." His breath drifted away in the cold air. He stood beside the steps with his hands stuffed in his pockets, not coming any closer.

"What's wrong? Is it Morgan?"

He looked up sharply. "Hunters intercepted the refugee group. They followed them to the Safe House, ambushed them before they took off toward the Centre. I just got word an hour ago."

"But they're okay, then? If you got word?"

I fumbled for a grip on the stairs' railing, panic rising up my throat.

"Morgan's fine. The group is fine. The driver managed to run two of the Hunters over and escape unscathed. They took an alternate route back to the Centre, but otherwise made it without trackers. It was only a small team that went after them."

Relief blossomed in my belly. I closed my eyes and nodded. "So she's safe?"

Silas pressed his lips together, then looked out in the distance. "As far as I know. I'll have more information tomorrow." He fiddled with his hands. Something else was there. I saw it, even in the dark. Something hidden in plain sight.

"What else?" I whispered.

"Maura." Silas's voice was low; a warning. I itched in my skin.

"What is it, Silas?"

"Before the truck took off...they captured someone from the group."

And I knew it before he said it. He wouldn't have been so worried about telling me if it hadn't been *him*.

"Who?"

Silas turned his chin and finally met my eyes. "It's Eli. They have Eli."

I shook my head, sure I had misheard him.

"Eli? Eli shouldn't be out on rescue missions."

"He's been going out on them for the past few weeks," Silas revealed. "He—"

"*What?* Why didn't you tell me?"

He gave me a knowing look. "Did you need to know?"

No. "Yes!"

"I just...thought it would do more harm than good. You've had enough to worry about."

"I can't believe..." I stuffed my hand into my hair and paced along the top step. "Why would he go out on rescue missions? He was injured when I left. What was he *thinking?*"

"He's a grown man, Maura. He knew what he was getting into. He's been a great asset."

I paused and stared at him, my lip curled. *"Been?"*

Silas opened his mouth, then sighed. "Sorry. *Is.* I just don't...I don't know where they're taking him."

"You have *no* idea?"

"I mean...I have a suspicion."

"So we can go get him, then?" I said. I wiggled my ankle, pulling up my pant leg to reveal my ankle monitor. "Get this thing off me, and then we can go get him."

Silas didn't move.

"That's the other thing, Maura," he said, looking up toward the sky. Even in the torturous silence, I read the betrayal before it came. "I talked to nearly everyone I could, but all the information I got back has been that the only people who can take that thing off have the highest clearance. Luke. Your Father. Few others will be granted that kind of access. I tried..." My ears rang, drowning out his voice. His excuses.

He had promised. I had banked on his promise. My sanity and resilience, my ability to deal with Andrew, had all hinged on knowing I could leave this place and partici-pate fully in the rebellion.

"Silas," I croaked. He met my eyes again, and they were full of pity. "Andrew thinks I'm *pregnant.* He's going to take me to the doctor, and they're going to realize I lied."

"I know," Silas said, putting his hands out as if that would quell my fear. "I can work it out with one of the doctors who can fake an image scan—"

"And what then?" Hysteria rose in my tone. I was

aware I was getting louder, and that I needed to calm down. Andrew might not hear me, but Abigail was close enough to. I sucked in air through my nose, working to lower my voice. "What next?" I hissed. "How long will I have to wait? I'm going to be stuck here while the Hunters have Eli? While everyone's out there fighting this rebellion?"

The fear inside my chest exploded. I gripped the railing tighter, the stair beneath me spinning as I tried to accept what I was being told.

"We're working on figuring out where Eli is, Maura," Silas said. "And…maybe it's safer for you to stay here for now."

"How can you—? How dare you—?" I said, unable to find words. "How can you expect me to stay here?"

"Maura, we don't have a choice."

"You *promised* me." My voice shook. My throat went dry. Silas took a step back.

"I'm sorry." He sounded apologetic, but I didn't care. I was so tired of being lied to. On every path I walked, someone I trusted would inevitably lie.

My breathing slowed, even though my heart pounded through my shirt. I was in awe of the blend of emotions cascading through me. Like bullets from a gun, they pierced me all the way through, leaving me weakened and exhausted. The rage I had felt earlier was only a glimmer, a small, dying ember inside of me. Now, all I felt was hope-lessness.

"I can't…" I gasped, impulsively reaching for him, grasping the front of his Hunter suit. "I can't stay here, Silas. I can't."

"Maura." He pressed both of his hands on top of mine. "You must. You have to stay here until I can figure this out. Tomorrow, I will have Dr. Mullen working in obstetrics.

He'll help you out on this visit. Then we'll figure out a schedule from there."

"Silas, please." I was desperate, and he knew it. I tightened my grip on his Hunter vest. "Please don't make me stay here."

"It'll only be a few more days," he promised. "I'll figure it out. I pro—"

"Don't you *dare* promise me if you don't mean it," I seethed.

"I mean it."

"And Eli?" I imagined him on the stretcher in the Centre. His white skin stained with blood. How dirty and weak he'd been. The idea of him being at the mercy of Father's Hunters set my anxiety on fire. "How...how can we find him? How can we help him?"

"I'm so sorry, Maura." Silas shook his head. "I don't have any more answers for you right now."

The last of my fury rose into my shoulders, and I pushed him as hard as I could, so angry at his words, so frustrated by the situation, so fearful of what might be happening to Eli in that moment. He stumbled backward, eyes wide in surprise.

"You never cared about me," I spat. "You only cared about getting your rebellion. And now you're going to leave me here to rot."

I couldn't catch my breath. Silas hung his head, and immediately I felt a deep sense of guilt at my outburst. All the emotional turmoil since I'd stepped out on the porch spilled out of me at once. The sobs came too fast, like rolling thunder, and I curled into myself, ashamed.

"You know that's not true," Silas said. "I'll fix this, Maura." His promise drifted away in the cold air.

I shook my head, unable to speak.

"I'm so sorry, but I have to go." Silas's quiet voice hung between us for a few seconds.

Of course he did. I knew he couldn't be gone from his post long without raising suspicion. But I hated him for it. I sobbed, watching him disappear into the shadows beside the house. Free to walk the commune. Free to communicate with the Centre. Free to walk away from my torment inside this god-forsaken house.

I buried my face in my hands and cried.

8

ELI

I WOKE to the buzz of electricity. The hum triggered an ache over my left eye, which forced pain down into my cheek, teeth, and jaw. But I kept my eyes closed. I hadn't yet worked up the courage to face the light head-on because even without moving, I knew I was in rough shape.

Beneath me, a thin mattress. My sore back rubbed against the plastic material as I shifted. It was so fucking bright. No matter which way I turned, I couldn't avoid the light. I lay flat, looking for my last memory. Heavy weight on my back and shoulders. Francis driving off with the trailer into the distance. The trailer that had Maura's sister inside it. The trailer I was supposed to be in.

Fuck.

It had been a Hunter that caught me, that I was sure of. My blood ran cold at the memory. His voice had sounded *so* young. We had been living off half rations for the last few weeks and being weak had taken its toll. That goddamn Hunter and his goddamn flashlight. Had Francis made it? Had he outrun the Hunters? Or had they shot out his tires and forced everyone out of the trailer?

I tried swallowing. My throat was so dry it induced a series of coughs. Each time my muscles tensed, my entire body ached. My ears rang. I tasted blood.

God.

I inhaled a labored breath. Choked it down. Then, I opened my eyes.

The light seared my retinas and forced my eyelids closed. Tears leaked down the sides of my face. I blinked, turned to the side, then tried again. This time, it was easier to gain focus.

My surroundings came to me in pieces. The room was bleached white with a long rectangular fluorescent light overhead. White linoleum tiles covered the floor, spotted with scuff marks.

Could this be a hospital? Could I have somehow made it out of that mess with the Hunters and come back to the Centre? I tilted my head, searching for some kind of medical equipment. A solid metal door was in the center of the opposite wall. A square hatch suggested someone could open it from the bottom. In the corner, a toilet, a small sink, and an empty shelf. The shiny metal reflected the light, and I forced myself to close my eyes again.

My heart sank. No. This was no hospital.

This was a prison.

After a year of hiding, months of trying to help Maura, and weeks of smuggling refugees out from the commune, the bastards had finally caught me.

I sighed, defeated and exhausted. I needed to move to see what kind of shape my body was in, to see if I could even think about trying to get out of here.

After a few excruciating minutes, I found enough energy and leverage to lift my body. I could not put pressure on my left shoulder. Every time it brushed up against the mattress, a sharp jolt of pain struck me, shooting up into my collarbone and ear to prompt a fresh headache.

I kept my left arm tucked into my side as I rolled. Black spots appeared in my vision as I sat upright. Bile rose in my throat. I closed my eyes, trying to quell my nausea. Accidentally, I tugged my left arm forward and yelped.

Oh, my God.

Agonizing pain flooded my nerves. I looked down at myself. Someone had taken my clothes, and a chill ran up my bare legs. A thin blue gown reached my knees. As far as I could tell, my boxer shorts still clung to my hips. Someone had put tight, white socks on my dirty feet. Beneath the gown, I saw a large, purple bruise in the crook of my elbow. The Hunter must've broken it. I was afraid to move it any more than I already had.

I tried my legs next, stretching each one out and letting it hang. Besides a slight twinge in my knee, everything felt as it should. I edged forward on the mattress, letting my toes touch the ground. My feet and ankles felt okay. I tried putting weight on them next, relieved to find no further pain. I sat back down. This was a good sign. Even with a broken arm, possibly a broken shoulder, at least I could walk.

Which was all well and good, except for the fact that I was sitting in a prison. The facility was clean. They clearly had running electricity and water. The world beyond the door was silent, but whether that was from a soundproof barrier or lack of life beyond it, I had no way of knowing.

When our scavenging team had returned to the Centre, they'd spoken of dismal conditions while they were imprisoned. This place was too clean. Too clinical. This couldn't be the prison at the edge of the Coutts' borders, so I was definitely elsewhere in the commune — but where?

How long had I been unconscious? And more importantly, why did they keep me *alive*?

I had watched the Coutts Hunters kill countless people, keeping others alive for seemingly no reason. That I was alive and my mother wasn't was proof. That very question had kept me up at night for months after Mom died. Why me? Why not her?

Of course, they also might know *exactly* who I was. Perhaps they recognized me as an accomplice who hid Maura, and they were planning on doing what they'd done to Nathan. Torturing me for more information — about the Centre, about people I needed to protect, about the rebellion. It was a crushing weight of responsibility I couldn't yet handle. Even though I was certain I'd identified my surroundings, I needed to be sure.

The room had finally stopped spinning. I braced with one hand on the bed and pushed myself to stand. The room couldn't have been larger than twenty by twenty feet. I started with slow steps, my pristine socks gliding against the floor like a pair of goddamn ice skates. The door was both tall and wide, and as I came closer, I realized why it looked so strange.

It had no handle.

I put my good shoulder up against it and pressed, some small part of me still holding onto hope that it would swing forward and a nurse would come tell me to get back into bed. But the door didn't budge. It was a solid piece of metal, enclosing me in a bright white tomb. My teeth clenched as I tried again with more pressure. Then, a third time, with a running start. My battered body slammed into the solid barrier, and my headache started all over again.

Defeated, I slumped to the floor.

The hatch at the bottom of the door was about as wide as my hand. It looked like a vent, with its slats pointing down, making it impossible to see beyond them. Like the door, I could not push it outward, but if I hooked my fingers into the slats, I could pull the hinge up. It took some finagling, but I finally managed to get the damned thing open.

I lay on my stomach, trying to adjust myself without hurting my arm. The circular room outside was just as white and pristine as my cell. Bright blue doors lined the curved walls, each with a number and a small white square. Some squares had black writing. Some were blank.

I squinted, trying to make out the writing on the boards, but between my strained eyes and throbbing headache, I couldn't make out more than a couple of letters. All in all, I counted eleven other doors. Seven of them had writing on them. Did that mean seven prisoners were here? Or seven empty rooms? Were there others as weak, bloodied, and bruised as I was? Could they be the refugees? Francis?

Against my better judgment, I pressed my face up against the window frame.

"Hello?" I called, keeping my voice low. "Is anyone there?"

The light's quiet hum permeated the small circle.

"Hello?" I tried again.

Silence. I sighed, letting my head fall forward against the cool metal, which brought momentary relief to my relentless headache.

"Hello?" A woman's voice. Soft. Hoarse. *Exhausted.*

I looked up sharply and glanced around, hoping to see a face.

"Hi," I said, hating how desperate I felt. I had so many questions. "Who are you?" I was afraid to give my name away willingly.

The person hummed. "I'm…" A pregnant pause. "Judith," she said.

Okay. I didn't know a Judith.

"Hi Judith. Do you know where we are?" Silence. "How long have you been here?" I tried. "Did you see me come in? Do you know how long I've been here?"

Questions flooded from my mouth. I felt both frantic about my situation and relieved to hear someone else's voice. Whether that was ultimately a good thing was yet to be seen. But at least I wasn't alone.

"Shh," the voice said, fear coating their tone. "Not too loud or they'll come."

"Hunters?" I asked, pressing one eye into the small square. There was no face I could see attached to the voice.

"Shhh."

She was afraid. But not so afraid that she wouldn't talk to me. Maybe she felt as desperate as I did. Maybe she'd been alone for a long time.

"Where are we?" I tried again, my voice a whisper. It drifted into the circle.

"It's a medical facility," she answered.

That had been my first thought. But it didn't seem right.

"Is it? Feels more like a jail cell."

"It's that too." Her voice hardened.

"Are you hurt?" I asked.

"A little."

Frustration prickled my spine. I needed more to go on.

"What kind of medical things do they do here?"

"Tests and stuff."

"What kind of tests?"

"I dunno. Shots and scans and stuff. They give us drugs to keep us calm."

"Why are they testing you?"

"I don't know."

Not helpful.

"Have you ever seen the outside of this place?" I asked, my heart hammering. My throat clenched. It was painful to swallow. "Do they ever let you out?"

She gave a dry laugh. "Only for the tests," she said. "And sometimes not even for that. I've been here since they captured me."

"When was that?"

"Five days ago. I think. It's hard to tell. They keep the lights on."

I gave the overhead light a fevered stare before taking a deep breath. "Are there others you've talked to?" I eyed the other doors. "It looks like there's more than just us here."

"Yes," she said. A long pause. A sniffle. She was crying. "Someone talked to me when I first came here. But then two days later, he just stopped. I—" Her voice cracked. I should comfort her, maybe. But how could I? We were both in the same impossible situation. "I don't know what happened to him," she finished.

"You didn't hear anything?"

"They give us drugs," she said. "Sometimes I fall asleep without realizing."

I felt cold.

"Do they ever unlock these doors?"

"No," she said.

"So how do they administer the drugs?"

"You don't feel it?" she asked.

"Feel what?"

"The thing they hooked to your chest."

I sat back. The metal flap swung shut with a *clink*. Horror struck my nerves. Careful to move only my good arm, I peeled away the gown's collar from my neck and peered down at my bare chest. All was as it should be. A smattering of dark curly hair. My thin ribs. The tattoo down my shoulder.

But there, unmistakably attached to the area near my heart, was a thin, beige piece of plastic. A green dot blinked at the top. Panicked, I reached for it. It was smooth, wider at the top, the bottom blending seamlessly into my skin. I hooked my fingers near the blinking light and tried to lift it.

I winced, sucking air through my teeth. Pinching pain forced me to drop the device. I looked down. The light blinked. This *thing* wasn't just taped to me. The device was entrenched in my flesh. I suspected that if I'd had the strength to pull the whole thing off, my skin would come away with it, too.

More than anything else, this was a huge problem. It meant the Coutts had access to my body. They could flood my veins with poison, and there was nothing I could do about it. My head ached. The room began to spin again.

"Do you see it?" called the woman, her voice a haunting whisper.

"Yes," I answered. "I fucking see it."

9

MAURA

EVERYTHING WAS WRONG. Cold night air stung my swollen face. I should move. Go back inside. But I couldn't get up. Perhaps I deserved this. I'd disrupted the order and unearthed the lies, and this was my penance. For the chaos. The pain.

The Hunters caught Eli. They'd infiltrated the Safe House and captured one of the people I cared most about in the world. One who knew *everything* about what had happened to me since the moment I'd fallen into the creek. My heart ached for him. The way he'd taken care of me. Even when he knew the risks. Even when he'd been afraid.

Our friendship had blossomed into more. It was meaningful, unconditional, and terrifying. But I knew now that I loved Eli. I loved him for who he was. Not because he'd saved my life. Not because he was nice to me. I loved him because he was kind, empathetic, and reliable. Because he had humility and integrity. Because he was a good man.

And now he was in trouble, and there was nothing I could do to help him.

Wind swept through the porch and I finally stood at the

chill. I felt removed from myself, like I was watching my body from a distance. I crossed the porch. Re-entered the house. Closed the door quietly, hung up my jacket, and took off my boots. Then, I pulled the snacks from my pockets and clutched them in my hands.

Eli could be hurt.

Could be dead.

There's nothing you can do to help him.

I walked to the kitchen, passing blurry objects. Fleeting thoughts clouded my mind, none of them sticking. I followed the warm glow that came from the stove light. Stopped in the doorway.

Morgan?

But no, the kitchen was empty, and I remembered. She had almost been captured, but now she was gone.

Eli could be hurt.

He could be dead.

There's nothing you can do.

I put the snacks neatly in the pantry, just the way Abigail had shown me when I'd first come to live in this house. Everything in its place. Everything as it should be.

Eli might be dead.

I closed the pantry door. My breath still came in short bursts, sometimes a shuddering draw. I pressed my icy hands against my warm face.

You deserve to be here.

Stupid child.

Worthless sinner.

This is what happens to children who disobey.

Was it my voice? Someone else's? I could no longer distinguish. Somehow, I'd made my way to the kitchen island, where Morgan and I had last cooked dinner together before Silas took her. Silas, who had left me here. Silas, who I'd pushed away. Silas, who had protected

Morgan, who had given us hope, who had started the rebellion I couldn't.

Shame flared in my chest.

Nothing you've done matters.

You deserved to be lied to by Andrew and Abigail.

You deserve to be stuck here.

You deserved it all.

I gripped the side of the counter, unable to sort my thoughts.

Mother's dead because of you.

My fault. My fault. My fault.

Eli might be dead.

Andrew and Abigail knew.

I twisted my ankle. The light caught on the ankle monitor's metal. This stupid thing. I should never have let this happen. I should never have let Father get to me after I'd returned. We should've figured out another plan. I had trusted God, or Silas, or fate to help me out of my messes one too many times.

Eli is probably dead.

They knew you couldn't conceive.

Silas will forget you.

You will never escape this prison.

I sank to the floor, knees drawn up to my chest. My fingers touched the ankle monitor, feeling the smooth metal and the seamless seal. It was loose enough that I could spin it around my ankle just above my bone. The metal slid neatly across my skin, not catching any hairs. A flawlessly executed piece of hardware. I dragged my thumb under the cuff, looking for the break Father had shown me when he had first revealed the monitor to me. At first, there was nothing but smooth metal. But eventually, I found the small crook, no bigger than the head of a pin.

They knew.

I slid my fingernail into the crack.

They laughed at you.

The result was instantaneous.

Mother's dead because of you.

A slit appeared in the metal, a small black sliver that broke the tracker in two. With it came the metal teeth.

You deserve this.

A pop of pain.

I hissed as the sharp metal bit into my flesh, instantly pulling my fingernail away. I was aware I should smooth the skin, check for blood. Instead, I just looked. The metal teeth had made small divots in my skin. They should have hurt, but they didn't. Everything was numb. My heart thudded dully in my chest.

Mother is dead.

Your fault. Your fault. Your fault.

Eli's next.

And all the others.

Morgan. Sid. Holli. Mia. Silas.

We can't win.

My fault. My fault. My fault.

Shame fired on all cylinders, convincing me of these truths. They weighed on me until my limbs felt impossible to move.

I should get up. Go back to bed. Sleep this off. The numbness might leave me. I might feel better tomorrow. I knew these things were rational and true. But my ankle throbbed. It was the only other thing I could feel.

And it felt good.

I had been an impostor my entire life. I wasn't devout; I wasn't holy. I was part of a community that thrived on others' destruction. And now, I was trying to be someone I couldn't. I was trying to be a hero. I was trying to fight a war we couldn't win. And even if we won, if everyone I loved died, what would be left for me then?

I had worked hard to push it all down. It had been necessary not to think about these things. It had been part of surviving. But the pain had woken something vicious and terrifying inside me. I pressed down in the crevice again with purpose. The teeth jutted out farther this time, and I steeled myself against the burning sting, feeling my jaw pop, and my ears rush with blood. Cool metal pierced through flesh and muscle, so deep I was sure it would hit bone. But I didn't pull back. I leaned into the agony.

They all knew.

They all laughed at you.

They're coming for every person you've ever loved.

Their deaths are on your hands.

My fingernail sank deeper. Pain finally registered, causing me to gasp. I bit my bottom lip. Warmth pooled down my ankle — slow at first, then quicker. It flowed until my hand, ankle, and pants were slick with it.

I didn't let go. I wasn't sure I could anymore. The sharp iron smell of blood filled the room, and I focused only on the deep, aching pain that matched what I felt in my chest. A scream worked its way up my throat, but I swallowed it, gasping against the impossible thing I was doing to myself. I was helpless to stop it.

It's what you deserve.

"Maura!"

I jolted awake.

Everything was slow and murky. My eyelids felt heavy. A dark figure hovered in sunlight. My eyes closed involuntarily. I couldn't keep them open.

"Maura, wake up!"

Hands on my shoulders. Urgency in Andrew's voice.

I moved my shoulders, rubbing up against the cool wooden floor. Which was wrong. I wasn't in the basement, and I wasn't in the guest bed. My fingers moved next. As I lifted them from my calf, they came away with something thick and crumbly.

I wanted to speak, but my mouth was so dry.

"Maura, please!"

I blinked. Struggled to open my eyes. Andrew knelt beside me and tried to lift my body.

I moaned. Nausea rolled in my stomach. It was unbearable, rising in my belly and burning my throat. I couldn't hold it. My stomach contracted, and I vomited up last night's dinner.

I couldn't breathe.

Andrew dropped me back onto the floor. My head hit the wood, and I moaned. Turned to lie on my side. Vomit spewed from my mouth again, splattering across the wooden floor and cabinets, the rest of it down my shoulder and arm. With it went the last of my energy. I collapsed into my own sick.

"God, Maura." He left my side. I let my eyes close. I smelled the horrendous stench of what had been in my stomach, and I heaved again, but I couldn't get the energy to lift myself. Spittle dribbled from the side of my mouth. I felt it, warm against my cheek. I was so tired. So unbelievably tired.

A crackle of static came from above me.

"Help!" Andrew's voice was frantic. On the verge of tears. "—someone from Medical. NOW!"

I wanted to open my eyes.

"Good Lord in Heaven, Maura." Andrew was back beside me. "What did you do?"

I tried to open my eyes. The world was gray. All I could smell was vomit.

A moment of awareness found me. My brain registered the pins and needles traveling from my feet up into my ankles. There was pain. Excruciating, crushing pain that made the world feel hazy and pliable. My ears rang. Andrew shouted something else into the radio, and someone answered calmly. Static lulled me back into the dark world behind my eyelids.

My ankle.

The monitor.

At the thought, I remembered each sharp tooth in my skin. The metal cuff radiated heat. What *had* I done? I needed to get back to bed. I needed to go back to pretending. But when I tilted my head and looked down at myself, I was horrified to find everything covered in dark, dried blood.

"Andrew?"

My voice sounded small and far away. My consciousness rippled dangerously. My body felt so heavy, so frustratingly uncooperative. Andrew kneeled beside me again, gently placing his hand beneath my head. I looked up and met his familiar blue eyes. He looked so tired, so haggard, so much older than I remembered him from before I'd fallen into the creek.

"It'll be okay," he soothed, his other hand resting on my belly, where he thought his baby was. "We're going to get you some help."

I inhaled. Closed my eyes. Gave myself over to the darkness.

The next thing I knew, there was a canvas beneath my back, and I was being lifted unceremoniously toward the ceiling of Andrew's kitchen. Light beamed through the window, washing across my face. Suddenly, we were outside.

Men carried me. I saw their jawlines from where I lay, the sun making it difficult to discern their features. Feet shuffled against the driveway. Andrew's ragged breathing followed somewhere behind.

A mattress appeared behind me. Antiseptic burned my nostrils. Someone sat me up. My head lolled against a thin pillow. A bright light shone in my eyes, and I blinked, writhing away from it.

"Do you understand what I'm saying?" someone asked as they let the light drop. Tears leaked from my eyes, and I shook my head yes, then no. A pinch in the crook of my arm. Warmth in my shoulder. A tender hand on my leg.

"Did you ask what we're supposed to do with this?"

Someone grunted in response. The hand pulled at the monitor around my ankle. I screamed, the pain waking every nerve still firing in my body. I reached for the side of the bed. Something to ground myself.

Someone gasped.

"Oh my—!"

"Get her down."

A pair of hands pushed me against the mattress. A series of straps worked their way across my chest, pinning my arms in place. Another pinch in my arm. Warmth spread through the rest of my body, coating me in a blanket of bliss.

The pain eased, like someone had pulled it from me.

Finally.

10

MAURA

A RHYTHMIC BEEPING lulled me from sleep. The comfortable fog around me bled away slowly, waking my senses. Antiseptic stung my nostrils. Tightness gripped my ankle. A thin, scratchy blanket lay beneath my fingers. My last memory was chaotic. The world around me now was anything but.

I blinked away the film in my eyes and let them adjust to the dark room. The beeping came from a machine on my left, which was attached to a pole. At the top hung a large bag, half-filled with clear fluid. From that, a wire led to a needle piercing the crook of my elbow beneath a clear piece of tape.

A dim glow radiated from a nightlight plugged into the far wall. On my left were two windowless doors. Across from me, a set of wooden cabinets, a metal rolling tray, a single chair, and a ceiling vent made up the remaining objects in the room. All the walls were blank. I lay in a thin bed, covered up to my chest with a blanket. The clothes I'd been wearing at Andrew's were gone, replaced by a gown.

My breathing quickened.

What had I done?

I knew I should feel shame that I'd let Andrew find me the way he did. But the cloudy feeling I'd gotten in the ambulance was still in my veins, dulling any guilt my brain pushed forward. I sat up, surprised to find my body cooperative. The blankets came away easily, and I edged my leg out. All the blood was gone. Someone had cleaned me up. My ankle was bandaged. Blue socks covered both feet.

I turned my ankle, curious how far I could stretch it until it hurt. I felt an ache, little twinges of discomfort, but nothing like I had when I'd released those teeth into my leg. I wondered how bad the damage was beneath the bandage…

The monitor.

It was gone. It had to be. The bandage was wrapped too tightly for anything to be beneath it. Frantically, I yanked my other leg from under the covers.

Bare.

My stomach flip-flopped, making me lightheaded. It was the feeling of knowing something I shouldn't. The feeling of being bad. The chain that had tethered me to Father since I'd been back was gone. Even if it was only temporary, it still felt freeing. But I knew Father. I knew he wouldn't have allowed the doctors to take the monitor off if he didn't have another plan for me before I walked out of here. I wanted to understand where I was and what I might be dealing with.

I swung my legs over the side of the bed and pressed my feet to the cool ground. The bottom grips on my socks stuck to the floor. Carefully, I braced myself on the mattress and stood.

The shock of the new weight made my right ankle bow. The room spun. The drugs in my system seemed more potent when I got up. I gripped the bed's edge and shifted more weight onto the other leg. Better. I let go and steadied myself on both feet.

Okay. Progress.

I grabbed the pole with the hanging bag and used it to balance myself as I stepped forward. Walking became easier with every step I took. I traveled the entire room from corner to corner. In the cabinets, I found my boots. My blood-covered clothes were missing. I deduced I was probably in a medical center somewhere in the Sciences and Innovations area. I had always imagined these places to be comforting and warm. Not a cold, dark room devoid of any character.

I approached both doors, letting my hand travel over the smooth wood. The handles were made of brushed metal, and I let my fingers rest on one. I could press down, see if it would move.

Something disrupted the quiet beyond. A voice. Metal against metal. Footsteps, getting louder.

My stomach dropped to my knees. Quickly, I scurried back to the bed and eased myself beneath the blanket, careful not to rip the needle out of my arm. The footsteps paused outside my door.

I leaned back against the pillow and tried to steady my breathing. The door's rubber bottom swept against the linoleum. Someone opened one of the doors wide. Beyond, a brightly lit hallway disappeared behind the silhouetted figure, the shadow of a large automatic weapon unmistakable in his arms. He wore no helmet, and the shadows hid his features, but he was definitely a Hunter.

A smaller figure appeared behind him, holding a tray. The thin, mousy-looking man hurried into my dark room like he was late for a meeting.

"You're up!" he said brightly, putting the tray on top of the rolling cart and pulling it up to the side of the bed. He paused, glancing at the monitor, then back at me. He was older than he'd initially appeared, his hairline receding at his temples. "Some food for you, when you feel up to it." He looked down at the tray — a plastic-wrapped plate, cup, and a single utensil lay on a plain piece of paper. "The doctor should be in shortly."

"Thank you," I tried saying, but my voice was so hoarse it came out muted. My throat was on fire. I forced a smile.

"Drink up," he said, eyeing the cup. "They've been giving you fluids, but your throat needs the liquid." He reached forward suddenly and grabbed my hand. "You might even consider a shower."

I narrowed my eyes at the peculiar behavior. He patted my hand with his, then turned and left the room. The Hunter nodded at him before he closed the door. The distinct clink of a lock came from the other side. Well, that answered that question. I was not free to leave, and that handle certainly would not open.

Resigned to my fate, I unwrapped the plate of food to reveal eggs and toast. Breakfast. Did that mean it was morning? Without windows, it was hard to tell. Had I really been out a full day? Or were they trying to confuse me?

My stomach decided it didn't matter. I stuffed my mouth with food, forgoing the fork and using my hands. Every bite burned my dry throat, so I turned my attention to the drink. With both hands gripped around the cup, I gulped liquid down. Gulp after gulp after gulp until… something hard hit the back of my throat.

I coughed, then choked, forcing the foreign object up with my tongue, wondering if I'd lost a tooth. Pounding panic hit my chest. But no. The object felt too large. I spat it out into my hand.

A coin.

Confused, I stared at it for a moment. What was it doing in my drink? Had someone dropped it by accident? Or had they…put it there? My breath hitched as I turned it over between my fingers. It was small and silver, with markings carved into the material. I recognized it as an old coin, one they'd used decades ago. We didn't use coins in the commune, but I had learned the Outsiders did. It was their way of making transactions. Instead of trading things, they would trade coins for things they needed.

My gaze traveled up and over the coin, toward the door. Had the man put this in the cup for me? And why? There was no more time to wonder. A new voice came from outside the door. I tucked the coin under my leg just as the door handle turned.

The Hunter with the gun held the door as a tall, broad-shouldered man entered. He was bald and wore wide-rimmed glasses that made his eyes seem bigger than his face. He gestured to the Hunter, who did something outside the door. The lights came on in the room. I squinted, shielding my eyes with my hand from the sudden brightness. The doctor seemed undeterred.

"Good morning, Maura," he said. "I'm Doctor Dabrowski. How are we feeling?"

He approached my bed, tucking his hands into his white coat. I sensed he was attempting to be calm. He was no rebel. And if he was, he was likely being watched. I needed to maintain my composure.

"Tired," I said. It was a lie. Despite the drugs they were feeding me, I was on high alert by both the doctor's tone and the gift left in my cup.

Doctor Dabrowski nodded. "We've been giving you some pain medication to keep you comfortable," he said, eyeing the monitor. "You made quite a mess of yourself, Maura." He shifted his gaze to my leg beneath the blanket.

"Which, in your state, is incredibly irresponsible, to say the least. This is no way for an expectant mother to behave."

I tensed at the accusation and felt shame's familiar flame climb high into my chest. I wanted to tell him it was irresponsible to force me to wear a tracking device that could slice my leg clean off.

"Yes," I heard myself say.

"Andrew is devastated," he continued. "The state he's in?" He clicked his tongue. "No husband should be made to feel that way by a wife."

Heat rose to my cheeks.

"Are you sorry?" he asked.

"Am I—?"

"*Sorry?*" His nostrils flared.

"Yes. Of course." I didn't sound convincing.

He looked away from me, disgusted. "Well. Your father has requested to see you himself. You should be so honored that he is coming all the way down here to confirm that your health is in good condition. Typically, Doctor Mullen does our ultrasounds, but your father insisted on doing it himself."

"An ultrasound?"

The doctor's eyes narrowed. "Yes," he said, like I was a dim child. "A scan of your uterus. To make sure everything's going well with the baby."

My blood ran cold. I met his eyes, tried to steady my gaze, but I could feel my limbs start to shake. A sneer crossed his face. Did he already know there was no baby? My fingers curled into the blanket.

"Sit tight," Doctor Dabrowski said with a smile. "I'll be back with the Prophet when he gets here."

I nodded, fighting through the tense muscles in my neck and shoulders. The doctor left the room, leaving me in silence.

Holy God above, please protect me.

I grasped the coin beneath my leg and held the warmth in the palm of my hand. There were no windows to escape through. The door was locked. The hallway was guarded. There was only one thing I hadn't tried.

Adrenaline shot through me as I stood, dragging the monitor, bag, and pole along with me like an unresponsive limb. I made my way to the doors, turning the handle of the one that hadn't yet opened. Lights flickered on with a small hum, revealing a large, tiled room. A toilet and sink were attached to the far wall. To my left, a shower.

You might even consider a shower.

I held my breath, letting it bottle in my chest as I approached the curtain. Its rings squealed on the pole as I pushed it aside, exposing a tiled area with a shower head, a drain, and a vent.

I exhaled. The vent was attached to the wall, painted over with the same white paint as the rest of the walls. At chest level, it was easy to inspect. Four screws held it in place. I opened my palm and eyed the coin.

Now it made sense.

The wire attached to the monitor and pole tugged painfully on my arm as I got to work. But I wouldn't remove it. Not yet. I was sure the minute I took it out of my arm, someone outside the door would be alerted and come running. I needed all the time I could get.

The coin's side slid easily into the large screws. Paint flecked off the edges as I worked to turn them left, loosening their hold in the wall. My hands sweat. The coin slipped in my grip. I wiped my fingers against the gown and adjusted my hold. The bottom right screw came loose, and I grabbed it, tossing it into the shower drain before I went to work on the next one.

This one was tighter. It took a few tries to get the coin

between the indents, and I grunted with effort as I pushed to free it from its position. The coin slipped. Connected. Slipped again. Finally, it sat right. I felt the threads give way, and the screw began to turn. Relieved, I brushed my sweaty hair out of my eyes, turning until my fingers ached and the whole thing came loose. The edge of the grate popped out from the wall.

I heard a noise from somewhere outside the bathroom. My heart beat in my ears as I went back into the hospital room, listening. A deep voice outside the room rumbled unintelligibly. The Hunter spoke with someone, and I didn't want to wait to find out who.

I crossed the room to the cabinets, removing my boots. I slipped my socked feet inside, tugged at the laces, then tucked them into the shoe. The pole dragged beside me as I ran back to the bathroom, my breath heavy. A new voice joined the conversation. Someone chortled.

No. No!

I tore the sticky bandage off my arm. The needle came next. The monitor's beeping quieted, and my vision tunneled. I sucked air through my teeth and grasped the sore area of my inner arm just as I heard the distinct *clink* of the door unlocking.

Now or never.

I yanked the vent away from the wall, revealing a hole that disappeared in darkness. Behind me, rubber slid against the floor. The door handle rattled. The monitor issued a series of emergency beeps.

I threw myself inside the metal vent. It was dark and tight, but with some effort, I managed to pull myself forward, my legs following until I was completely enclosed in the grate. I didn't have enough room to look behind myself, so I kept the course and shimmied forward, using my hands to push along the grate.

Behind me came a yell. Urgent, angry voices. A door slammed against a wall.

I cried out in fear, unable to hold it in. If that Hunter used his gun to shoot at me, I was dead. And I resigned myself to the chance. But I kept moving, crawling into the darkness, blind and desperate to just get *away*. There was no tracker on my leg. Nobody could follow me, as long as I got out of here without being seen. I could join the rebellion. I could—

It didn't matter. An angry growl echoed behind me, and my heart squeezed in fear. In the dark, I nearly went headfirst into the vent ahead, where it separated into a T.

Hurry up and choose.

Left.

Blindly, I turned the corner, leaving the light and the shouting behind me. I was waiting for the bullets, for the piercing sound of a firing gun, but still, I crawled. The walls closed in around me. It was so dark and so tight that my arms began to ache. What if the vent didn't have an exit? What if I got to the end and needed to turn around to come right back through the bathroom I'd escaped from? I didn't know if this was going to work. They already knew I wasn't pregnant. If capture awaited me, then I could only expect a life of pain. They could do anything they wanted to me now.

Just as my tears welled, I made another turn and gasped. A sliver of light rose from another break in the vent. I pushed myself forward, reaching toward it as the tears came anyway — not from fear, but from relief.

Down this path, a series of vents led to different bathrooms, similar to the one I'd left. I couldn't risk going back into another room with locked doors. My tender arms pushed me onward. I could feel the drugs they'd pumped me with start to leave my veins. The world was becoming clearer. My head was losing its cloudiness. But most concerning, I felt a deep ache in my ankle.

The vent tilted at an incline, and I was forced to hook my boots on either side to climb it. The effort was well worth it. The next vent looked down into a well-lit hallway.

Three people walked it, one holding a thin, digital device, the other two chatting in hushed voices. I released a slow breath. They hadn't issued a building-wide lock-down yet. I kept going until I reached another dead end. From there, I turned left. Crawled down to the last vent on my right. I was sweating. My heart was racing so fast I was sure it would never calm. But at the end, I was relieved not to find a bathroom.

This vent looked out into a mostly concrete room, filled with shelves of what looked like cleaning supplies. Six massive rolling laundry baskets filled with linens and clothes lined the vent's wall. But most importantly, there was a door on the far wall, with a glowing red EXIT sign hung above it.

My muscles felt weak. I bowed my head before crawling to the end. This was it. I might make it out of here. I reached the vent, jammed my fingers through the slats, and pushed.

It stuck.

No.

Ugly, relentless defeat crept up my shoulders, and I nearly shouted out in frustration. I couldn't turn around in the tight space. I was here at the end. I could *see* my freedom.

No, no, no.

I reached around, pulled off one of my boots, and used what strength I had left to push all of my weight up against the vent with the boot in my hands. With a crack, I saw the edge give way.

Emboldened, I did it again, struggling against my racing heart. I swore I heard people behind me, coming through the vents, their eager hands ready to grab me. But I pushed again, and again, until finally the vent cover gave way. It dented outward, the screws yanking out dusty drywall that landed softly inside the laundry baskets below.

I vaulted myself forward and through the hole, aiming for the laundry cart. My body landed awkwardly, tilting the basket so that I fell out of the side, clothes and linens falling on top of me. I eyed the door, then the clothes. The shirts and pants were all the same color of navy blue with suspicious stains and smells. It didn't matter. They were better than the gown I wore. Quickly, I stripped and redressed in new clothes. When I got to my feet, my ankle ached, but I pushed through it. I just needed to get out.

Adrenaline fired me toward the door. The lights flickered in the room. An alarm began to blare. I reached out, pressed against the door's thin metal release bar, and smelled the cold outside air. I stumbled into the sunlight, squinting against the brightness and wincing against the pain in my ankle.

I braced myself to run.

A strong pair of arms caught me around the middle, stopping me in my tracks.

11

MAURA

THICK FINGERS GRASPED MY JAW, covering my mouth and nose. The force muffled the guttural scream that came out of me. In the distance, I saw the forest, covered in bare trees and dead grass. Beside us, a series of buildings. This was the back of the Sciences and Innovations area. The way I'd come in weeks ago. I'd been so close. The person behind me took a step backward, and I saw the edges of a green suit. I briefly considered biting their fingers.

A Hunter.

"Stay quiet." The voice was hushed but…familiar. He released his hold, and I broke away, stumbling against the building. The sun made everything difficult to see, but as my eyes adjusted, I made out blonde hair. A tall figure. A boyish, guilty smile. Not Silas, but—

"Gabriel?"

His eyes darted from side to side. He kept his right hand tight over the strap of his gun, which hung from his back.

"Geezus, Maura. You need to go—"

"—what are you doing out here?" I interrupted.

We stared at each other. "We were called in," he explained. He looked over his shoulder. "To look for you."

My vision tunneled. I braced myself against the building.

"Silas told me what happened," Gabriel said. "Said you were found all bloodied up. Are you alright? Andrew didn't hurt you, did he?" His worried eyes grazed over me.

Embarrassment flushed up my neck. "I'm fine," I said.

"How the heck did you get out of there?"

"I don't know." I shook my head, thinking of the man who'd brought me food. "Someone left me a coin. I was able to get through the vents."

He pressed his lips together and nodded. "Smart."

"Yeah, well, that was the end of my plan."

"You're lucky you ran into me, then," he said." The Auto Shop Safe House is compromised. You'll need to go through the forest, east to the Waste Center. There's a small collection of buildings out there that are all demolished. They're being monitored, but not that heavily. There's some friendlies on that patrol. Hide there. We'll get someone to come look for you. It's a straight shot from here along the river. You have to put some distance between yourself and the border. I can let friendlies know to expect you," Gabriel said, speaking so fast his words ran together. "Just *don't* get caught."

His bright eyes were full of fear.

"The Hunters know," I said matter-of-factly.

He raised an eyebrow.

"They know I'm not pregnant."

He nodded, his face somber. If I thought the Hunters had been dangerous before, they'd be out for blood now. Lying about a pregnancy wasn't just blasphemy. It was the most heinous crime imaginable. They'd use the lie against me. They'd tell everyone if I could lie about a baby, I could lie about being a martyr. They would make an example out of me and not feel an ounce of regret.

"Go. Friendlies will use code 287. Alright?"

"Psalm?"

He nodded. "The Lord is my strength and my shield."

"I hope so."

Frantically, he looked around again. The longer I stayed here, the more danger I put him in. I swallowed. Shifted on my heels. Tightened my muscles. Got ready to run.

"Okay."

I reached out and squeezed his arm. He rewarded me with a smile.

"Go. Be careful."

I nodded, releasing my grip on him, and stumbled toward the forest.

Everything felt too large; the trees too high, the terrain too long, too wide, and too open. A door slammed, and as I looked over my shoulder, I saw Gabriel was gone. The alarm blared from somewhere deep inside the building. Where they were still looking for me.

Anxiety sparked. My stomach rolled. I focused on a point in the distant forest and ran.

***

Trying to stay hidden among sparse trees was a tricky endeavor in the frigid landscape. I was relieved I'd had the sense to change out of the hospital gown, but the thin material of my outfit provided little warmth. The pants were too large, and I kept tripping over them. I missed my winter coat.

The landscape was vast and brown, with occasional green pines scattered between. Fall's overgrowth created tangled nests of branches and decay. The forest was quiet this time of year. Dead. Which amplified every sound.

Every so often, I'd snap a branch or accidentally crunch a pile of leaves too loudly. I'd scurry as quickly as I could on my injured ankle to the closest hiding place — over-turned tree roots, dips in the terrain, or a thick branch. But no Hunter came. Gunshots did not pierce the air. No shouts echoed in the distance.

My boots kept my feet dry, and the bandage around my ankle secure. The pain medication had fully worn off, and the result was a deep, painful ache every time I took a step. At least my training in Abigail's basement was paying off. I had walked for hours and barely worked up a sweat.

Scattered clouds blotted out the sunlight, but the sun remained a clear navigator. I followed my course east, putting more and more distance between myself, the Sciences and Innovations area, and the Auto Shop Safe House. That was probably where they'd captured Eli. I wished I knew where he was now.

The trees finally began to thin when I heard the first gurgle of water moving over rocks. Despite the cold, the river was thawing as spring approached. I smelled damp earth and hurried to the edge. Here, the cliff drop was shallow, and I got to the creek without much strain on my ankle. I cupped my hands in the frigid water and drank deeply.

It felt strange being back at the edge of the creek I'd fallen into when Eli and I first discovered each other. Almost poetic, in a way. I had once found this river to be my salvation when I was a Scavenger. It gave me peace. Made me feel connected to God. Maybe I had known all along that it would lead me to the truth.

I sat and watched the slow-moving water cut through the valley, disappearing around a curve in the distance.

There was no way I would make it to the Waste Center today. I would need to find shelter and rest, and keep moving tomorrow.

Even though being on the run wasn't ideal, I had done it before, and I could do it again. I had made it. I'd gotten away from Andrew with no one's help but my own. But now, I faced endless uncertainty. I knew my next move, but what came after?

Suddenly, I regretted stopping. The moment of solitude had felt calming at first, but I could feel the other things I hadn't yet addressed fighting for my attention. They had killed Mother. They had captured Eli. Silas had abandoned me. The Hunters knew I wasn't pregnant. Abigail had known I couldn't conceive. Father was an evil man. My chest tightened as my thoughts ricocheted. I dug my fingers into the dirt beneath my legs.

Survival made it easy to keep those things at a distance, but sitting down and having to confront them was something I was not yet prepared to do. Grief and rage gathered together like kindling, just waiting for me to set the spark.

No.

Blood rushed to my ears as I tucked my face between my knees.

How had I missed the signs? How foolish had I been not to see through such lies? How had I not seen Father for who he truly was? Andrew? Luke? It was maddening to go back through the past, to pick up on the details that could have — should have — clued me in.

It was all you knew.

That was a new voice. A gentler one I hadn't heard before. I *had* only known what was in front of me. Eli had said it himself. Father was a master manipulator and had formed our thoughts and beliefs like a baker kneading bread. There had always only been one path forward. One way we were meant to live. One man we were taught to follow.

Not anymore.

There was no sense in dwelling on these things I couldn't change. If I wanted to be part of this rebellion, I needed to stop feeling sorry for myself. I needed to stop sitting in regret. I needed to reveal these truths to the rest of the commune. *Everyone* deserved to know the truth.

I lifted my head, smelling the dirt, the air, and the crisp smell of melted snow mixing with the river water. I inhaled, closed my eyes, and let myself feel the cold. The ache in my ankle.

Then, I got to my feet.

12

ELI

It had never been clearer to me that time was an enigma. The lights never went off in my cell. It had been a long time since we'd had any source of reliable electricity, so it fascinated me. I'd forgotten how lightbulbs buzzed. How artificial light could trick your senses and make you see spots. That sometimes bulbs crackle, dim, or brighten without reason.

The mechanism on my chest was in complete control of my behavior and habits. Although I tried to keep track of the hours I spent in my prison, the injections made it impossible. Without warning, drugs would flood my veins, enveloping me in a warmth I couldn't climb out of. Sleep came quickly and easily, and when I woke, I had no idea how long I'd been asleep.

Food came intermittently. It was enough to keep me from starving, but never enough to satisfy. A lone hand delivered the tray to my cell. I had tried to look through the small flap, but both times I'd been kicked and my food had spilled. After the third time, I wasn't willing to risk losing my food again.

The woman I had spoken with when I'd arrived had stopped responding after our first and only conversation. The only other noise I heard besides the buzzing of the bulbs was the occasional door opening and closing in the center circular room.

My door never opened.

I was stuck. I'd resigned myself to being imprisoned, but it didn't help the guilt I felt at not being there for the people I'd promised to help. I had two options. One, someone would come for me, and I would be a victim of whatever it was they did to these prisoners down here. Two, someone would come for me, and I'd try to escape. The second option was getting less and less likely the longer I sat here. I began to think my captors had forgotten me.

I lay on my thin bed, unsure if I had just been asleep or not. I might have been. Might not have. Moments bled into each other. Footsteps came from the far door. I stared at the wall, ears perked and straining to listen. I expected more of the same, but today something beeped outside my door. The sound was close. Closer than anything had been before.

I sat up.

My head throbbed from the sudden movement and whatever drug cocktail was in my veins. My heart had the good sense to start beating quicker, but I barely felt it. My vision swam. If I'd had anything in my stomach to puke up, I might've.

Someone pulled my door wide.

I squinted to steady my gaze. A man dressed in Hunter green stood in the doorway, blocking my view. Like all the others, he held a large gun. But that wasn't the thing that scared me most. He also wore no helmet. I had come to realize that Hunters wore their helmets to conceal their identities. That way, nobody could blame them for their atrocities. If this man wasn't wearing his helmet, it meant he didn't care if I saw his face.

Which was bad news for me.

I'd once had the irrational thought that the Hunters weren't real. That they were robots or some form of artificial intelligence dispatched to round up the people who didn't agree with Peter. Somehow, that had made it easier to stomach their cruelty. Of course, after watching them closely for over a year, I knew that wasn't true.

The Hunter that stood in front of me was a boy, no older than sixteen. Spots of acne covered his chin. A sneer crossed his face as he pulled the large weapon into his hands and pointed it at me.

"Get up," he barked.

The weapon could rip a bullet clean through my middle before I even knew what happened. I should've been scared. But instead, I considered that death might be better than whatever awaited me.

I stood up nonetheless.

I towered over the young man, but he seemed undeterred. He kept the weapon on me as he came around to my back and grabbed my wrists. I hissed with pain as he yanked my bad elbow backward at an unnatural angle.

"Hurts?" he asked.

I didn't answer.

He yanked again, with intention, and I moaned, the pain so great I nearly fell to my knees. I heard him snicker as the metal cuffs clicked together around my wrists. All of this seemed unnecessary given how heavily they'd medicated me, and I had the sudden urge to tell him so.

He moved down to my ankles, shackling them, too. I wore nothing more than a gown and underwear, and it made me feel cold and exposed. Humiliated. Still, I held my head up as he stood, came to my side, and jutted his chin forward with a sneer.

"Let's go."

I stepped forward, walking slowly, as I tried to remember every detail of the room outside. It was circular, as I'd deduced from the hatch, but smaller than I'd originally thought. The Hunter closed my door behind himself, then crossed the room.

The writing I had seen on the doors was clearer now, and I quickly read everything I could.

Female. 24. Strain F.

Male. 17. Strain B.

From the bottom of the door with *Female. 21. Strain C.*, I glimpsed a pair of blinking eyes. I startled in surprise, feeling a glimmer of gratitude as we met each other's gaze. A friend. My friend? She had faded, tired, green eyes.

A beep broke my focus. Another door opened.

"*C'mon,*" the Hunter said impatiently, prodding my shoulder with the neck of his gun like it was a plaything. I winced. "Come. On." He poked me twice more. I clenched my jaw and refocused away from him.

The door he ushered me through led to a long, gray hallway lined with metal doors. Dim lights illuminated a cold, concrete floor. My socked feet shuffled along, the chain restraints clinking together as I walked.

Another guard stood at the end of the hallway, guarding a set of stairs. Well, there went Option One. Even if I did somehow break free, the stairs leading out of here were guarded. They would kill me in seconds.

As we moved along the hall, the air grew colder. Did these metal doors all lead to similar prisons? Other places? The medical testing rooms my friend had mentioned?

The Hunter brushed ahead of me, reaching for a door on the right. I was vaguely aware of how weak I was. I hadn't gotten any exercise. I'd barely been eating or drinking. My disorientation especially concerned me. I knew that whatever waited for me behind that door would not improve my situation, and it made me shiver.

"Man," I said. "Where the hell are we?"

The question was a desperate last-ditch effort to find some humanity left in this kid. At sixteen, I had done some stupid stuff. Smoked too much weed. Broken a girl's heart. Lied to Mom. I was still figuring things out. Maybe this kid was too. If I could get him to question his motives, maybe I'd have a shot at appealing to his compassion.

The young man's face spread into a wide, sinister grin. He gripped his gun and pulled it into his puffed-out chest. He looked ridiculous, but it didn't matter. The guy was on a power trip, and anything I did or said would only encourage the behavior.

"You've got a one-way ticket to the Pit," he said, his eyes narrowing. "In you go."

The Pit? I scoured through my messy memories, trying to remember if Maura, Silas, or Gabriel had ever mentioned a place called the Pit. I couldn't think of one. I knew the Peak. Sciences and Innovations. The Waste Center. Scavenging Zones. The Island of Repentance. But the Pit didn't ring a bell.

Was it a medical facility, like my friend had mentioned? Were they going to do strange, experimental tests on my weak body? It seemed improbable that they knew I was a rebel. And they had to know, didn't they? They'd caught me off the back of an escaping caravan.

The cuffs felt heavy around my extremities as I entered the new room. It reminded me of a police interrogation room from old movies. A mirror on one side. A single light hanging from the ceiling above. A table with two chairs on either side. Everything else, like my cell, was blank. A cold, unwelcoming room.

Definitely not a medical facility.

"Have fun," the Hunter said from the doorway. He gave me the same creepy ass smile he'd been throwing me and yanked the door closed with a slam.

I wavered on my feet, steadying myself on the table. In the mirror, my reflection haunted me. I looked like a ghost of myself. Pale white skin. Large bruises under both eyes. Matted hair. An overgrown and unruly beard. Chapped lips. Sharp collarbones peeked through the hospital gown.

It hurt to look at myself. My body had kept me alive through the unthinkable, and now it looked like it was failing. I had been strong. I'd been a protector, a hunter, a survivalist. But the past few weeks had been cruel to me. These past few days, even more so.

I settled in one of the uncomfortable seats, taking care not to bump my broken arm on anything. All those pain meds and the damn thing still hurt.

Voices came from outside the door. The handle turned. A figure entered.

He was tall and broad, with receding blonde hair. He looked eerily familiar, though I couldn't place his face. I inspected him quickly, afraid to look at him too long. But his features weren't the thing that caught my attention. It was the number on his breast pocket. The number 11.

I knew that number well. I would never forget it. Because that number — Number 11 — belonged to the man who had ruined my life. It belonged to the man I was sure had killed Mom.

13

ELI

THE MAN CLOSED the door behind him, straightening as he studied me. If I weren't so tired, I might've felt embarrassed by my appearance. In two strides, he made it to the opposite end of the table and pulled out the chair so that its legs squealed against the floor. His eyes caught mine in the mirror, lip curled in a perpetual sneer — cold, calculating, and full of hatred.

Great.

He gripped his hands on the chair's back and tilted his body forward, lifting his head. The gold cross he wore around his neck hung off him, glinting in the light.

"So. Are you enjoying your stay with us, rebel?"

His voice remained even, as if we were discussing the weather.

I cocked my head. The question was rhetorical, and I wasn't about to give him the satisfaction of an answer. I clenched my jaw and stared into his dull blue eyes.

He sighed, pushed back from the chair, and crossed his arms over his green uniform. "You know, when I hear about rebels, I often wonder what led them astray. You,

you're from the Outside. So you've been living in sin for… what?" He spun on his heel and looked at me. "Your entire miserable life?"

I pressed my tongue to my cheek and let it slide around my teeth.

"But for the most part, we've left you all alone, haven't we?" He shook his head and looked at the ceiling as if this were the truth. "You made your choice when Peter opened the doors to our commune, and you decided not to follow him. You *wanted* to stay out in that wasteland." He paused and gripped the chair again. "So why, pray tell, were you trying to steal innocent people from our land? Children? Women?" His nostrils flared, eyes widening. "You sick animals."

I breathed slowly, fixing my gaze on the corner of the mirror.

"Once you stole these people from us, what was your plan?" He raised his brows. "You would take them out into the world, convert them to whatever sick teachings you believe? Help them stray far away from God? From the Prophet?"

I felt his gaze on me. His back tensed in the mirror. I kept my features neutral.

"Of course, you feel no remorse. You took children away from their families. You've confused them. Put them in harm's way. You've condemned them to hell unless they repent."

My eyes slid over. His face was red, dark brows narrowed, deepening the lines on his forehead.

"They're *children*," I sneered.

"Exactly," he spat. "Children!"

The word echoed in the room, bouncing from wall to wall and around my brain. I twisted my neck and tried to shake it. Number 11 finally took a seat in the chair opposite me, but I kept my eyes fixed on the corner of the mirror and bit my bottom lip, hard.

"So," he said, his voice calmer now. "You're working with a man named Avi."

I froze in my chair.

"What do you know about Avi, hm?" His voice was light, even a little gleeful. "Probably not much," he deduced. "He probably kept his history a secret to the people he surrounded himself with, isn't that right? Otherwise, I'm not sure you'd be following his orders."

I licked my lips. Tried to focus on my breath. I hated how curious I was.

"You may not have known that Avi was a combat engineer for the United States Army," he continued. "He worked mostly on developing plans to cut off the Coutts commune from the rest of the country. The thought at the time was that if they starved the Coutts of resources, the community would fall." He sighed, leaning back in the chair. "How wrong they were, right? They didn't realize we had God on our side.

"One year into his service, Avi got cancer — Hodgkin's lymphoma. And you know what the United States government did for him? Nothing. After years of service to them, they did *nothing* but tell him to submit an insurance claim. Avi saw the writing on the wall. He was a young man with plenty of life to live. He realized who was actually in power. So, your leader, Avi, became a spy — a rebel, if you will — for the Coutts when Peter developed the Coutts Organization Non-Profit. He was among the first to directly benefit from the free medical care there. They treated his cancer. They saved his life. And he provided them with invaluable information about what the government was aiming to do. He was even awarded honors for his role in helping the organization expand."

These were lies. They had to be lies. Avi would have told us if he had helped the Coutts.

"You're lying," I said, my voice hoarse. But my heart beat wildly against my claim. Everything this man was saying had the potential to be true. Didn't it? Or was I just delirious after spending so long in my cell?

"Am I?" The man stuck out his bottom lip and raised his brows. "After Avi recovered, he realized the benefits of the commune were too great. He had access to excellent medical care. Engineers. Materials that the United States no longer had when trade partners had been disrupted. He joined the cause, and..." he chortled, "for a while he was a great asset.

"But Avi was hungry for power. He wanted a higher position in the organization. He petitioned Peter many times about how he would benefit the commune with a higher rank. But Peter, at the time, only believed in his own blood working at the highest level of power. Avi didn't like that. So he retreated back to the Outside to build a group of rebels. And that, unfortunately, included you."

The room was spinning now, and I couldn't keep my focus on the mirror.

"And I'm supposed to just take your word for this?" I asked, shaking my head. "I'm not that stupid."

"Oh no," Number 11 said. "I had a suspicion you'd like to see proof." He turned toward the mirror. "Isaiah?"

Silence hung momentarily before I heard footsteps in the hall. The door opened. The young Hunter who had led me here entered, a white folder in his hand. He smiled at me before he plopped it down on the table between us.

"Let me help you there," he said maliciously, opening it.

Photographs spilled out. Black and white features,

colored images, and newspaper clippings of all different sizes. I didn't want to know. I didn't want to look.

But I did anyway.

On top, a black-and-white photo depicted a younger and trimmer version of Avi alongside a small group of men. His dark skin and features stood starkly against the white men surrounding him. But on the left, clear as day, stood Peter Coutts.

There were other photographs. Avi in meeting rooms with men in Hunter uniforms. Avi waving out a car window with a Hunter in the driver's seat. Avi visiting Coutts Peak.

The proof was there. Clear as day. I closed my eyes and looked away, heart pounding. What did this mean? Surely, Avi was still coordinating the rebellion for the good of the Centre, wasn't he? Plenty of people made bad choices, realized their mistakes, and changed.

But deep within me, I knew this was bad news.

"That man you're following is going to get you and all of your friends killed," the man said, more softly this time. He dipped his chin and caught my gaze. "It's not too late, you know. To help us."

The cuffs around my hands and legs said otherwise.

"He's a smart man," I countered, leaning back, away from the pictures. "He knows what he's doing."

"Ah." The man nodded, looking down at the table. He drummed his thick fingers against it, and it made a *thud-thud-thud* sound. "If he were so smart, he wouldn't have let his own men be captured now, would he?"

I looked up. A knowing smile spread slowly across his face, distorting it in a way that made me squirm in my seat.

"You're not going to get anything from me," I said sternly, narrowing my gaze.

"I'm not?" He phrased it as a question. "Now what

makes you think that?" He was baiting me, trying to corner me into a response I didn't want to give.

"Because I'm not gonna tell you shit."

I felt firm in my decision. It was something Avi had taught us, and something I was more than willing to do. Coutts apologist or not, without Avi, without the Centre, my group would be dead. Mia would not have a father. Holli, Sid, Maura, and I would never have survived. I owed Avi and the Centre for keeping us safe, for giving us a life and a purpose in the horrible world we'd been thrust into.

"I think you might," the Hunter said, his voice light and airy. "Under the right circumstances, that is."

"Abso-fucking-lutely not."

His eyes narrowed. "Look at you," he said, studying my face. "What leverage do you think you have here?" He raised his eyebrows and then laughed. "I, on the other hand, have all kinds of tools at my disposal. I would have no issues finding out who you were before you came here. What kind of loyalties you have, the people you care about. I could have them all killed one by one, while I sit here and rip out your fingernails." He smiled.

"I. Won't. Tell. You. Shit." I spit each word.

The man leaned forward, pressing his chest against the table. "I am a *merciful* man," he sneered. "I believe in giving everyone a chance before we do anything too…irrational. Now, maybe you've been led astray. Maybe you've been fed lies and come to believe them. Avi is a convincing man. You know, we Coutts can be very forgiving."

"Forgiving?" It was my turn to laugh, and I threw my head back as I cackled, eyes watering from the absurdity of it all. "How the hell do you define *forgiveness*? You denied people help when they needed it. You let them die. You *kill* people. I've seen you. That's not *forgiveness*. That's insanity.

All under the name of God? You're as bad as the people you condemn — hell, you're worse!"

His nostrils flared.

"You dare question the word of God? Peter's word?"

"Peter is nothing more than a clown dressed up in a priest's clothes," I snarled. "He's a con man. A man who's always been out for his own self-interest. He has no desire to make the world a better place or to help the common man. He has no desire to spread the good word of God. GOD would not have done what he did. He wouldn't have left millions to die because they disagreed with him. There is no God I know that would bless that—"

I felt my nose crack, the warm drip of blood begin from somewhere inside my broken capillaries. I sputtered, stunned by the impact, choking on the steady red flow that dripped out of my nose, onto my chest, arms, and the table in front of me.

"You're sent by the devil," the Hunter hissed, caressing the knuckles that had just made impact with my face. "You're a blasphemous, wicked soul. And you deserve what will come to you." The smile was back. I could see it through my watering eyes. "You just wait. I'll get the information I need, one way or another. By the time I'm done with you, you'll willingly give up every single rebel you know."

He stood, scratching the chair backward across the floor as he stood to his full height. The only point of victory I had was that he still massaged his knuckles as he left the room.

I moaned, letting my head fall backward, swallowing the sharp iron taste of blood that coated my throat. My face ached. But I couldn't focus on that. Worse things were coming my way, and fast. I had little idea of where the rebels were now, but I knew it was likely a matter of hours before they began infiltrating the commune and revealing how many Hunters they'd turned.

I couldn't wait for that. I'd be one of the first they tortured for information. Desperation led to violence, and I'd be caught in the middle. I needed to get out of here before any of that happened, or else I faced certain death.

I just wished I knew how.

14

MAURA

The vantage point at the top of the hill gave me a clear view of the crumbling office buildings and the Waste Center. To my right, empty farmlands disappeared against the dark sky. From the Waste Center, a spotlight cast out bright, artificial light, washing over the buildings and into the darkness beyond from left to right, then back again. Everything else was bathed in a strange, blue light that radiated from the Waste Center's central structure.

The light illuminated a handful of guards patrolling the area, marching up and down the cracked sidewalks, their shadows dragging behind them like oil stains. Gabriel had mentioned the patrols, but he'd failed to mention the huge spotlight. Standing between me and the closest building was a wide open hill I'd need to cross. By my count, the spotlight came around every sixty-two seconds. A guard rounded the end of the buildings every three minutes. I would need to time my run down the hill *exactly*.

My body was beginning to fail. Every muscle ached, every bone crackled with pain. My ankle had gone numb, which was most likely a bad sign, but I had no time to worry. If the Hunters found me now, there would be no surviving it. There would be no chance of ever seeing Morgan again. There would be no chance of saving Eli from whatever fate awaited him.

I pushed away from the tree I had hidden behind, finding my footing. Just one more run and then I could rest. The spotlight did its sweep, starting at the middle of the hill, washing down across the Waste Center and brick buildings beyond. It shone against broken glass windows, the collapsed ceilings, the sunken awnings over doors. It highlighted green moss growing between the bricks, the forgotten cars, and the cracked road littered with garbage from another time. It bounced off the Hunter's helmets, weapons, and fancy trucks, slowing as it reached the end of the short row of buildings.

Then, it swung back the other way.

I counted five Hunters on patrol in the broken roadway. Friendlies or not, this was an incredibly risky plan. But what choice did I have? I couldn't stay hidden in the trees, and I couldn't go elsewhere. This was where Gabriel had said to go, and I had no other option but to trust him.

The spotlight reached the hill again. Swept left, then right. The guard rounded the corner. I inhaled deeply, bracing myself against the tree. The spotlight swept over the buildings to the other end, then came back. I eyed the back exit door I planned on running to. The spotlight stopped at the hill, then went right.

I bolted.

The spotlight moved so fast it was impossible to chase, even as the slope helped me pick up speed. It was steeper than I remembered, and I felt my legs and feet get away from me. They moved too fast, too uncontrollably for me to stop, until…

My foot caught on something — a branch, a rock, a

cluster of dead grass — I'd never be sure. I tripped in slow motion, watching the ground roll beneath me as I tumbled over my legs. I landed harshly on solid earth, scraping up my arms and face as I bounced down the hill. My bandaged ankle hit solid ground.

I heard myself scream.

No!

I grit my teeth together, trying to muffle the yell, my neck muscles straining as I fought against it. The pain was blinding, a rush of agony that filled my nerves. I skidded to a stop at the end of the hill, desperate to find my bearings.

The spotlight. Where was it?

I saw it in the distance, its glow rushing back over the buildings as though it were eager to expose me. I lay out in the open, pain filling every empty crevice in my body.

Get up, get up, get up!

I grunted, moaning as I got back to my feet on wobbly legs. My body burned, ached, and protested. I tasted dirt. A stitch in my side made it impossible to straighten, but I had enough adrenaline left to hobble to the door.

The light's edge shone upon the hill, lighting up the dead grass. With horror, I saw I had kicked up dirt and left a long, indented trail. It didn't matter. There was nothing I could do to hide it. The light came, and I pressed myself up against the back of the building, squeezing my eyes closed as if that would help me blend in.

This was it. Either they would see me under that spotlight or they would miss me. Would they notice the trail? How it led right to the bottom of the hill, close to the EXIT door where I stood, trembling?

I tried to stay flat, but my chest heaved as I struggled to breathe against the pain of my injuries and the exertion I'd put my body through. Tears leaked from my eyes. I was inches away from the door, and I stuck my hand out for the handle. Maybe. Maybe…

But the light hit me. I saw it creep up against the side of the building, washing over my side. At this angle, I was halfway hidden, but I was still outside the door. I should've gone slower. If I hadn't fallen, I'd be inside right now.

Time slowed. I heard chatter from somewhere in the distance. Some mechanical thing in the Waste Center made a strange call into the night. I could've sworn the spotlight stayed on me for a minute, and I held my breath.

Think, Maura.

What would be the punishment for a rebel wife, the daughter of the Prophet, who made herself into a martyr, and then pretended to be pregnant? What would be the punishment if she ran away a the third time?

Death.

There was no other option. Father would never forgive this. His men would never forgive this. Andrew, Abigail, and the entire slew of loyal Hunters would chase me down and make an example out of me. They wouldn't hesitate. They would find ways to justify it. And in the midst of fear, they would use me as the scapegoat to get everyone to comply with whatever they decided came next.

The rebellion would die.

For a moment, I resigned myself to this being the truth, and then the light faded. It swept away, past the edge of the building, covering me in darkness. The breath came out of my mouth and nose so fast I could've vomited along with it. I yanked the door open and fell inside the dark interior of the office building.

My heart beat in my ears, but otherwise, the world was silent. I crept along the back wall of the room, careful to avoid any glass. My leg ached. The wound pulsed beneath my bandages and boot. The scratches from my fall were wet with blood. But there was no place to rest. Not yet.

With no windows, the office was pitch black; the spotlight remaining like an aftershock in my peripheral vision. I steadied my breathing while my eyes adjusted and the cubicles came into view. It felt like years had passed since I'd been here, even though I knew it had only been months. And at once, the ache in my heart unfurled, reminding me of how fragile things always seemed to be. We had been together once, running from the same enemy. And now, we were back, fighting them in our own separate ways.

I swallowed, wincing at my dry throat. How long had it been since I'd had water? Food? Would a rebel Hunter find me and help me, or was I doomed to be trapped here until I starved?

Enough.

These compounding thoughts were unhelpful. I needed to stay alive. Wasn't that enough to focus on? Why did my mind insist on thinking about things I had no control over at the worst times?

Focus.

I needed to get to a window so I could see what was going on outside, to know if I needed to run again. And where would I even go? The next building? Back up the hill? My body was in no shape to even think about moving that far. I desperately needed rest.

One. Thing. At. A. Time.

The window. I edged along the hallway that led to the center of the building, careful to keep the direction of the EXIT door in mind. Smashed windows lined the front of the building, giving a clear view into the rest of the structure. If I moved from the hallway, I'd be immediately visible. The spotlight swept through, illuminating thousands of glass shards scattered across the carpeted floor.

I waited, watching the guards move up and down the sidewalk outside. Had the person with the spotlight seen me? Would they direct the Hunters to infiltrate the building and sweep it until they carried me out? I thought about running. I thought about the energy it would take to get my body to a different floor or building, and I knew instantly it wasn't feasible.

As dangerous as it was to stay on the ground floor, it would be more dangerous to risk putting my body through more. Rest was a priority. Without it, I wouldn't be able to do anything.

So, I retreated into the hallway, finding refuge in one of the blue cubicles. Under the desk, I curled up on the dirty carpet, watching the spotlight seep into the building's crevices with hypnotizing rhythm.

Back and forth. Back and forth.

The floor was rough beneath me. I felt every throb of pain climb into my nerves, reminding me of how poorly I'd treated my body these past few days and how grateful I was to still be alive. Sleep came like a gentle wave, and I welcomed it, letting my body give in to the rest it so sorely needed.

WITH A GASP, I woke from my deep slumber, nearly hitting my head on the desk I'd fallen asleep beneath. Something had pulled me from my murky dreams. Despite the frigid air, sweat clung to my armpits, back, and upper lip. My ankle ached. I barely had enough saliva in my dry mouth to swallow.

Voices split the quiet. Men. Laughing, then talking. I couldn't make out what they were saying. It didn't sound like they were inside the building, but they were still too close for my liking. I hadn't hidden myself very well. Anyone could walk through this building with a flashlight, turn the corner, and find me.

I needed to move.

Gingerly, I got to my feet, careful not to put too much weight on my bad ankle. Keeping myself in a low squat, I peered down the dark hallway toward the lobby of shattered glass.

Empty.

Good.

I needed to get closer if I wanted to see anything.

Using the cubicle walls as my support, I tip-toed down the hall, trying to focus on the voices, on the way the textured wall felt beneath my fingers. Anything to avoid thinking about the way my ankle ached. Once the cubicles ended, I passed two rooms with glass windows until I was far enough to peer into what had once been an office lobby.

Standing near the front, a few feet away from what had once been a set of glass double doors, were two Hunters.

God help me!

I shot backward on my heels. Pressed my back up against the wall. Lost the ability to breathe.

"— get your facts straight, Murphy." One guard chuckled. I watched his shadow move as the spotlight swept in front of the entryway.

"I'm not kidding," came the response from the other.

I exhaled. Rubbed my hand down my face. I peered out the lobby doors, careful to keep myself hidden in the shadows. A truck passed the building's entrance, the sound of its engine disappearing in the distance.

"They would've radioed."

"They're trying to assess the situation," the man named Murphy insisted.

"Alright, then don't panic until they say to panic."

"But who would be approaching the borders?" Murphy questioned.

"Probably some folks who left and want to come back. They saw how sinful the world outside was and are coming home with their tails between their legs to beg forgiveness. Is that really so hard to believe?"

"That's not what they said when I heard them over the radio."

"Murphy, you're not even authorized to be on that channel. You shouldn't be listening to it, alright?" The voice was stern. Accusatory. The man named Murphy didn't respond.

A body shifted. They were too close. I eyed the stairs. I couldn't climb them without being completely exposed.

The guard sighed. "Listen, I know for a fact they've captured some of the rebels already. The Prophet knows what to do; he's commanded interrogation of the rebels to figure out their positions and plans. One of them was from an actual caravan taking people away from our holy lands into their god-forsaken hellhole. Can you believe that? He's down in the Pit now."

My heart slowed. It might've stopped beating. Because I knew that story. Silas had told it to me the other day.

They have Eli.

"Really?" The responding voice sounded so young and eager, so fresh and willing to believe. I had once sounded that way, I was sure.

"Yes." And that voice, the knowing, certain voice, eased the doubt with just its tone. "Trust they know what they're doing. The Prophet sees all. He knows all. We're not always privy to that knowledge, but faith goes a long way. You'll see."

"Praise God. Praise the Prophet," the young man said.

"Indeed," agreed the older Hunter.

The Pit. I had never heard of it, but it sounded like a place the Hunters monitored. A prison, where they kept rebels. Rebels like Eli. But something else was happening. Something the Hunters didn't want to publicize or make known to all. That meant it was something they hoped to contain and hide.

That sounded like the beginning of a rebellion.

Hope blossomed in my chest. Avi, Silas, and Gabriel had come up with detailed plans and timeframes for how to infiltrate the commune most effectively. They would take it by surprise. In moments, Father's own Hunters would turn against him — aiming their guns not at his enemies, but at him. The abruptness would give them little time to react or prepare.

So we hoped.

"Who has you out here?" I heard the older Hunter question.

"Hunter Silas," Murphy responded.

The older Hunter scoffed.

"Is there a problem, sir?"

"Hunter Silas." The older Hunter spat on the floor. "I didn't realize he was still calling stationing orders."

"Why's that?"

The older Hunter shifted his stance. "Let's just say, just because he's Luke's son, doesn't mean he supports the cause. I believe he achieved his position without the right intentions."

"You mean—?"

"He is not a righteous follower of God. Now, you didn't hear it from me, but I'm not the only one who's suspicious. He's been making strange disappearances, trips nobody has authorized. He flies under the radar, or at least he thinks he does. But there's been plenty of talk. So watch your back and watch what you say. Remember, if he asks anything of you that goes against what the Prophet proclaims, you must reveal this to the heads. Any blemish on the team is a blemish on us all. We can't have that kind of cancer spreading through our ranks."

"Wow," the young Hunter said. "I had no idea a high-ranking Hunter would be capable of such disloyalty."

"You'd be surprised," the older man said with a sigh. "The Devil is a trickster. Not everyone here is as pure of heart as most of us. God tests us all in peculiar ways."

"Mm-hmm."

My heart beat in my ears again. Pain rose up my calf. I desperately needed water. But all of that was dulled by my fear.

I needed to warn Silas.

I needed to rescue Eli.

But without a medical team or clear friendlies to partner up with, I was a sitting duck. I had critical information that might save their lives, and there was absolutely nothing I could do with it.

15

MAURA

WITH THE STAIRS not being an option and the guards lingering by the front door, I had no choice but to retreat to my cubicle. I used some of the furniture to create a makeshift barrier before curling up under the desk, so exhausted not even my adrenaline kept me awake. I drifted in and out of sleep. Occasionally, a truck's rumble would startle me, only to fade away, and then, I'd drift once more.

Dawn came, lightening the room. New voices echoed from the sidewalk, forcing me out of my exhaustion. Someone coughed. The sound was so close.

Too close.

Footsteps came next, crunching glass beneath heavy boots. I shot up. My heart was off again, pounding in my chest. I peered through the piled-up furniture, seeing nothing but rows of cubicles. Icy fear gripped my neck.

Heavy footsteps echoed down the hallway. I eyed the EXIT sign in the corner of the room. How long would it take me to run out the door? Would they see me? Could I make it up the hill? Back into the forest? My ankle twinged as if to tell me the thought was ridiculous.

I inhaled a shaky breath and got to my knees, gripping the side of the cubicle.

"287," whispered a voice. A *familiar* voice.

I pushed aside the furniture and crawled out from beneath the desk. The person approaching was just a shadow, but his wide frame was a dead giveaway.

"287," he called again.

"Zeke?"

He craned his neck toward my voice as I emerged fully from the cubicle, stumbling toward him. A slow smile spread across his boyish features.

"Maura," he whispered. "It's good to see you."

"What are you doing all the way out here?"

He chuckled. "They've got me out here lookin' for you."

I fell into his arms, squeezing him, my muscles quivering as I let the tension of the last few days go. A familiar face. A friendly. Someone I knew. The comfort brought me to tears, and I shuddered against him.

"Hey," he soothed, patting the back of my head. "It's alright, yeah? You alright?"

He gripped my shoulders and held me at arm's length. I pressed my trembling lips closed and nodded.

"Good," he said. "You're alright. It'll all be alright."

I had so many questions, so much information to give to him, but all I could do was cry. I was so tired. So sore. So relieved. Zeke slid his arm around my neck as he moved us both through the office, back toward the hallway.

"It's lucky you made it out when you did," he said. "They've been ramping up security almost everywhere. But you'll be safe here. Friendlies outnumber loyalists in the Waste Center, so the risk of you being found is low. Silas asked me to bring you here."

We stopped walking. I looked up at a bathroom door.

This was where Holli and Mia had once hidden, back when we had sheltered here months ago.

"In here?" I asked, already hating the idea of being back in total darkness.

He nodded apologetically, then dug through his pocket to produce a flashlight, which he handed to me. I took it, running my fingers up over the ribbed side.

"There are provisions in there. A small knife. Some clothing. I couldn't take much without being noticed, but it should hold you over for a few days if necessary."

"A few days?" My voice crackled. "I don't have a few days."

He raised his thick eyebrows. "You need to wait for transport, but we can't have anyone moving out right now since the rebels have moved in. Too many eyes watching."

"But *Silas* is in danger. My friend, Eli. He's been taken." I had finally found my words, and they all came pouring out too fast. "I overheard a Hunter last night speaking about how they can't trust Silas, how he got his position just because he's Luke's son, and that he's not devout enough. That his behavior is suspicious. And, and, and, Eli. They took him." I gestured wildly toward the front door. "He was rescuing the refugees from the commune, and the Hunters captured him, and they're holding him somewhere called the Pit, and we have to find him—"

"Maura," Zeke said, his tone calm and understanding. "Breathe."

"I can't just…they're out there…in danger!"

"I know. They know. Rebellion *is* dangerous. Silas knows the risks he's taken."

"But Eli—"

"Also knew the risks. I know this is hard, but we have to let the rebels move in first before we can do anything. The Pit is highly guarded, highly secretive. I know very little about it except that it's heavily guarded inside the Waste Center. Trying to get in would be futile."

"So let me join you!" I pressed. I didn't want to stay here alone. "I can fight."

He glanced down at my leg but said nothing. "You can't. It's…too dangerous."

"You *just* said it was fine that people put themselves in danger if they knew the risks." Anger rose in my chest, drowning the pain in my body. "So why can't I? Why can't I fight?"

"Maura, you're too valuable."

I scoffed. "Too valuable, and that's why you're leaving me here, alone with no protection?"

Zeke shook his head. "This is the safest place for you right now. I *promise* we'll be back for you once we've cleared a safe area. Then you can help us fight."

I groaned in frustration. "How *long*?" I heard myself whine, but couldn't help it.

He sighed. "Not long now."

The realization dawned on me. "So Avi has moved in?" I asked. "They're at the gates?"

"Further out," Zeke confirmed. "Sciences and Innovations is in chaos right now. Peter called for all the high-level Hunters to retreat to the Peak so they can coordinate. They know something's going on." He shifted his weight. "Right now, it sounds like they don't think the rebels are much of a match for the Hunters. They probably think they can subdue them in a few hours. But come morning, the Hunters will begin to turn. You'll need to stay hidden at least until then."

I knew I needed to accept my defeat. But staying here felt so useless and meaningless after everything I'd been through. I wanted to help. I wanted to know what was going on, not be kept in a dark little box until someone told me it was safe.

But I was not in charge.

"Will you make sure Eli is a priority?" I begged. "Please. I don't know how long they've had him or what they've..." My voice cracked, and I swallowed my fear. "...what they've done to him." I blinked back my tears and grimaced.

Zeke took a deep breath. "I can't make *any* promises, Maura. But I'll relay the information to Silas, okay? You know he'll do what he can."

I wanted to feel relieved, but I knew Silas could only do so much. I couldn't expect an individual rescue from him. Not with the entire rebellion on his back.

"Thank you," I said, anyway.

Zeke nodded and then opened the door, revealing the dark room. I clicked on the flashlight, bouncing light off the walls, stalls, and mirrors, and stepped inside.

"Rest," he said. "You need it. We'll check in on you as much as we can."

"Okay," I answered, watching in the mirror as he closed the door.

I placed the flashlight in one of the sinks so that it beamed off the ceiling, brightening the room. Radio static came from outside the door. I heard Zeke's heavy footfalls disappear as he left the building.

Three stalls, sinks, and mirrors made up the bathroom. A cobweb-covered bucket and mop stood in the corner, and I approached, looking inside. Stuffed beside the mop was a canvas backpack.

I pulled it between my legs as I settled on the ground and opened the flap. Inside were a thin blanket and a canteen of water. Binoculars, a small pocket knife, and a beige jumpsuit that seemed slightly too big but preferable to what I wore now. A pair of socks, gloves, and a knitted hat. Provisions they often sent the Hunters out with.

I ate and drank first. I tried to go slow, to relish the calories my body so desperately needed, but before long, my hunger took over and I blew through three bags of provisions and half of my water.

Next, I peeled off the dirty clothes I'd found at the hospital, redressing in the jumpsuit, new socks, gloves, and the hat. Even though I had the privacy and time, I resisted looking at my injuries. There was nothing I could do for myself right now. So I lay up against the wall and tried to rest.

It was futile. My mind moved a million miles a minute. Despite the cold outside, it felt stifling in here, which had nothing to do with the weather. Urgency ached in my limbs. I knew what my instructions were. I knew I was safe here. But how could I sit here and wait for things to happen?

I couldn't.

Experience had taught me not to wait for someone to come and rescue me. Chances were, nobody would come. What had waiting ever brought me? Pain? Misery? Disappointment? The only person who could save me was me.

I got to my feet. The backpack felt light on my shoulders. I kept the knife gripped in one hand, the flashlight in the other. Carefully, I approached the door. Light spilled through the crack, and I paused for a minute to allow my eyes to adjust. I clicked off the flashlight and stuck my head out.

Bright sunlight shone through the entryway's windows. I paused, breathing through my nose as I listened for noise. A steady hum of movement came from somewhere beyond the building, but there was nothing inside. Just to be sure, I turned back to the bathroom, found a loose piece of tile, and chucked it out into the hallway. It clattered against the dusty linoleum. I sucked in a breath and waited for footsteps.

None came.

Good.

I slipped through the crack and into the hallway, testing the balance of my bad ankle. It was fine enough. I could, at the very least, make it up the stairs now so I could see what was going on beyond the buildings. Zeke had mentioned the Pit was guarded in the Waste Center. I wanted to see if it was feasible for me to get there.

I crouched as I traveled the hallway, stepping lightly, careful to position my weight on my good leg. The EXIT door was behind me, if I needed it. A truck rumbled by outside, passing without incident. Someone's voice carried with the wind, their words indistinguishable. I kept moving until I reached the lobby area.

Glass covered the floor, but if I was careful, I could avoid most of it. My heart thudded in anticipation, and I wiped my sweaty palms against the legs of my jumpsuit. I glanced at the street, then back up the wide open stairs. All it took was one loyal Hunter to pass those doors to see me.

I'd need to run.

A muffled voice came from the street. A loud laugh. Then, silence, again.

Waiting didn't make this any safer.

I shot out from the hallway and darted up the stairs, taking them two at a time. The sound of my boots on the floor bounced off the high ceilings and shattered window frames. I worried about the noise, but couldn't very well take it back now.

The world slowed. The stairs felt too long, too high, too endless. The second floor loomed far. I imagined a shadow coming around the corner, gun drawn, aimed at my temple. The sound of my body thudding down the stairs. What pain awaited Eli and Silas if I didn't get to them in time.

I reached the top. My boots skidded around the corner as I fell to my knees, hiding behind a half-wall that surrounded the stairs. This floor had a wraparound hallway, leading to offices on all sides. I chose one that looked out toward the street and scurried inside. Half-drawn blinds covered two large windows. I kept my body close to the wall. A truck drove back up the road, passing a few ambling Hunters on the sidewalk. I held my breath. Made my way to the blinds. Tugged at the cord to let them uncurl to the bottom. The room darkened. I released my breath.

After closing the door to the office, I used a spare chair to lock the handle from the inside, then settled on the ground near the window. Step one: complete. At least now I had a visual of what was happening. Even though I knew Silas and Zeke were looking out for my safety, I felt ignored. Was I simply a person of convenience? Utilized when useful and then hidden away until I came in handy again?

The men had no problem putting me front and center when they needed a martyr. I'd put myself in harm's way. I'd confronted my greatest fear. I'd made it known that I wanted to fight. But now I was expected to sit in a dark bathroom waiting for rescue?

No. I was tired of being the damsel in distress.

I adjusted the blinds for an inconspicuous view out toward the Waste Center. I didn't need help. I had shown myself to be powerful, brave, and determined.

I would find Eli and get that information to Silas one way or another.

16

MARA

THE DAY PASSED SLOWLY. I spent most of it lying flat against the wall, peering through the binoculars. I could see between two of the buildings if I situated myself just right. Indents began to form around my eyes from where I held the binoculars up. The rug scratched through my jumpsuit, rubbing my knees raw. My neck ached from strain.

But I had information.

I'd scribbled everything I'd discovered on a blank notepad. Hunter trucks drove through the town and followed a route. They drove in from the left, all the way down the single road until they had to turn around. Then, they drove back out the way they came, doing the same thing in the empty area between the office buildings and the entrance to the Waste Center. The whole route took just over three minutes.

Two new Hunters had joined the existing patrols, and they followed a route, too. Two walked through alleyways. Three stayed on the sidewalks. Two more were stationed at the Waste Center's entrance.

But beyond the building was more interesting. Since I'd

started watching, dozens of trucks had driven in and out of the Waste Center area. Indistinguishable from each other, the trucks revealed a path. They drove in the entrance, rounding three large piles of waste. Then, they vanished somewhere behind the building blocking my view. They reappeared between the spacious alleyway, then disappeared between two high mounds of trash. All the trucks went in and exited from the same area.

Something was there, and I believed it was a way in.

By the time the sun lowered in the west, I'd finished another pack of rations. My body felt stronger and well-rested, even though every time I twisted my ankle, it throbbed. But it supported my weight. I could likely run a short distance on it. And that's all I needed. I still refused to look at the injury. Better to wait. Better not to know.

Too much time had passed. But Zeke had been right. Rushing in before the rebels came would be foolish. Even if I *could* sneak past the guards on the sidewalks, the trucks patrolling the roads, and the security inside the Waste Center, I did not know what waited for me beyond. A bubble of frustration came with the realization that he'd been right, and that there was simply nothing I could do for Eli right now.

A deafening bang rang out, strong enough to rattle my window. I startled, pushing away from the glass and pressing up against the wall. The world slowed, the space around me warping. My breath came in bursts. Every muscle tightened. I couldn't place the source of the noise, and I waited for someone to come crashing up the stairs, through my measly barricade, and hold me at gunpoint. With shaking hands, I reached for my pack, fumbling for my singular weapon.

The knife felt futile and pathetic in my grip. Nothing like the gun Sid had armed me with when we'd run from

Coal Creek. It didn't matter. Gun or knife, I wouldn't be able to defend myself against a Hunter with an automatic weapon. They held all the leverage, and they knew it.

Another bang came, this one not as loud. Behind the blinds, the glass shivered in its frame. I inhaled through my nose, listening for danger over the noise of my thudding heart. I should get on my feet. I should look out the window. But I was frozen with fear, clutching the knife handle for dear life as if it would do anything to protect me. What would I do if someone burst in here? I had no exit strategy.

I needed to move.

I gathered my courage and peered out through a break in the blinds. Smoke billowed from the building on my left. More came from the Waste Center. Even from inside, the air smelled acrid.

Shouts came from below the building, from the street, and beyond. Another bang rang out, even farther this time. I exhaled through my mouth. The noise hadn't come from inside my building, but it'd been close. Something was happening at the Waste Center. I lifted the binoculars and peered out.

Everything had changed. My breath caught in my throat as I tried to make sense of what was happening. Nearly twenty trucks had arrived at the gate of the Waste Center, and men in Hunter uniforms and regular clothes poured out, spreading themselves thin, then converging as they traveled down the truck route.

The rebels.

Below, Hunters struggled against each other. Three on two. One on one. It was hard to tell who was who. Were there more rebels or loyalists? The combat had happened so suddenly; they swung at each other, guns forgotten, grunting and yelling through the chaos. I watched one man take another out at the knees, subduing him with his hands behind his back. Another man put up a good fight, but after a hit to the face that knocked him out cold, the other Hunters secured his arms behind his back and left him face down on the sidewalk. One spoke into his radio. A truck barreled around the corner, stopping in front of the tied-up men, who were both put into the back seat.

At the entrance to the Waste Center, trucks began to move, forming a barricade at the gates, while the rest disappeared behind the mounds of trash.

Another bang, accompanied by flying waste. Someone yelled. Someone else fired a gun.

My heart rattled. This was it. The rebellion was here.

I PACKED MY BAG. With everyone distracted, I knew if I wanted to move, I needed to do it now. Whoever was guarding the Waste Center would either be subdued or friendly — I hoped. If I could find my way inside, Silas and the rebels would have no excuse not to let me be part of their plans. And then, I could make sure I got to Eli.

First, I needed to get closer.

The Hunter patrols had abandoned their posts on the sidewalks below the building to join whatever was going on inside the Waste Center. I was free to get across to the other row of buildings for a better visual. From there, I'd figure out a way into the Waste Center and find Silas. If all the fighting was happening out in the open, nobody would spare me a second glance.

The plan was flimsy at best, but I couldn't stay here. I needed to do *something*.

I slung my backpack over my shoulders, keeping the knife in one hand. I removed the chair from the door and opened it, traveling into the well-lit hallway. It was freeing not to have to worry about noise, but my tight muscles protested every movement. My ankle throbbed, but I didn't mind. The dull ache reminded me I was still here. Still alive. That my body, despite all of its injuries, still worked.

A deep rumble shook the building. I stumbled down the stairs, clutching the railing for balance. The noise settled as I approached the lobby, trying to keep my feet light across the glass. I crossed the threshold into a shattered waiting area, keeping myself halfway hidden by the receptionist desk. From here, the street looked empty.

Someone shouted in the distance; an urgent, panicked yell. My heart squeezed, and I took a few shaky breaths before approaching the front doors. I rose to full height, then peered out under the awning into the bright sunshine.

The road was empty. No trucks. No people. Across the street, similar buildings with sagging roofs and shattered windows reflected the one I stood in. Ahead, a wide alleyway provided ample shadows to hide in. I just needed to get there so I could see the entrance to the Waste Center, and if there was a way I could get inside.

I just need to cross the street.

I pressed my toe against solid ground and rotated my injured ankle, gritting my teeth against sharp stabs of pain. It hurt, but not enough that I couldn't run.

Just get across the street.

I readied my muscles, my head on a swivel as I inched out onto the sidewalk. The putrid scene of rot and garbage filled the air, so strong it made my eyes water. I swallowed my disgust and tucked my nose into the jumpsuit's collar. The long street was empty. But it might not be for long. Now was my chance.

I looked left. Looked right. Looked up at the Waste

Center between the buildings. Electricity crackled somewhere in the distance. An engine revved. The distance between where I stood and where I needed to go felt like miles. Someone shouted in the distance. Another rumble came.

I rose on the balls of my feet and darted out into the street.

It was like running through molasses. My legs weakened as I dragged myself across the crumbling pavement, my ankle like an anchor in water. I was so exposed, and the realization sent my stomach plummeting with fear. I gasped for air, too aware of how pitiful the knife was in my hand. I was so vulnerable. How could I have thought this was a good idea?

The shadowed alley loomed ahead. Anyone could be waiting for me there. I had assumed the Hunters who subdued the others were the rebels, but I could have been mistaken. I could be running right into my enemy. After everything, one foolish mistake and my desperate need to rescue Eli would give them exactly what they wanted.

I waited for bullets to pierce me. For someone to shout into the wind that they'd found the heathen, Maura Coutts. I waited for strong hands to pull me back by my hair. An angry voice to snarl in my ear. But miraculously, the tips of my boots met the opposite sidewalk, leaving behind the faded yellow lines and weed-infested pavement.

My heart thundered in my chest, throat, and ears. Carefully, I slipped into the shadows between the buildings, willing my eyes to adjust faster so I could see if there was a threat. I pressed my body against the brick. Potholes and trash that had blown over from the Waste Center settled in the alleyway's cracks and corners. Faded graffiti lined the brick walls, forgotten words and symbols that had once meant something to someone.

I traveled down the well-worn path toward the Waste Center's border, eager to get away from the open space. Dirt and debris nearly concealed the road I approached. From here, it was maybe fifty feet to the Waste Center's fence. I gripped the edge of the brick building, the texture gritty beneath my fingers, and peered around.

A truck barreled through the entrance, making a quick turn so fast it kicked up dirt beneath its tires. I gasped, instantly pulling myself back into the shadows. My mind went blank with fear.

I'd been visible. Someone looking this way would've seen me. It would've been a miracle if they hadn't. A panicked breath rose up my throat, making my eyes water. I couldn't catch my breath. The world spun around me, and I lost my footing. My shoulders hit the wall behind me.

What now?

The world felt too big, too open, too exposed, even in the dark alley. I couldn't stay here. I commanded my legs to move, and they obeyed too slowly. With the world unsteady around me, I stumbled against the side of the building, back toward the street I'd run from. Silas had been right. I should've just waited in the bathroom for rescue. This was stupid. Reckless.

I knew in my heart that I'd been caught.

At the edge of the building, I peeked my head out into the sunlight. The roar of an engine came from my right. They were coming, and I had a decision to make — wait to see if they were friendlies or retreat into the building. My limbs trembled. Fear encouraged me to cross the street back into the familiar building.

As I crossed the road, the sun was hot on my sweaty neck as if telling me to turn around. I couldn't now. I hurried across the pavement, glancing over my shoulder for the truck. The building stood in front of me, shattered glass glinting in the sun.

An engine roared. Tires squealed as they rounded the end of the buildings and sped down the pavement toward me. I felt its presence, the eyes inside the car. If they hadn't noticed me before, surely they noticed me now. I hadn't gotten inside in time. The only hope I had left was that the people driving the truck were friendlies.

It was useless to hide now. My ankle couldn't support any kind of running. I turned on my heel, steeling myself to face whatever awaited me head-on. The Hunter's truck rolled to a stop in front of me. A shadow shifted behind the tinted glass, and I heard the handle open on the passenger side. The door popped open, and the person inside pushed it outward, revealing the inside of the truck.

A man dressed head to toe in a Hunter's uniform sat behind the driver's seat. I stood, frozen and uncertain.

Friendly or not friendly?

As if to answer my question, the Hunter took both hands to the side of his helmet and lifted it, revealing his features in slow motion. Features I had become so intimately familiar with. The strong jaw with loosening jowls. The stubbled chin. The familiar blue eyes.

The Hunter in the driver's seat was Andrew.

17

MAURA

NOT FRIENDLY.

I went stiff. Every thought I had about getting to the Waste Center, about rescuing Eli, and joining the rebellion popped like a balloon. Right up there with Father, Luke, and Abigail, Andrew would be the least forgiving of my transgressions.

Finding me would be a *blessing*. A blessing he would keep chained up in his house for the rest of eternity. A blessing he would allow Father to make an example out of for what happens to women who pretend to be pregnant.

I felt cold.

"Get in," he said, his eyes flashing wildly. He looked out of his window toward the Waste Center. "Hurry up."

The urgency in his command prompted my body to move against my will, and I found myself climbing into the plush leather passenger seat and closing myself in with the man I'd been so desperate to run from.

Bile coated my throat as he hit the gas, using one hand to turn the steering wheel around so that the truck instantly turned back toward the Waste Center. My head slammed against the headrest, hands searching for purchase on the door to steady myself against the speed. The buildings became brick blurs against the blue sky. We followed the road around the Waste Center's fence, traveling toward the back of it and into the open fields.

The truck bounced as we left the road behind and edged up onto uneven dirt terrain. Rocks leapt up, dinging the sides as he made a sharp turn. I struggled to find words as terror once again clawed its way up my throat. He was heading toward the Waste Center's fence. We were going to hit it.

At the last second, he tugged the steering wheel, guiding the truck's nose through a break in the barrier that scraped the sides of the truck. We flew into a space between the mounds of trash. He hit the brakes, and we skidded to a stop so fast I needed to put my hand out to stop my body from vaulting forward through the windshield. He pulled the car into park, then slumped back in his seat with a sigh.

I looked at our surroundings, expecting to see more trucks. To see other Hunters ready to collect me. To see Father coming around the corner, dressed in his most holy robes and most sinister smile.

But we were alone and hidden from view.

"What's going on?" I heard myself ask, the question lingering between us. My body remained tense, my senses on alert, waiting for the surprise to come out of nowhere and destroy me.

But Andrew just sat there. I felt a hot pang of rage as I remembered what he had done to me and the secrets he had kept. The way he'd talked about my sister. Mother's last moments. The hatred Luke had harbored and used to excuse her murder. The grief he'd left me with. The grief nobody had ever mentioned again. I had a gaping wound that would never heal. Andrew knew. He had to have known.

What was he *doing* here? I wanted to rush him, to beat him with my fists, to jam the knife deep into his throat as I demanded an answer as to why *my* life had been filled with such suffering, when so much of it was unnecessary. And though I knew my rage was warranted, it would never come into being. Doing so would make me just as bad as him.

"What are we doing here?" I asked again, my voice more stern this time. Andrew put both hands on the steering wheel, then let his forehead rest against them.

"I don't have much time," Andrew said flatly. Much time for what? Getting me to Father? Killing me? Letting the loyal Hunters know where I was? "But I'd like to apologize."

I leaned into him, certain I'd misheard.

"What?" I asked.

Andrew lifted his head but did not meet my gaze. His eyes lost focus, and I watched him in awe as he continued speaking.

"I haven't been a good husband," he admitted. "I know you've been through many difficulties, Maura. And I am sorry for them. We weren't truthful to you because I don't believe in the eyes of God that it made a difference. And I thought there for a while—" He ran a gloved hand over his face, then shook his head.

"The truth is, I have struggled a great deal these last few months. I have always revered my brother's word. I have always been loyal and devout. A true follower of Christ and of the great Prophet of the Lord. I had been so blessed for so long. With wives. With children. With high-ranking positions and great men to command. We succeeded in a world that had been destroyed by sin. By radical ideology.

By people who hated what we believed in. And I rallied for our cause. My entire life, I rallied for my brother and this community.

"But then my loyalty was brought into question, as it pertained to you, Maura. You see, I had no control over our marriage. I had simply been brought a gift by my brother, and I was pleased to accept it. You held so much promise. And he was sure I could make you a mother. Our family had been used as an example for others — for what true holiness looks like. And we were prepared to make you our miracle."

He turned toward me. "But I had no control over you. Over what happened when you disappeared all those months ago. Even though my brother commanded me to control you and dictate the appropriate punishment, I learned I couldn't contain you. You were determined to sin. To commit blasphemy against your family. To leave."

Anger grew hot in my chest at his words, but I continued to listen anyway.

"I thought God was punishing me. I thought I had done something wrong, something to anger Him, though I couldn't figure out what. We were a devout, loyal family. Did we have things to improve? Sure. But that's what makes us human. And God can be forgiving, so long as we follow his Word. So what was my sin? That I felt slighted that my brother gave me such a disobedient wife? Someone who I struggled to connect with, someone who struggled to be submissive, to be a decent wife to me?"

Resistance danced on my tongue, and I clenched my jaw to suppress it. I wanted to defend myself. I had done *everything* in my power to be devout. To be a good wife to Andrew. I followed his rules. I laid with him. Prayed with him. Served him. I turned the other cheek while my sister-wives shamed me.

"You *lied* to me," I seethed, nostrils flaring. "You let me believe I could get pregnant. You blamed me!"

"I know," he said, and had enough decency to let his head fall in shame. "But the Prophet—"

"I don't care," I growled. "I trusted you. Lying to me wasn't God's plan. It wasn't making you devout. You don't need to search far for your sins. Isn't that enough?"

"You don't understand—"

"Oh, I understand plenty. Women are less than, is that right? We are simply vessels for life? A servant? Expected to obey and have our lives dictated for us?" I shook my head, knowing what I was saying went against every teaching Andrew believed. It didn't matter. I was at his mercy now. I was marked for death. I wouldn't make it out of this rebellion alive, but I'd be damned if I didn't get to tell him how I felt.

"I believe women must be subservient to men, yes. I believe a woman's purpose is to bear children. But I have also come to understand that the tighter I hold those who want to leave, those who want to believe something different and follow a different path, the more misery it brings me. I have confronted the question many times. Why does someone else's blasphemy reflect upon me? If someone wants to leave, why shouldn't they?" He pressed his lips together and shook his head. "But this is where the conflict arises."

"Meaning?"

He met my eyes now, his bleary and wet, mine narrowed. "You must understand that I care for you. That I care for all my wives, all my family. That even though you and Morgan chose to leave, I still hope for your souls to be saved. For your safety. If you want to leave, then I must let you, and hope you one day find your way home to me."

My stomach turned. All he cared about was himself. I

had always known it. But it was a different thing entirely to hear it come out of his mouth.

"But that's not all," he said.

I raised my eyebrows. What more could there be?

He sighed. "There are rebels at our doors, and I think they're yours. But I know that if they succeed, they will find the thing my brother has been trying to hide since the first pandemic hit our shores. It is something I have struggled with for a long time." He looked up, eyes shining. "But God has led me here. He allowed me to find you. And I think He wants me to tell you the truth so that you understand what you're battling."

I felt like the breath had been knocked out of me as I studied his lined face and the sweat clinging to his brow. The craggy skin against his jaw made his face look distorted, like cracked earth. It was the first time in my life I'd ever seen him look deeply troubled.

"Beneath us," he said, "is a place called the Pit. The Prophet's most coveted secret. The scientists from Sciences and Innovations have been working on this project since the first pandemic. It was our mission to gather non-believers and bring them here. From them, the scientists would inject certain virus strains and harvest cells for immunotherapies necessary for the vaccines and cures Peter brought to the market to combat the different sicknesses. It was how they were able to get a jump on curing people so soon and how they maintained a steady supply.

"But as the viruses became more frequent, and people kept falling ill, they developed a vaccine that gave near-perfect immunity. The caveat was that the donor for each vaccine needed to be the same sex and similar age as the recipient. The success of each vaccine relied on multiple donors giving their lives to protect against different strains of different viruses. And because the process was so intensive, we only saved people of a beneficial age. My brother called it a necessary sacrifice for the greater good."

My throat tightened as I tried swallowing his words. Giving their life? I could barely breathe.

"At first, we took this as proof that we were righteous. That our community alone had God on our side. Why else would he allow the scientists to discover this cure? For us to collect enough sinners to offer themselves for the holy? After all, God sacrificed his only son. Sometimes, these things were necessary. We accepted that God had sent these Outsiders to be sacrificed. And for a while, the vaccines worked exactly as intended.

"But people continued to get sick. The demand for the vaccines increased. As we ventured outward with our scavengers and Hunters, people came back with new, mysterious illnesses. The scientists had a hard time keeping up. We needed more vaccines to improve the ones we'd already made, which had become quite tricky..." He cocked his head and shook it.

"Because they started running out of donors," I assumed.

Andrew nodded, his eyes glassy again. He rubbed his hand under his uniform, massaging the side of his neck. "It was difficult not to question why this was happening, even as my brother tried to explain around it. That we had allowed Outsiders to join our ranks, which tainted our devoutness. That we had not prayed hard enough. We needed more time at church. More time speaking to God." He paused, seemed to think for a moment, before he said, "This is what made me question the righteousness of what The Prophet was doing. Why would God send more diseases to our community if what we were doing was based on His Word?"

"God help us," I murmured.

A tale as old as time. It was the exact thing I had been told when I was trying so desperately to conceive. I wanted to hit him. This was the thing that made him question Father's tactics? The idea that they couldn't use defenseless people they deemed sinners to save their own? It was a disgusting realization. If they had found me with Mia, they might've taken her. They might've deemed her a sinner by association. By the fact that she hadn't repented. And then they would've killed her, without mercy. Used her to save someone else.

That wasn't God's word. That was Father, playing God.

"As time's gone on, the Prophet has gotten more…questionable in his methods of finding donors. Of keeping people within the borders. He started using followers as donors, citing some sin he himself had discovered. And then when you escaped again…" He rubbed the space between his eyes. "He told me he was planning on doing the same to you."

My blood ran cold as I thought of how close those voices had been behind me in the vent at the hospital.

"The Prophet has commanded us to do things I feel misrepresent how I understand God." He bowed his head again. "So, I no longer feel righteous. I truly believe God is commanding me to do something different. To make a different choice."

"That's the right thing to do," I said softly. "What Father is doing isn't right. He's not God. He was never meant to be God. He's just a man."

Andrew looked up sharply, and I recoiled. Was he planning to hurt me? To kill me himself? He had just given up Father's most precious secret. And now, *everything* made sense. The stories Eli, Sid, and Holli had told me. How secretive the Hunters had always been. The strangeness that surrounded the Waste Center — the Pit.

And then I remembered those Hunters, talking.

He's down in the Pit, now.

"It's a holding place," I said, voicing my realization out loud. "The Pit isn't just where they *make* the vaccines. It's where they hold the donors."

I looked up and met Andrew's eyes. His dry lips turned downwards in a pout, but his eyes — filled with regret and uneasiness — told me everything I needed to know.

I grasped for the door handle, desperate to get outside. I needed to get to Eli, and I needed to get to him *now*. Before they did something to him that was irreversible.

But there was no time. Because just as I opened my mouth to tell Andrew I was leaving and there was nothing he could do to stop me, the driver's side window shattered.

18

MAURA

"Out of the car."

Zeke stood beside Gabriel, both dressed in dark clothing. Zeke discarded the long piece of wood he'd used to break the window. From his hip, he pulled his gun and aimed it at Andrew's head. Gabriel pocketed his radio.

Andrew put his hands up in surrender, eyes widening in horror as he looked over his shoulder at the weapon. I grasped the passenger door handle and stumbled out into the bright sunlight. The festering, spoiled heaps of garbage made me gag, and I took a minute to collect myself as Zeke wrestled Andrew from the car.

"You okay?" Gabriel asked, sliding around the truck's hood to reach me.

I nodded, feeling scrutinized under his gaze. His eyebrows drew together in worry, and for the first time in a while, I considered how I must've looked. I had worn my body to its edge. I was scraped up, limping on my bad ankle, and on the brink of collapse. Even my throat felt hoarse. The only things that had kept me going this long were adrenaline and fear.

"Did he do anything to you?" Gabriel demanded, coming closer.

I rubbed my hand across my face and shook my head. "No, we were just…talking."

He raised his brows, but didn't comment further.

"Hands behind your head. On your knees." Zeke's voice was stern. He had always been a commanding force, but now that his rebellion was out in the open, he had fully settled into that role. We had agreed at the start of this that violence was not on the table unless it was absolutely necessary. So what would he do with Andrew now?

Andrew got to his knees carefully, his age showing as he rocked his hips back and forth. Guilt reared its ugly head, startling me. Guilt? Remorse? For Andrew? I reminded myself of all the bad things: his drunken slurs, his propensity to take me to bed, to mix me up with my sister, to tell me being childless was my fault. He had stood by the wayside in my most terrible moments. Never once had he protected me.

He didn't deserve my guilt.

Zeke searched Andrew for weapons before handcuffing his hands behind his back. Then, he hooked his arm beneath his and pulled him back to his feet.

"Let's go," he grumbled.

We walked in duos, Zeke and Andrew in front, Gabriel and me behind. I fought hard not to focus on anything in particular, but even so, my stomach churned at the sight and stench of the trash around us. It would permeate my clothing and live in my hair. But all of that could be solved. At least I was alive. At least I was with the rebels.

My ankle throbbed viciously as we left Andrew's truck behind and rounded another high pile of trash. The large oversight building came into view, its two-story windows glaring out across the gigantic waste complex. Below were more trash piles, but as we got closer, I saw where we were headed.

Tire marks had dug rivets into the ground over time, showing it was a well-traveled path, leading to two massive mounds of garbage. Between was a wide silver garage door, framed by concrete columns. It looked otherworldly and out of place; well-hidden unless you came around to the right angle.

This must've been where all the trucks I had seen at the office complex came in and out of. The door rose at least two or three stories high as we got closer. Gabriel paused about ten feet away from it, then raised the radio to his lips.

"S, I've got her. We're in front."

The radio crackled, and the door gave an almighty lurch before it rolled upward. The metal crinkled like paper, disappearing into the space above, revealing a dimly lit concrete space. Zeke and Andrew entered first, with Gabriel and me on their heels. Inside, the ceiling arched upward, supported by concrete beams. It reminded me of the warehouse in the Centre.

Was this the Pit that Andrew described? A few Hunter trucks, two-pickups and an ambulance were parked neatly against the left wall, and besides a few doors on either wall, most of the space was empty. It didn't look like a medical facility. It looked like a storage facility. Maybe that was the point, especially if the Hunters had worked to conceal it. It didn't have the modern architecture of the Sciences and Innovations area, and it didn't have the ornate designs like Father's church on Coutts Peak. This was something different. Something I was never meant to see.

We crossed through the space as the garage door closed behind us, our footsteps echoing into the high ceilings.

"There's a storage closet, just there," Gabriel said to

Zeke, pointing to a door near the ambulance. "Here." He unclipped a keyring from his hip without breaking pace. "Silver key. Lock him in. We'll deal with him later."

Zeke caught the key Gabriel threw him, dragging Andrew off in the other direction. Our conversation had confused me, and I was glad to see him go.

Gabriel guided me to the back left, through one of the unlabeled doors, which opened into a stairwell that only led up. Together, we climbed three flights of stairs.

Voices bled out of the room as soon as the door opened — distinct tones, a cackle of laughter, and radio static. The space was half the size of the garage below us, and a glass wall on the left offered a view out over the Waste Center.

We were in the lookout building.

Desks and computers filled the space. Hunters and rebels hurried around, speaking to one another, pouring over maps or computer screens. The central focus of the room was a massive television screen, surrounded by smaller monitors.

I barely had time to process my new surroundings. Two figures leapt to their feet. A tall, blonde woman with fair, familiar features grinned at me.

Nadia.

Behind her, a large figure with dark skin, bright eyes, and a scar across his nose rushed forward with open arms.

Sid.

He swept me off my feet before I could find words, squeezing me in an embrace I was quick to return. He smelled of sweat and earth and gunpowder, but familiar in his own way. Warmth uncurled in my belly at his touch; at seeing someone I considered family. Relief. If anyone would help me find Eli, it was Sid.

"A sight for sore eyes," he said in my ear, pressing a kiss to my temple before he released me.

I grinned up at him. "Hi."

"It's good to see you."

"Likewise."

"Hey, you," said Nadia as she slid her arm around my shoulders and squeezed.

"You alright?" Sid asked. Silas approached from the other side of the room, his eyes narrowed on me.

"I'm *fine*."

"What the hell were you doing out there? I'd heard you escaped the hospital and were in the Safe Zone."

"I—"

"Why didn't you stay put?" he pressed.

"I couldn't—"

"You could've been killed, Maura!"

"Because *Eli's here*!" I yelled, hating the tears forming in my eyes at my outburst. "He's in the Pit. I heard the Hunters talking. And I'm tired of sitting on the sidelines while everyone else does the work!"

"Maura." Silas stopped at Sid's side. An embarrassed flush rose up my cheeks, and I wiped the tears that had fallen before I faced him. "We know," he said.

"You know?"

Silas nodded, his features impassive. He looked like he'd aged a decade in the last few days. "It's partially why this team is here."

"I'm sorry," I said. "I know—"

He placed a hand on my shoulder. "I'm glad you're here. I'm glad you're safe."

"You're—?"

"Listen. I got confirmation that Morgan's safe at the Centre. They're sending the medical team, and new Centre arrivals will make camp in the office complex in case the Waste Center gets compromised. For now, we're using this as our base of operations so we can utilize the technology.

Peter and the other Hunters have retreated to the Peak. Once I can get you safely out of here and back to the office complex, we'll do so, but—"

"No," I said. "If Eli is here, I'm staying. I want to help. I need to get to him."

If he's still alive.

"*We* will get to him," Silas corrected me. "There are still loyalist Hunters downstairs in the lab, medical area, and holding cells. They'll have no idea what's going on up here. Those shifts are designed to be taken in isolation. We're gathering a team to subdue them first, but we need to be careful. If anyone gets a whiff of what we're doing up here, they could use the prisoners as hostages. Which we don't want."

"Right," I said. A sob rose up my throat, and I was helpless to stop it. "Right."

"Once we have the medical team at the complex, we can safely move them out and over there. They will likely all need medical attention." Silas tilted his head and met my eyes. "I don't want to lie to you. Eli will most likely be in very rough shape."

I could read between the lines. I knew what he was trying to tell me. There was a chance that Eli was dead.

"Alright?" he asked.

I nodded, unraveling his words. Of course there was a plan. Of course they knew about Eli. I had been foolish to think they wouldn't. But Eli…

I couldn't swallow. I shivered as sobs overtook my body, curling my hands around my middle as if I could disappear within myself. *What if* he was dead? What if the Hunters had killed him? What would I do then? There was no world I wanted to live in without him.

Sid wrapped his arm around me from behind and pulled me into his chest.

"Hey," he whispered, rubbing circles into my back. "Eli's strong. He can survive a *lot*." I sniffled, wiping my nose on my sleeve, and looked up at him. "Don't you give up on him, Maura. We'll get him back. He's a stubborn son of a bitch." He cracked a smile. "Have a little faith, would ya?"

I laughed, despite myself. There was still fear behind Sid's eyes, but he was hiding it well enough. And he was right. Expecting the worst was helping no one, least of all Eli. He *was* strong. Fearless. Smart. If anyone could survive the Hunters, it was him.

From the far end of the room, static erupted from multiple radios. It crackled before a clear voice came through.

"Explosions!" it cried. "At Sciences and Innovations! The hospital—" The radio crackled again. "The whole damn building—!" In the background, I heard gunfire. Static. "Who the hell—?" Static. Someone yelled.

I froze. Beside me, Sid stiffened.

"Explosions?" Sid questioned, looking at Nadia. She shrugged. "Peter?"

"Unlikely," Silas said. "Why would they blow up their own medical center? Unless..." He lifted the radio to his lips. "Team A, come in?" he said, then waited. "What's going on?" Silence. "Hello?" he yelled impatiently. "Someone?" He looked around the room at all of the eyes trained on him.

"Silas?" A new voice. Static.

"Julian?" Silas asked.

"I'm over at the cooling towers," the voice answered. "I just watched three explosions decimate the damn hospital."

The hospital?

"WHAT?" Silas's face distorted into panic. His eyes widened. He looked for Gabriel, who approached him slowly. "Why? Who? What happened?"

I searched for Sid's gaze, but his focus remained on Silas, brows raised, his jaw clenched. The room was silent, save for the radio's static. I dug my nails into my palm.

"There's a caravan of Jeeps," Julian said. "They're coming around the front. I can't quite see…"

"Can you get any closer?" Silas asked, turning away from us.

I looked back at Sid and Nadia, who shared an apprehensive look. My chest felt heavy as the realization settled. The Jeeps. The Centre had Jeeps. It was how they traveled in and out of the old shopping mall.

Silas spun on his heel. "Is it our people?" he hissed into the radio, his face turning a dark shade of red. "Please tell me it's not our people."

His fear was palpable, and I felt it, heavy in the air around us.

The voice on the other end hesitated. Static came again. "You'd better get someone down here," Julian said. "It's not loyalists."

"Shit," said Sid.

Silas released the button on the radio and gripped it in his hand, pressing his forehead against it. He squeezed his eyes closed and took a deep breath. Unease filled my bones. This was *bad*.

"This was not what we agreed to," he whispered.

"Silas," Nadia said, taking a step forward.

"We *agreed* there would be no violence unless it was absolutely necessary. Why would Avi use bombs? He can't —" He shook his head. "We haven't evacuated people. Most of the commune probably doesn't even know what's going on. We need to…oh God." He ran his free hand over his face.

"What can we do?" asked Nadia. "How can we help?"

Her face had gone pale white, but she was all soldier and looking for a solution.

He turned to Nadia. "Right." He composed himself and cleared his throat. "Get Abraham down here. Call Kaufman if you can reach him," he said. His glazed eyes were far away, lost in thought. Abraham was Father's brother, I knew, who ran the communications systems. Dr. Kaufman had been the newly appointed head of Sciences and Innovations. "Who did Avi have with him?"

"Darius's team," Sid said. "Francis's team. A bunch of the security team."

"Try to get in touch with them," he directed the group of rebels over by the computers. "Where the hell did he get access to a bomb?"

"I—" Sid shook his head. "I don't know."

"We need to evacuate the rest of those buildings," Silas said. "Get someone down there to reason with him. He can't go into the farmlands or residential areas. Those are all occupied by innocent families. Kids," he said, his voice hoarse with desperation. "He can't just blow them all up. He *agreed*. No violence."

I felt lightheaded. How could Avi have done this? He'd been so determined to have a cohesive rebellion, and now he was just going rogue? Something else must've happened. Something that forced him to use force.

"Silas!" The radio crackled again. "Jeeps are on the move."

"No," he whispered, his face screwed up in horror. He lifted the radio to his mouth. "Where are they headed?" he asked.

The radio crackled again. The voice came through low and certain.

"To the Peak."

19

ELI

I couldn't pinpoint the pain. My entire body throbbed, every pulse agonizing. Someone had brought me back to the flat metal board they dared to call a bed. Breathing was a labored struggle, and I wheezed with every exhale. One of my nostrils was closed, crushed by force. My nose was definitely broken.

I didn't want to open my eyes. Too painful. I knew my face was swollen; my eye sockets felt bruised, my lower lip had split, and I could feel the gap where Number 11 had knocked one of my teeth loose. Every time I swallowed, I tasted blood. A persistent ringing in my left ear suggested it was damaged. Which was fitting, I supposed. Sid and I would finally have a family resemblance.

My arms were sore, and it was impossible to move my shoulder without crying out in pain. I stretched my fingers, feeling the scratchy, laughable excuse for a blanket. My thumb joint ached. The spots where he'd torn my fingernails away ached in the air.

But it was my leg I feared for the most.

A persistent ache in my lower back led to numbness in

my left leg. My toes could wiggle, so I knew the vicious Hunter hadn't paralyzed me, but I definitely had some kind of nerve damage. My knee was the size of a balloon. When I'd gathered up enough courage to lift up my gown, I saw the gaping wound the Hunter had made in my pale, hairy flesh. Where he'd pounded a thin knife deep into my thigh until he hit bone. I could see the marks from the hot iron he'd used to cauterize my flesh so I wouldn't bleed out. My wounded skin looked like ground beef, all unnatural angles, and bloody flaps of skin.

I hadn't looked again.

My prison was mostly quiet, aside from the fluorescent bulb's hum and the occasional influx of climate-controlled air. Every so often, I'd feel a cool sensation in my chest, coming from the device. Something flooded my veins, and I would sleep. Wake. Assess my pain all over again.

I stopped caring about time.

Dreams bled into reality. I was in my cell, then back at Mom's. I was in the cell, then back at the Centre. Mom came, her warm hands soothing my feverish face, cupping my chin between her thumb and index finger. She sang to me — a lullaby I hadn't heard since I was a boy.

Soon, I wondered if I was already dead. Maybe I was in the morgue, on the cool slab of metal, waiting for some Coutts doctor to carve me up and harvest my organs. For a Hunter to come and taunt my corpse, assuring a watching audience that this was what happened when you tried to fight the Almighty Prophet.

But inevitably, the pain came flooding back, and I knew I was still alive.

I had sat with Number 11 for hours. Days, maybe. He'd known all about the rebels and how the Centre was infiltrating their precious commune. He'd known about Avi, the way he worked, and drew several concerning parallels between our community at the Centre and the Coutts commune.

I'd refused to believe it. Avi hadn't wanted to be violent. He'd sided with Silas and Gabriel, who had been adamant about approaching the infiltration with as much peace as possible. He'd wanted to focus on compromise, not ownership. He'd promised he was different from Peter.

I'd told the Hunter he was wrong. I'd told him there were more rebels than he could've ever dreamed of. That they were everywhere, even within the ranks of his precious Hunters, and he'd be surprised when they turned on him.

I'd told him they would lose this war.

That had earned me my broken nose.

After that, he hadn't stopped. He'd asked the same questions again and again, keeping my wrist in his grasp, snapping my bone when he'd had enough of my defiance. I had bitten through my lip and spat blood across the table at him. He'd asked me for names. I'd told him to go to hell. He'd ripped out six of my fingernails.

By the time he'd finished with me, I was on the floor, breathing in my own blood, the world around me a hazy gray. Distantly, I'd heard a door open and a new voice insist that he'd needed to let me rest and recover. That I was the only rebel they had in custody.

I'd smiled at that, even though I was in agony.

But my resolve had weakened.

They hadn't tended to me. They had left me here to rot. After I'd assessed my injuries, I wished for death. Releasing myself from this physical pain would be better than sitting in it, even knowing my family might find me this way. I couldn't make it through another round of torture. They would understand, given my state.

Wouldn't they?

It hurt to think of Sid, Holli, and Maura, but they were the only things that eased my mind away from pain. They hadn't been caught. They all still had a chance. I wondered if the rebels had infiltrated the commune yet. If the refugees made it safely. Silas and Avi still had so much to do. So many things needed to be set in motion for the rebellion to be successful. But I knew they could do it. I had to believe it. It was the thing I was going to die for.

I coughed up blood, tasting it, smelling the iron through my crushed cartilage. I rolled away on my side, every tendon, muscle, and nerve on fire.

I had given up hope of being found. But I still hoped for some things. I hoped my family would know I died not divulging any of their secrets. I hoped they knew I died trying to keep them safe. I hoped people believed in Maura, Avi, and Silas and followed them toward whatever came next.

But most of all, I hoped they burned this whole fucking place to the ground.

20

MAURA

"Avi's going to go after Peter." Silas sat straight-backed in a rolling chair near the large black screen. He wiped a hand across his mouth, his distant eyes staring out the windows. The sun was lowering in the sky, casting a fiery red hue over the trash mounds. Hunters and rebels conversed in clusters, nervous gazes flickering toward Silas. I recognized a handful of the Hunter rebels, including Joseph and Jonah, who had led me into the commune when I'd first arrived.

Sid crossed his arms and paced the floor in front of Silas. One hand he held up to his mouth, his other clutched his elbow. "And he won't care who he plows through in the process?" He phrased it as a question, even though we all knew the answer.

"It's pure stupidity," Nadia cried. She leaned against the front of the television monitor's control panel, her long legs crossed over one another, threading her blonde hair around her finger absentmindedly. "Above all else, the loyal Hunters are going to protect Peter to the death. And they're all armed. Better than we are." She looked up at Sid. "What the hell is he thinking?"

Sid shook his head.

"Not just that," I said wearily. "His followers will try to protect him, too. He's basically been preaching about this since I came back. If you're loyal or devout, you must protect him in his time of need." I sighed, meeting Silas's gaze. "We've been told since I can remember that the Prophet must be protected at all costs. It's not just the Hunters we need to worry about."

Silas nodded. "You're right.

"They're innocent civilians," Sid said.

"Not to Avi," Nadia said.

"Someone needs to get down there," Silas said. "Cut off the trucks, get him on the radio. Talk some sense into him." He glanced around the room full of people who were relying on him. "I can't—"

"I'll do it." Nadia lifted herself off the console.

"Nadia." Sid took a step toward her.

She raised a flat hand, pressed her lips into a thin line, and nodded at the rest of us. "You need to be here for Eli and to protect our team if the Hunters come back. I'll take a small team for protection. Avi and I have been together a long time. He'll listen to me."

Silas moved his head as if the thought were bouncing around. "If you're sure, then—"

"I'm sure," said Nadia.

"Good. You'll want to—"

"Silas," Gabriel interrupted his brother, his voice tense with worry. He approached, his chin tilted forward, eyes glued on the screen behind us.

We turned our attention toward the once-black screen. Only now, a familiar figure stood in the center, his hair neatly greased and combed. My stomach dropped to my knees.

My father.

It had been some time since I'd seen him. He had handed down his commands through Abigail and Andrew in an effort, I assumed, to show how much control he still had over his commune. Over me.

I had expected him to look worried, maybe even a little afraid. But his appearance left me disheartened. He looked healthy and strong, flanked by Luke, his brothers Isaac and Gabriel, and a handful of young Hunters.

They stood on the altar of the church on Coutts Peak. The table had been exquisitely decorated, with white and gold accents. The standard portrait of my father's face hung on the wall behind. Sunlight filtered through windows we couldn't see, shining against their faces. My father and his men were all dressed in long robes, standing in a V formation with my father at the head.

The Shepherd and his sheep.

His lips moved, arms raised in prayer as if he were addressing a congregation. To the average commune member, he might look passionate. Excited. Happy, even. But I saw the fiery rage blooming in his eyes. To me, he looked crazed, hungry, and deranged.

"Someone turn on the volume," Silas said, his voice low and weak. "Please."

I glanced at him. His face had gone white, his mouth slightly parted. He looked so far away from the man I saw scoop up my sister a few nights ago. He had the weight of this rebellion on his shoulders and now not even Avi's word to embolden him. We were at risk of losing every-thing, but Silas most of all.

Nadia fiddled with something on the console.

"—devils are here, in our home." My father's voice filled the room in its booming, deep tone. He narrowed his eyes. "And we must pray them out."

The feed cut to the Sciences and Innovations area. A great boom filled the speakers, echoing outward. The sound of gunfire. We watched in horror as a fireball engulfed the bottom of the tallest building. The hospital. The building where I had narrowly escaped. Another explosion blew out the front windows. Distant screaming was barely audible. The third and final explosion took out three floors in the middle.

The building gave a mighty tremble. Dust and smoke plumed outward as one of the internal support beams collapsed. Brick crumbled like sand, tumbling out of the structure. Metal screeched, rubbing against itself as it struggled to fight against the blaze from the bomb someone — *Avi* — had planted in three different places inside the hospital.

I thought of the man who had slipped me the coin. Of the rebel obstetrician who would've risked his life to lie about my fake pregnancy. Of the patients waiting for care, not knowing what was happening outside. Innocent people. Rebels who would've rallied for our cause. Children. Babies.

The feed did not cut away as faces pressed against windows. As hospital beds rolled out of rooms and into the fire. As bodies teetered on the edge of the sills, socked feet dangling as the building tipped precariously.

"My God," Sid hissed under his breath.

"This is what these devils are doing to us." My father's voice overlaid the video. "They want to kill us for what we believe. They want to infiltrate us. Ruin us. They will stop at nothing until they have gathered us all under their control. Look at what they have done to our most defenseless."

The feed cut back to my father's face. I could see his chapped lips, the lines indented into his aging face. His eyes had softened. He lifted cupped hands up to the screen.

"But I am here to save you," he said, the corners of his lips lifting into a smile. "We are stronger than this evil. And if you *truly* believe, you will stand your ground. You will protect this land. For it is ours, and it is holy!"

For the first time in my life, I saw the full picture of what he was doing. The manipulation of what he was saying and showing us. He probably hadn't even told the families of the people who died in the hospital. Instead, he broadcast it live to his followers. To get them angry. To scare them. To feed into the existing chaos.

He was no leader. He was willing to throw his loyal, innocent followers into the path of an incoming war. And they would gladly go. Blood pounded in my ears. I couldn't take my eyes off the screen.

"Today is the Day of Reckoning. The one we have been waiting for. God is testing us, and I have asked him to spare the innocent and the devout. In order to do your duty, you must protect his most loyal servants. Me and your Hunters. We saved you and your families from the horrible plague, from the evil that lingered outside our doors now for decades. We have kept you safe. We have kept the devil at bay. And now we are being tested. We are being hunted. We are being asked to show our loyalty to God.

"Do not disappoint me. You will know these rebels when you see them. They are the ones who will claim to want to save you, while blowing up your homes. They are the ones who will promise a better life. Safety. Freedom. But my brothers and sisters, I ask you. Are you not free? Are you not given a holy, blessed life on these mountains? Our commune thrived in the midst of death and destruction! And now they want to bring it to our doorstep. And I say, no more. For we will fight for what we believe in. For we have God on our side. And…" A full smile now spread across his face. "God. Is. Good."

The camera focused on his blue eyes. And now I was sure he was speaking directly to me.

"Remember, my loyal followers. Do not trust those who claim to be more powerful than God. Those who have claimed to have come back from the dead, who claim to have seen him in forms we could only dream of. Beware of false idols. For they will not save you. Only I can. If you prove loyal, I can promise you a place in heaven. A place where you will know nothing but everlasting peace. You know the one true way home. And that is beneath my wings."

The screen cut to black.

I couldn't breathe.

"Oh, this is *bad*, bad," I heard Sid say.

"He's rallying the troops," said Gabriel.

"—discrediting Maura."

"—forcing them to sacrifice themselves."

"—the day of Reckoning—"

The words scrambled, and I turned away from the murmuring crowd, retreating toward the door we'd come through when we first arrived. I couldn't leave. I didn't want to. But there were too many things happening at once. I pressed my forehead against a cool piece of wall and tried to steady my breathing.

In.

Eli could be dead.

Out.

Avi had betrayed us.

In.

Father would sacrifice innocent people to ensure his survival.

Out.

Things were looking just about as hopeless as I ever thought they'd be.

21

MAURA

THE CONTROL ROOM's door banged against the wall as Zeke barreled through, breathless.

"You'll never believe this."

He crossed the room, clutching a large blue canvas roll under his arm. I pulled away from the wall and followed him. His brown eyes shone with success as he approached the console where Silas sat.

Silas looked at him, then at the roll he carried. "I hope it's good news."

"Oh, it is." Zeke unravelled the canvas, letting it spread wide across the desk. Inside were a series of what looked like small maps, each labeled with a different floor level.

"Blueprints?" Silas asked.

"Of the Pit place?" A disbelieving smile crossed Sid's lips as he looked over Zeke's shoulder. "Where the hell did you find this?"

Zeke flashed me a worried glance.

"Actually...it was Andrew. He told me exactly where they were."

So much had happened since my conversation in the

car with him, I hadn't yet paused to wonder *why* he'd told me about the Pit. And why he'd brought me right back to the place where the rebels were coordinating. He must've known the Waste Center was overrun. So why take me here? Why not take me to the Peak? And why on earth was he helping Zeke?

"He also told me there are two guards on each floor, plus two floaters that patrol the stairwells. It confirms our estimates," Zeke said, glancing at the small monitors around the larger screen.

Silas looked at the blueprints, then back up at the screen multiple times, his fingers tapping his lips. He seemed to be thinking exactly what I was, but didn't want to say it out loud. He met my gaze, and I shook my head. I didn't know why Andrew would help us, either.

"Sir?" Jonah approached our group, still wearing his vest with the number 3801. He gave me a small smile. "Abraham's team is on their way."

"And I'm heading out," Nadia interjected. The two men beside her were both young security personnel from the Centre. Each of them had a hunting rifle slung across their backs.

"Good, good, good." Silas nodded. While he seemed to have a newfound sense of energy now that things were moving, all I felt was anxiety. I wanted Nadia to stay safe. I didn't know what to expect from the communications team. I desperately wanted Eli to be okay. I had wanted to be here so badly, but now, I felt helpless amidst the chaos.

"What are we doing with Abraham's team?" Sid questioned after Nadia and her team departed, his voice low enough not to be overheard by the busy rebels. "Obviously a communication of some sort?" I swiveled my head to listen to the answer.

"We're going to film what we find down there. If Peter

wants to play the propaganda game, this is how we combat him. Video doesn't lie. If he wants shock and awe, we'll give them shock and awe. We'll show his followers exactly what he's allowed to go on beneath the Waste Center, in this so-called *Pit*. They can see his crimes firsthand. What it cost to keep us all healthy while the rest of the world burned. Based on what we know so far, it won't look good."

"Whoa." Zeke's eyes widened. "That's one way to shock them."

"That's what we need," Silas said. "They won't be convinced on words alone. Not anymore."

"And when he tells them it's all a lie?" Sid pressed.

Silas met his gaze. "Some people will never believe it. Even if they watched Peter shoot a room full of children, they'd find a justification for it. Those aren't the people we're trying to reach."

I breathed in newfound enthusiasm. *This* was why Silas needed to be in charge of this rebellion. His plan was brilliant and something I never would have thought of. I had been on the defensive since I'd arrived here. Silas was meeting Father where he was and playing the same game.

"Look at these," Silas said to no one in particular, hunched over the blueprints. He rifled through them, taking a moment to scan each one. "Eight floors below the garage. A full medical facility on seven and eight, but it looks like..." He pulled one blueprint out from the rest. "The fifth floor houses explosives. Weapons." He shook his head in disbelief, handing the paper to Zeke, who looked it over, too. "There are full bunkers on the fourth — look how they labeled them. One for each Coutts brother and his children. High-ranking Hunters." He looked up at us. "And no space for anyone else."

"Did they think the commune would be attacked or something?" Sid asked.

Silas shrugged, his eyes not leaving the papers. "They probably prepared for everything. I can't believe all of this was here without anyone knowing." He looked up at me. "Andrew must've known, right? And my father?"

There was a waver in his tone, one I knew well. He felt hurt. Even though he wouldn't have wanted to be there. Even though Silas would never have left others behind. Even knowing how ruthless his father was. Understanding your own flesh and blood would leave you to rot without blinking an eye, was never a good feeling.

"What do the lower levels look like?" Sid asked, looking eager to shift the conversation.

Silas blinked and ruffled through the papers, pulling out the ones labeled *Floor B7* and *Floor B8* and laying them flat across the others. "Stair access only," he said, trailing his finger to the spot where they would enter. "Only one exit, one entrance. There's a bunch of medical rooms off this hallway on 7." He lifted his finger and tapped against its label, *Medical Facility & Equipment*. "On 8, there's a bunch of rooms with small—" He looked up at the small blue monitors. "Huh. There's only two guards there?"

"Plus the two in the stairwell," Zeke said.

Silas shook his head. "Two guards just doesn't seem like it'd be enough security."

"For?"

Silas looked back down at the blueprints. "Eight is where they're keeping people. It should be heavily secured."

"Well, they had all the Hunters up here," Sid said.

"But Peter..." Silas pressed his fingers against his lips. "He wouldn't take that risk. If there were enough prisoners, he'd want to make sure there was enough force to keep them where he wanted them to be. How would he ensure he'd get a cooperative patient to go get tests done?"

I thought about the Island of Repentance. How, even though there were no guards, the waterlocked island threatened death if you tried to escape. He was right. Father would've built something else into this system to ensure compliance.

Sid shook his head. "I don't know, S, but didn't you say the shift change starts at dusk?" He eyed the window. The reddish glow was fading to purple. "Answers or no answers, we gotta get down there."

Silas looked up and nodded.

"Jonah?"

The young man hopped off a chair and approached us.

"How far is Abraham's crew?"

"He said it'd take them about half an hour to get in."

Silas checked his watch. "Should be here any minute, then." He looked back at Sid, Zeke, and me. "Get geared up. Flash bombs to subdue. Handcuffs. Keycards. Walkies. Headsets." He turned to Gabriel. "Show Maura how to use the control panel."

I straightened, surprised, but pleased to be included.

"Who else are we sending down?" Sid asked.

Silas's eyes scanned the room. "I need two for each floor," he announced, then paused, doing the math in his head. "Fourteen total. Practically our entire crew. You and Zeke and whoever they send from comms will take the bottom floors. Gabriel and Maura will stay up here, watch the monitors, and direct you as necessary. I'll keep the team up here accessible to guard the entrance and keep communicating with Nadia."

"You got it," Sid said.

It was all hands on deck. I'd wanted to be there when

they found Eli. To comfort him and help how I could. But the rescue mission was meant for trained soldiers. People who knew how to use guns and flash bombs. I'd be more useful up here.

The rebels coordinated a team, each assigned to a floor, while Gabriel showed me how the monitors worked at the video screen's control desk. We could access each feed manually, or the system would switch between floors automatically. It was a simple system. We would watch the guards on the screen and let our team know when it was safe to move in.

The room hummed with heightened energy as we anxiously awaited Abraham's team. I had only met Abraham personally a handful of times, but he had been a constant prominent figure in the commune since I was a child. He was one of Father's full-blood brothers, like Andrew, and had been a commanding force in the Coutts hierarchy as the supervisor of all communications in the commune.

Media was one of those things that was used when necessary. We had one television in Andrew's home, where it hung in the living room, only switched on when Father had something to communicate. Every home was required to have one. Viewing was mandatory. Sometimes we would gather at the church for the same purpose. Father would give a sermon, we would watch on the large drop-down projector screen, and then be on our way. For most of my life, these videos didn't seem significant. Just another part of life — mundane, boring, and required. But understanding them with fresh eyes made my skin crawl.

We watched videos talking about Outsiders, showing how they would steal, rape, and kill if given the chance. Their only hope of salvation? Joining our cause. We watched videos about other religions that existed across the globe, and how filled with sin they were for not believing in our Prophet. Their only hope of salvation? You guessed it. Joining our cause. There were videos on how to be an obedient girl. How to be a faithful wife. How to be submissive. How polygamy gave our righteous men more opportunities to spread the good word far and wide. How our one and only true purpose was to build the ranks of our community through childbirth. How any word against Father or against our beliefs would send us straight to the fiery depths of hell.

Abraham had other responsibilities back when the Outside world was still alive. He'd been tasked with drawing more Outsiders into our mission, of enticing them to join the cause. I remembered Leo mentioning books and other media that the Coutts had distributed into the world, and how angry he'd been at their existence.

It was terrifying to think how easily we'd taken those videos as truth. It was put in front of our faces, and we lapped it up like dogs. No questions. No thinking. We just retained the information and let it dictate our beliefs.

A heavy rumble came from the floor, and I looked up and over at the large windows. A barely visible truck rolled around the waste piles and into the garage below us.

"Sub-level floor teams," Silas called, "ready to assemble in five?"

"Sir, yes, sir—"

"Ready—"

"Armed and ready, sir—"

Agreements rattled off in quick succession. Footfalls hit the stairs, and I heard movement before the door opened cautiously, letting in the voices from the stairwell.

"Tell him to run whatever Peter says," said the newcomer. "Don't push back. He'll know something's up."

A crackle.

"Got it. Over."

A tall, thin, middle-aged man appeared in the doorway with a radio hung from his belt. His dark hair was cut in a traditional crew cut, and he had a clean-shaven, narrow face. He carried a formal presence and entered the room as such.

"Elijah," Silas said, stepping forward. "I'm glad you're here."

"Silas," Elijah said, shaking his hand. Behind him, a shorter young man with round, red cheeks and a bad case of acne entered. He wore a backpack and held two large equipment cases. Elijah took them from him and set them neatly on the floor.

"James," he said, "this is Silas. Silas, James." He glanced around at the rest of us. Sid, Zeke, Gabriel, and I introduced ourselves by name.

"Abraham sends his best," Elijah said as he squatted down to unzip the cases. Straight to business. "He'll be ready for us when we need him."

"That's great," Silas said. "Are you armed?"

Elijah tilted his hips, showing a gun in his holster. I shouldn't have been shocked by it, but I was. Being part of Abraham's team had its advantages, it seemed.

Silas explained what we knew about the Pit and that it was crucial to get first hand footage out to the public as soon as humanly possible. As he spoke, Elijah put together a very complicated-looking recording device, while Gabriel and I sat at the control desk flipping through the different feeds.

It was eerie watching people who didn't know they were being watched. The Hunter guards on each floor roamed their hallways, back and forth. I flipped from Floor 4 to Floor 5. I knew Hunters. I'd grown up with boys who dreamed their whole lives of being fitted for their green uniforms, just as I had dreamed of having babies. And while some of them were awful people, like Luke, there were others who were good, like Silas. Did these men still have good inside them? Did they know what they were guarding?

"We'll have a team managing each floor," Silas promised. "Gabriel and Maura will monitor the screens up here and relay any important information back down to you. Guards go down with the flash bombs. We subdue with handcuffs."

Elijah nodded, looking down at the camera he'd assembled.

"All sounds good," he confirmed. "James will stay here to ensure everything gets broadcast back to our hard drive. Quick turnaround, alright?"

James nodded, settling beside Gabriel. I stowed my guilt about the oblivious guards away. Rescuing Eli and whoever else was down in the medical facility was the priority. It had to be.

"Here," Sid said, handing Elijah a heavy, bulletproof vest. He slid it over his head and tightened the straps on each side. At the same time, Silas brought the blueprints to the middle of the room, spreading them across the floor.

"Sub-floor team?" he called.

Fourteen suited-up rebels, Sid, Zeke, and Elijah, all crowded around the maps on the floor. I watched Silas in awe as he directed these men into what felt like a real battle. He commanded them like a general, like a *Hunter*, and I had to remind myself that he was one. He'd gotten that training as a boy. He'd been raised in the commune, the same as I had, only on the other side. He was raised to be a fighter. To use violence to coerce. To murder if it served the purpose.

And like me, he chose a different path.

When he finished his instructions and safety protocols, he looked up, giving every face in the circle a lingering, grateful glance. I found my heart swelling with appreciation that he was here, leading this resistance.

We'd be nothing without him.

22

MAURA

I sat beside Gabriel, fiddling with the controls as I flipped between Floor 7 and Floor 8. The blueprints suggested this was where the prisoners were being held, but the singular camera showed nothing but a long hallway with a few doors. The guards walked the length over and over again. I searched for any clue, any sign of Eli. It was futile, of course. What did I expect? A live feed showing me that Eli was alive?

Thinking about him made my stomach hurt.

Behind us, Silas's radio crackled as he spoke with Doctor Mick, who'd arrived at the office complex with Holli and a few other reinforcements from the Centre. Knowing they were here made my legs restless. I knew we needed them. I knew they could hold their own. But all it felt like was more people to worry about.

James worked diligently to my left on a thin laptop with a bunch of wires. I watched him, desperate for the distraction. He straightened, looked up over my head, and found Elijah, who wore the contraption he'd put together on the floor. It fit over his head with two lenses raised at least three feet up off either shoulder, looking out on either side of him.

"Hey," he said. "Elijah. Turn the cams on."

Elijah fiddled with something at his hip, and a red light began to blink.

"There," James said. I peered over his shoulder at his laptop. "Now we can see what they see."

Our faces filled the small laptop screen from a bird's-eye view. Through the lens, I sat between Gabriel and James, staring at the camera. Exhaustion lined my frail face, my eyes plagued by worry. I knew I hadn't been hiding my emotions well, but I looked so unlike myself it was baffling. My stomach soured, and I turned away, feeling disoriented as I watched the back of my head on the screen.

On the laptop, Elijah turned the camera to focus on the rebels wearing their walkie headsets, ready to charge the lower floors. I was relieved not to have to look at myself anymore.

Silas used his finger to do a silent headcount.

"Alright, team," Sid addressed the group. "Let's head out."

He opened the door, and the rebels followed him through it, disappearing down the stairwell. As the sound of their footsteps quieted, silence fell over the room. I swallowed, looking up at the monitors, my heart pounding so loud I was sure the others could hear it too. My numb fingers hovered over the controls, and I glanced at Gabriel, whose pale face drew up in a frown. His Adam's apple bobbed as he swallowed.

"Check?" Zeke's voice came through the two radios in front of us.

Gabriel grabbed his radio, his hands shaking as he pulled it to his mouth. "Clear on my end."

"Back at you."

"I'll focus on the first couple of levels," Gabriel said to me, eyeing the three monitors on his side. "You monitor the last four. Okay?"

I nodded.

The radio felt too large in my sweaty hand. I gripped it, making sure I knew where all the controls were, before I fixed my gaze on the three small monitors on my side. Eight guards. I punched the button to switch the feed to the lower stairwells. One feed showed the stairwell between Floors 7 and 8, where one guard currently patrolled.

"Reaching stairs," Zeke said.

"You're alright," Gabriel answered, eyes fixed on the monitors. "Your first guard is outside on Floor 4's door, ascending to 3."

"Noted. Second?"

"Coming up from 8," I replied, eyeing my monitor, where a Hunter climbed a set of stairs at a pace as slow as molasses.

"Noted," Zeke answered. "Radio silence on my end. Keep them in your sights."

"Will do," Gabriel said. He placed the radio down, and we turned our attention to James's laptop. This feed was much clearer than the monitors. The video camera was intended, I assumed, for higher-quality productions like Father's propaganda.

A sea of black bodies crowded around one of the doors in the concrete garage. Sid and Zeke stood in the front, saying something I couldn't hear but wished I could. The two men looked at each other, nodded, then disappeared through the door.

On the small monitors, we watched Sid and Zeke travel down the first stairwell.

"Hunter coming up from Floor 3 to Floor 2," Gabriel said into the walkie.

Sid gave a thumbs-up to Elijah's camera. I reminded myself to breathe.

The Hunter climbed lazily, pausing on the landing between floors before moving to the next flight of stairs.

"He's stationary," Gabriel said.

The two men moved quickly. As the Hunter turned the corner, Sid charged him, grabbing him by the throat beneath his helmet. From behind Sid, Zeke pinned his arms against the wall. Immobilized, the Hunter desperately fought against them to move, but their hold was too strong. Sid yanked off his helmet, revealing a young man with wide, frightened eyes. Zeke used the gun handle on the side of his head, and the boy crumpled into a heap. They handcuffed, disarmed, and blindfolded him, and moved onward.

My stomach clenched with guilt.

"Next?" Sid whispered.

I swiveled toward my feed.

"He's passing Floor 6 now," I whispered into my radio.

The wide-set Hunter was visibly much larger than the boy Sid and Zeke had just brought down. He walked with precision, arms straight at his side. A true, loyal Hunter. On the laptop, I watched Sid and Zeke take the stairwells quickly, moving past Floor 3, then 4.

"He's on 5," I said, as they closed the space between them.

Another thumbs up from Sid. They hugged the corner of the stairwell. The guard reached the top of the stairs and paused at the door, lifting himself on his toes before he turned on his heel to go back down.

"Now," I hissed.

Sid and Zeke rushed him at the edge of the stairs,

toppling him face-first. They disappeared out of frame, and my heart accelerated. I stood up from my chair, leaning over to watch James's monitor.

On the screen, the Hunter had Sid in a chokehold against the stairs. Zeke charged down, using his foot to kick his helmet. The Hunter's head snapped back, his body stiff. Stunned, the large man searched for purchase, grabbing feebly at Sid's vest but catching only air. He tumbled backward down the stairs like a rag doll. The men raced after him, blindfolded, handcuffed, and disarmed him.

I tried to remind myself that these men were our enemies. That they would hurt us without asking questions. But I couldn't help but feel awful about anyone getting hurt.

"Done," Sid said, breathless into his headset. "Someone come help us get these guys outta here. Teams for all floors, move in, please."

There was a flurry of movement on the small security screens. Two rebels helped Sid and Zeke move the Hunters who had guarded the stairwells into the garage, where I assumed they'd be locked up with Andrew. The rest of the rebels found their floors and situated themselves in front of the doors.

"On my count," Sid said, as he, Zeke, and Elijah reached the bottom floor. "Throw. Hold the doors. Wait for the all clear. Gabe?"

Gabriel looked at me, his lip quivering. His fear matched mine. My whole body trembled. I clenched my free fist. Gripped the radio so tight I could feel its sharp edges against my palm. We both looked at our monitors, then back at each other.

Gabriel lifted the radio to his mouth. "All clear up here."

Sid counted backwards from three. My heart pounded in my ears, every second an eternity. On the same count, each floor door opened, and the rebels threw a small grenade-looking contraption down the hallway where the guards patrolled. From the radios came the sounds of slamming doors and the *clink-clink-clink* as the metal contraptions bounced down the hallways. I held my breath, switching my attention between my three monitors.

On Floor 5, the two guards barely looked up. On Floor 6, one of the guards took off his helmet and stepped closer to it. On Floor 7, both backed away, knowing it was trouble.

But on the last floor, the guards immediately ran toward the door.

I stood up, leaning over James's shoulder as I watched Sid and Zeke hold the door closed, unaware.

I should pick up the walkie. I should warn them.

But it happened so fast.

On my monitor, the guards rushed the exit, their bodies slamming into the door. The other side rattled violently, shocking Sid and Zeke, who changed their hold. My mouth went dry, fingernails digging into the control panel's overhang. If those Hunters got out…if they somehow charged through, what then?

Sid grit his teeth, shoulder up against the door, the handle tight in his grip. Zeke mirrored his stance on the other side. One of the guards took a running start and slammed into the door again. Sid and Zeke's feet slipped against the floor.

The devices lay motionless in the middle of the hallways. Did it normally take this long? I tried to think if Silas had ever said how long it took for them to detonate. I swallowed, my breath coming in short bursts as I watched, helpless.

What happened if they didn't work?

As if my thought was the trigger, the flash bombs went off.

The building shook from the noise, and I closed my eyes, my hands clenched tightly around the control panel. Blinding white light filled a few of the monitor's screens, so bright it forced me to look away. It took a few moments to steady my breathing.

"Fifteen seconds," came Zeke's voice.

On every monitor in the stairwell, the rebels pressed themselves against the doors. The blinding light had begun to fade on the alternating feeds.

"Floor 2, go," said Gabriel. "Floor 3, go ahead."

I stood, peering up at my monitors, at the crumpled, disoriented guards in Hunter uniforms. I swallowed, gathering myself as I wiped my clammy hands down the front of my jumpsuit.

"Floor 6, guards are down," I said, my voice shrill. "Floor 5, go ahead." I switched feeds.

"Floor 1," Gabriel said. "Floor 4, hold your position."

"Floor 7, go ahead," I said.

"Floor 4, you're good to move in," Gabriel said.

The screens filled with our rebels, handcuffing guards, removing their helmets and weapons. On the seventh floor, I watched two rebels handcuff a rogue doctor we hadn't seen as they swept through the hallway.

The light faded more slowly on Floor 8, and I stayed glued to the screen, the walkie at my lips. Sid and Zeke remained at the door, chins tilted upward as they waited for my command. In the hallway, I watched a guard pick himself up from the floor. He reached for his hip, drawing his gun.

"FLOOR 8," I yelled. "SEND ANOTHER."

My voice was wobbly and panicked. The door opened, and the small flash bomb bounced against the floor, the sound a distant *ping-ping* on the radio. The guard aimed his gun at the door just as the bomb went off.

A loud crack, then another.

My shoulders tightened as I turned my gaze to the laptop. Sid, Zeke, and Elijah stood curled around the side of the stairwell, faces peering out at the door. Desperately, I turned back to the monitors, squinting through the bright light.

Two huddled masses.

Both guards down.

"Floor 8, go ahead," I said, my voice cracking.

On the small monitors, we watched the men enter the long hallway and tie up the guards. Together, they got them into one of the side rooms. Sid emerged with a key ring and locked them inside.

I ran my hand through my sweaty hair, exhaled deeply, and took a seat. Everyone was in. All the guards were subdued. But I knew my relief would be short-lived. According to the blueprints, Eli was likely on this floor.

I needed to focus. I still had a job to do. As I reminded myself to exhale, I flipped through the other feeds, making sure all the rebels were safe and there were no additional threats coming from the stairwells. All looked clear.

I let my gaze travel back to James's laptop. Sid and Zeke had reached the end of the hallway, where two doors faced each other. They used the keyring near the door on the right, and a green light on the handle showed it was open. They swung it wide, revealing a circular white room with numbered doors. Sid and Zeke faced each other and talked for a minute before waving the keyring in front of one of the numbered doors. Like the other, the handle flashed green. Sid opened the door and disappeared inside.

"There's a woman in here," came Sid's voice from the radio. "Young, maybe early 20s. She's unresponsive. Once the rebels are finished on the other floors, we could use help getting her upstairs."

"Are all of these filled?" Zeke's voice came in the background before static took it over.

I glanced at the laptop. Sid entered the next door, then came out with both hands over his face. My stomach turned over as he looked up at the camera.

"Sid?" I cried into the radio. I couldn't help it. I needed to know.

He took a minute to compose himself, and I watched him, wishing I could hear his thoughts through the screen or that Elijah would move close enough so I could see what Sid had seen. If it were Eli, would they tell me?

Sid's eyes flashed to the camera.

"It's not him," he said, his whisper coming through the radio in a crackle. I took a shuddering breath, letting my hand rest against my mouth in momentary relief. My hands shook. I balled them into fists, then released them, unable to control my trembling. There were still so many rooms to go through. "But we need help urgently. Whoever can get down here, please do so immediately."

I went back to my monitors, back to Floor 7, where the blueprints had labeled it *Medical Facility & Equipment*.

"Floor 7?" I called into the walkie. "See if you can find some stretchers, or even some sheets. Something we can use to get people up and out of there."

"We'll take a look," the rebel replied.

Back on the laptop's screen, Zeke and Sid opened the rest of the doors, but the radio was silent as they worked. No people came out of the cells, and it made my stomach curdle with fear. These were not good signs. I remembered what Silas had said about Eli and desperately tried to push it aside.

"Silas there?" Zeke asked, finally coming through the radio.

Gabriel peered over to the other corner of the room, where Silas and two other rebels spoke over the radio with Nadia.

"What's up?" Gabriel asked.

"Do we have any commune medical staff we can spare?"

Silas lifted his head at the question. "I'll try to get in touch with Kaufmann again, but I can't make any promises. Avi bombed the whole hospital. What're you finding?"

A moment of silence.

"It's not good," Gabriel said. He lifted the radio to his mouth. "Sid, Zeke? What've you got so far?"

"I've got at least four in need of immediate attention," Sid answered. "One is conscious, but barely. The other three…" He trailed off, but we understood.

"Floors 2 and 3 coming down now," came new voices on the radio.

"We've got three canvas stretchers," the rebel from 7 added.

That was good, but I wanted to scream. My heart felt like it was going to burst. The skin around my knuckles ached as I gripped the control and switched my feeds from the stairwell to the hallway, struggling to stay focused and on task.

Where was Eli?

From the corner of my eye, I watched Sid and Zeke cross the hallway and enter the other room. One by one, they opened the doors with the keyring, and one by one, they gave us a report of what they found.

Female. Teen. Deceased.

Male. Teen. In need of medical care.

Female. Twenties. In need of medical care.

Female. Teen. Deceased.

Male. Twenties. In need of medical care.

There were only two doors left by the time they got to Door 8.

Zeke opened the door wide. I kept my eyes steady on Sid as he threw his head back and rushed forward into the room. I pressed myself up against the counter, my responsibilities forgotten, touching the screen with my fingertips. It was Eli. It had to be.

But was he alive? Dead?

"Maura," came Sid's voice. "It's him."

I began to cry.

"Sid?"

"He's alive. Barely."

23

MAURA

I couldn't breathe. I knelt in front of the console, the walkie still gripped in my hands as I cried into my shoulder. My heart pumped in my ears, muffling the world as I sobbed up relief. The unexpected release of the tension I held in my body was overwhelming, and I collapsed to the ground, pressing my hands into my eyes.

My body felt lighter, like I'd shed a hundred pounds I hadn't realized I'd been carrying. Eli was alive. Barely. But he was *alive*. That was enough hope to cling to. Holli was here. She could fix him. I knew she could.

The thoughts I'd suppressed bubbled ruthlessly to the surface. I couldn't have handled his death at the hands of my people. It was the thing he had tried to warn me of all those months ago. The thing I hadn't believed until I saw it with my own eyes. I had been such a fool.

A pair of hands found my back and nudged me timidly. Silas. He leaned forward and scooped me up, and I fell into him as I got to my feet, too unsteady to stand.

"Hey," he said. "Hey. Let's get down there, alright? Come on."

I nodded, wiping my face with the inside of my jumpsuit, trying to calm my hitching breath as I followed him to the door and down the stairs. As we moved, I heard the massive garage door lurch and open, and by the time we'd reached the ground floor, a large van had already pulled in and parked near the door.

Two figures approached from a distance, and I managed to find my composure as I ran to meet them. It was good to see Doctor Mick, the silver-haired, spectacled doctor who ran the medical team at the Centre. He wore a blue stethoscope around his neck, but every other item of clothing was black.

But seeing Holli behind him was another thing entirely. She met me with a wide smile and sparkling eyes that crinkled at the edges. We embraced without words, and she held me in a way that only Mother and Morgan ever had. It was the comfort I needed as I came down from Sid's news of finding Eli. Seeing, touching, and hugging Holli was like coming home. She understood how deep my love for Eli went because she cared for him just as much.

Her fingers threaded in my knotted hair as she shushed my cries, finally holding me at arm's length so we could get a good look at each other.

"Eli?" she asked.

"They found him," I croaked. "Sid and Zeke. He's alive, but barely."

Her face darkened, but she nodded at the news, glancing at Mick. "How can we help?"

Silas approached from behind, shaking both of their hands. "They're bringing up the first few now," he said. "We'll need to make some tough calls. Save who we can. How's the triage coming along?"

"Well," said Mick with a nod. "Kendra is nearly finished getting the beds lined up in one of the complex's apartment buildings. Shelly's sterilizing the cleanest room we could find for any temporary or essential procedures before we can get back to the Centre. We'll do our best."

Silas nodded. "Unfortunately, there's not much here and Avi...well..." He shook his head, breezing past the details. "The commune's hospital has been compromised. One of our men brought over the ambulance over there, which probably has some supplies in it. I've got some vodka for sterilizing that I can bring you. I'm sorry we don't have much else."

"That's not new for us," Holli answered. "We'll make do."

Silas gave a curt nod before heading over to the door leading to the lower floors. He held it open with his back. Voices echoed from within — shouts and commands, moans, cries, and whispers. I followed Holli and Mick to the ambulance, carrying bandages, gauze, medical tape, small glass vials, and syringes wrapped in plastic back to their van. I tried focusing on my task, but every few seconds my eyes drifted to the open door.

The first people to arrive from the stairwell were two women, carried in canvas stretchers by our rebels, who laid them gently beside the van. Both looked to be around my age, their features sharp against their gaunt faces. They wore gowns similar to the ones I'd had on in the hospital. Their matted hair collected in nests, as stringy as their thin frames. Though they had distinct features, there was a clear similarity between the two. Sisters, I guessed. Bruises trailed up from their wrists to the crooks of their elbows. Like someone had poked them with a thousand needles.

I couldn't tell if either of them was still breathing.

Holli tended to the sister on the right, leaning over her to check her pulse. She pulled back, checked again, before she looked at Mick with glassy eyes. She shook her head.

"Put her over there," he said, pointing near the vehicles at the far end of the garage. "Do we have blankets?"

"I'll find some," I offered.

Had I really felt relief just moments ago? All I felt now was dread. As if in a daze, I crossed the wide space between the van and the ambulance. The ground seemed to stretch, making the void feel endless, my destination impossibly far. But I managed it, even in my stupor, reaching to open the back doors. Inside, it was empty, so I stepped up to check the different compartments, trying to keep my emotions steady.

Alive. But barely.

Sid's words and description could mean anything. It could mean that Holli would need to make a call that he wasn't worth transporting back to the triage at the office complex. That he was better off taking his last breaths in this garage as we all circled around him, helpless to stop the inevitable.

No.

I was right back where I'd started.

Alive. But barely.

I curled my arm around my bicep and squeezed, forcing myself to focus on my task. I found a stack of sheets in one of the bottom compartments and gathered them into my arms. The rebels had laid the girl beside the truck and carried the now empty canvas stretcher back toward the stairs. More rebels had come up since I found the sheets, laying one more person down beside the girl Mick was now tending to.

The dead girl looked so small and so alone, it made my chest ache. I had the irrational thought of wanting to lie beside her, to let her know she wasn't here by herself. That I was sorry this happened to her. That she didn't deserve this fate. That if I could've changed these outcomes, I would've. I would've done *anything*.

Instead, I kneeled beside her and fixed her hair. I straightened her gown. And I prayed for her soul.

Urgent voices brought me out of prayer. The dead deserved dignity. They deserved to be remembered. But right now, Holli and Mick needed my extra pair of hands, so I set to work shaking out one of the white sheets and settling it over the young girl's corpse. I left the pile of blankets at her feet, hating that I knew there would be more beside her soon.

Another pair of rebels appeared near the van, holding another person in a makeshift stretcher made from sheets. Holli assessed him, then pointed toward the girl. I squeezed my eyes closed, took a deep breath, and approached Holli and Mick as more rebels and yet another prisoner arrived on the floor.

The place was about to turn into a madhouse.

"Water," Mick said, pointing at the girl as he got up, moving to the next patient.

I knelt beside the sister who had finally opened her eyes. She stared blankly at the ceiling as I leaned in to look at her face. Holli handed me a bottle of water, which I opened.

"Are you thirsty?" I asked.

The girl didn't respond. Gently, I placed my arm beneath her head, giving her a little leverage as I brought the bottle to her chapped lips. I let the water dribble around her mouth and down her chin, but she made no effort to drink.

"Can you hear me?" I asked.

The girl blinked. Her focus shifted. She met my eyes.

"Chest," she croaked.

I tilted my head and lifted the water bottle so she could see it. "Water?"

The girl squeezed her eyes shut, then shook her head. "My chest."

"Have some water," I encouraged her. "It'll help."

The girl sighed and let her head droop against my arm. I tried the water again, to no avail. Her eyes fluttered closed, and her breathing slowed. Had she fallen asleep? Maybe that was okay for now. But what had she meant by her chest?

I lifted the gown's neck and looked down past her thin collarbones, not wanting to invade her privacy but curious to understand why she'd mentioned that part of her body. And there it was. A small box hooked to the side of her breast. A green light at the top blinked every few seconds. Horrified, I dropped the fabric and got to my feet.

"Doctor Mick?" I said quietly, backing away. "Mick?"

He lifted his head and turned toward me, brows raised over his circular glasses.

"Their chests," I said. "There's something on their chests."

He furrowed his brow, then looked back at his patient, pulling the gown's neck back to look down. His eyes widened. He dropped the fabric and looked around at the prisoners on the ground around him.

"Rip everyone's gown down the front, please," he instructed, while tearing the gown of the patient he tended.

Mick leaned over him, studying the device from all angles. Carefully, he used his fingers to lift it from the man's skin, but when he pulled, the man's skin stretched upward with it. He let out a moan. The green light kept blinking.

"Damn," he muttered.

Another team of rebels came through the doorway. Not Eli, but another young man. Mick told Holli to cover him up as he left the patient where he was, tending to the new arrival. I couldn't help but admire him and Holli. It was like watching Silas command the rebels. They were born to take care of people. In this moment of such a crisis, they could keep their heads on straight. They knew exactly what to do. One step at a time.

Holli and I helped patient after patient, cutting through their thin gowns so the monitors were all exposed. The closer I looked at them, the less I liked them. Even though they looked different, they reminded me of the lethal metal cuff I'd had around my ankle.

Just as Mick had directed the rebels to take another young woman over with the dead, Sid's tall stature appeared in the doorway. He stood with his back turned toward us, all muscles pulled taut, his dark dreads piled on top of his head. He looked over his shoulder, guiding the long canvas stretcher they carried into the garage.

The world quieted. I felt numb. I didn't know what to do, where to look, how to help, how close I should get. I just stood there watching Sid and Zeke carry Eli over to the end of the long line of prisoners they'd rescued.

From here, I could see Eli's tanned skin, the red bruising of his knuckles. Dried blood clung to the side of his hand that fell over the side of the canvas. His feet were bare, legs bruised beneath his dark leg hair, one more bloodied than the other. He wore a thin hospital gown like the others, showing just how frail he had gotten. Bruises coated what I could see of the inside of his arm. And his face — dear God, his face.

I cried out. I remembered how to use my legs and raced toward him.

Sid kneeled beside his brother, and I matched him on

the other side. I felt the tears I cried, but couldn't focus on them. Only on Eli. He looked so wrong; unlike himself, his features nearly indistinguishable from his injuries. His nose was clearly broken, twisted in a way that didn't make sense. Dried blood clung in clumps in his overgrown beard, at the sides of his lips, and down his chin.

His lip was split. The skin leading down to one of his shoulders was an angry shade of red and purple beneath his tattoo. He breathed heavily, his chest labored and shuddering, the air in his lungs rattling with mucus or blood, or both. His eyelids fluttered.

"Eli?"

My voice came out in a whisper, and he reacted to it, blinking and struggling to keep his eyes open. Our gazes found each other, and I felt my stomach flip, my heart clench, and my adrenaline fire. Look at what they had done to him. To this wonderful, kind, and giving man. What my Father and his Hunters had done to others, to this commune, to strangers on the Outside had been horrific. But seeing the damage up close to someone I cared so deeply for was gut-wrenching. It made me see red. It made me want to tear someone limb from limb.

"Hi," he whispered, reaching out a hand. I grasped it, threading our fingers together, desperately clutching him against my palm. It was the only part of him I felt comfortable touching to be sure I didn't hurt him. But it was enough for now.

If we hadn't gotten to him today, he'd be dead. I was sure of it. Someone handed Sid a pair of scissors and instructed him to cut Eli's gown, which he did, revealing the device on his chest. The surrounding skin was pinched and pink.

"Hey," Eli groaned, letting his unfocused eyes trail back to his brother. "Take me to dinner first."

"Yeah, I'll take you to dinner," Sid said, using his thumb and forefinger to wipe his tears out of his eyes. "I'll make you whatever the hell you want."

"A cheeseburger?"

Eli smiled, sighed, then let his eyes close.

I looked up at Sid, who looked back at me, pressing his lips together as he laughed. Tears rolled down both of his cheeks. He pressed his hand against Eli's forehead, bowed his head, and whispered something in his ear.

Eli's fingers tightened around mine, and I collapsed on my side, lying next to him. I knew I was needed. I knew I needed to get up, to let Holli tend to him, to figure out how to get the contraption off his chest without hurting him. But I just wanted to stay here with him.

We rested our hands together on top of his stomach, and I watched the rhythm of his breathing take them up and down, up and down. Mick came by, checked his pupils, his pulse, and his lungs, giving us a nod of approval. That was enough. He was in better shape than some.

I curled closer to him, leaving enough distance so I wouldn't touch any of his injuries. After some time, his fingers went slack, and I let them go. His breathing slowed. It was time for him to rest.

After some time, I got up to help the others. We would save who we could. And then we'd go back to fighting.

We had to. *I* had to.

Because the people I loved couldn't.

24

MAURA

Sixteen prisoners came out of the Pit. Eight of them were dead or beyond saving. Two of them were critical. But we couldn't move them. I'd explained my ankle monitor to Holli and Mick — how it tracked my every move. How it would sever my foot if I strayed too far. I suspected the heart monitors would do the same thing. They agreed.

Now, Mick and Holli sat on the floor beside the most recent corpse — a male teenager — removing his monitor to see how it worked. Zeke had gone back down to the Pit to help the rebels look for more medical supplies and make sure they'd searched everything. Sid and I hovered at the feet of those left alive, listening for trouble. Significant changes in breathing. Seizures. New points of pain.

It was a disorienting, stomach-turning scene that smelled of rot, sour sweat, and blood. One of the patients wouldn't stop moaning, the sound bouncing from corner to corner of the high-ceilinged garage. I clenched my jaw, trying to drown it out.

Eli had curled up on his side, his hand absentmindedly hovering above his injured shoulder. After Mick's assessment, we'd learned someone had taken a knife to his thigh, damaging the nerves there. It was possible he might not walk on it again. It was devastating, and I knew how much it would devastate *him*, but after hearing how many others had fared, I was just glad he was alive. I hoped he would see things that way, too. For now, they'd given all the patients some pain medication while they tried to troubleshoot the device.

Across the room, Mick gave a triumphant whoop. Holli bounced to her feet, holding the contraption in the air. Long, thin needles were attached to each side, like some robotic spider. They flexed in and out, like it was running in midair before the whole thing froze.

A chill ran up my spine. I glanced back at Eli, at the small bulge on his chest, beneath the split gown, then up at Sid. His frown deepened as Holli and Mick approached.

"What the *hell* is that thing?" Sid asked.

"It's like a tick, only trickier," Holli said, holding the contraption up. I wrinkled my nose at it. "They're embedded deep in the flesh, but if we pull hard enough, it'll come straight out. Has to be quick, so the legs don't pierce anything."

"Let's hurry," Mick said, kneeling down by the first girl who'd come out of the Pit. "I need all the local anesthetic we can spare. We've got to get these patients moving over to triage and—"

The garage door lurched, and the room filled with mechanical whirring, drowning Mick's words out. Night had settled over the Waste Center, the outside entryway coated in blue light coming from the upstairs control room. The door pulled upward, revealing two trucks. They rolled forward. Stopped. Their headlights dimmed, and eight new people spilled out.

I recognized Dr. Kaufmann from when I'd arrived back

at the commune from the Centre, but the others I didn't know. They were all dressed differently, some in the same outfit I'd left the hospital in, some in regular clothing, but I could tell immediately that they were here to help Mick and Holli. The medical reinforcements, and quite possibly the only medical staff the commune had left.

"Oh, thank God," Holli said under her breath.

A door slammed, and I looked up. James crossed the space with wide strides, eyes focused on me. I stood, not wanting to leave Sid or Eli.

"Elijah wanted me to get you," he said. "To show you what we've put together."

I raised my brow.

"From the footage. He wants…well, you'll see. Come on." He turned back toward the door, but I hesitated, glancing back at Eli on the floor. Sid met my eyes

"Go," Sid said, his hand on my shoulder. He squeezed. "He's in good hands. I'll go with him to triage, okay? Don't worry."

I gave a dry laugh.

"Yeah, I know," he said. "Just go."

I nodded. James held the door for me, and together, we climbed the stairs to the main control room. For the first time, I understood where the blue light came from. It spilled from the monitors, bathing the room in its glow. Silas stood near the window, the walkie held to his mouth, hand threaded in his hair as static crackled through the air.

"Maura, Silas," Elijah said. He beckoned us over from where he sat in front of James's laptop. "Come on over."

I hated the feeling that came with being surrounded by men from the commune. These were rebels. My friends. And yet, I still felt an innate need to be obedient and submissive. I closed my eyes and tried to bury it.

Silas pocketed his radio with a sigh and stood behind

me as I settled into the seat next to Elijah. On the laptop screen, some kind of software showed a bunch of boxes, each with different still images.

"You saw what your father put out, yeah?" he asked.

I nodded.

"Okay. Our aim is to do the same kind of thing, only instead of your father speaking, it'll be you." His eyes searched my face for a reaction.

"We thought it might be impactful, kind of like you did when you first came back into the commune," Silas said. "Your voice can rally the people. Convince them of the truth. With Avi out there, I think our top priority is to get people to safety. To alert them of the danger and try to persuade them not to lay down their lives for Peter. If we can do that, it'll be enough for now."

I rubbed my fingers across my mouth. "What would I say?" I mused to no one in particular.

"Channel what you said into the camera when you were in the Sciences and Innovations center, when you'd first returned," suggested James. "Something from the heart. Something that speaks to the people and can turn the tide of loyalty. Let them know that you've been there, that you were once them. Convince them that the rebels aren't here to hurt them. We want to help them."

I took a breath.

"I'll need a little bit. To just…think about what I want to say," I said.

"That's fine," Elijah said. "James can write out the main points you should hit. The sooner we can do this, the better. We need to have something ready when Peter puts out another announcement, so we can override the broadcast and be sure everyone is watching."

"It'll help to show what we have," James said.

Elijah nodded, turning back toward the computer. With

a few clicks, he pulled one of the screens wide and hit the play button.

The video started outside the Waste Center when the sun was still high in the sky. It reflected off the trash piles, glinting on the different materials that rotted together. James and Elijah had obviously been in a truck while this was filmed, but Elijah kept the camera steady as they approached the entrance between the high mounds of trash. An overlaid text identified this place as the Coutts Waste Center, and then, in parentheses, The Pit.

In the video, we rolled up to the massive gate, the camera's position circling, so it was clear we hadn't changed locations. The truck rolled forward, revealing the concrete interior. It was empty on the video, save for a few patrolling rebels. The video cut to black.

All of this has been hiding beneath the Coutts Waste Center for years.

The next video showed the rebels crowding around the door that led down into the Pit. Sid and Zeke held the flash bombs in their hands.

"No violence," Zeke reminded the rebels. "Tie everyone up. Do not shoot unless you have to."

The video flashed next to their journey down the stairs, tying up guards, and keeping them alive. It showed Zeke and Sid throwing their flash bombs down the hallway, subduing the guards, and clearing the rest of the floor, just like we'd watched on the video monitors.

Elijah made it clear that the guards wore Coutts Hunter suits; their numbers zoomed in and visible to whoever was responsible for these men. But none of this mattered until people actually saw what they were guarding.

The video cut next to Sid and Zeke in the circular white room with the numbered doors. Sid waved the keys in front of the first door. Something buzzed. The lock unlatched. He pulled the door open.

The footage was damning. I had seen bits and pieces of things as they were happening, but it was nothing compared to watching it stitched together, with sharp imagery and clear angles. The room was bare except for a toilet, sink, and a flat metal board with a thin mattress. A woman was curled up in a sheet, tucked into the corner of the bed.

A gray foot peeked out from the thin blanket she was wrapped in, and as they came deeper into the room, her complexion did not change. Her bone-thin limbs showed the definition of her fragile muscles, the curve of her bones. And even though Elijah did us the favor of not zooming in on her face, one cloudy eye was visible, indicating she was dead.

The next room was no better, except that the subject was alive. Barely. A young man with patches of hair missing, a blackened eye, and a body that was failing him. My stomach churned as we went in and out of rooms in quick succession. It would be easy to look away, to close my eyes, to avoid the horrors. But we'd been doing that for too long. I had to look.

These atrocities were the fuel I needed to remember why I needed to fight, and fight hard. The men I had trusted, my Father, once a Prophet to me, had done this knowingly. To save himself. To save the thing he built. To keep those who obeyed him healthy while killing others. All of this against everyone's will, because he deemed himself the mouthpiece of God.

It had been easy over the past few months to distance myself from it. To think about these things theoretically. I hadn't known about the Pit. I hadn't known what he was doing with the people he was kidnapping. Naively, I thought perhaps he was giving them lives in the commune. Putting them to work, utilizing their skills and knowledge for something purposeful. I had lived that life forever. It was a half-life, I knew. But it was still a life. I was still alive, fed, and sheltered.

I had never in a million years imagined this.

The depths of Father's evil went so much deeper than I'd realized, and it filled me with a blind, hot rage. For the lies, yes. But more so that he had done this to strangers; to innocent victims who were no different from us. These people's only crime was that they were born in a different place to different circumstances. That they didn't share the same beliefs as us. And this was the sin he found unforgivable. The sin he used to justify this kind of punishment.

What he had done was more than ungodly. It was the work of a Devil.

On screen, overlaid text explained the medical room we saw next, how it was a place where the prisoners were harvested, their cells and life-force used to create vaccines for our people. Because in my father's mind, our lives were more valuable than theirs. Unknowingly, we'd all taken medication and vaccines that had signed others' death certificates. Father had played God. And we were exposing him for it.

James and Elijah had interwoven clips of Father talking about his innovations and vaccines to the broader public, promising health and medical care if the Outsiders would just give up their unholy ways. They showed him speaking to the government during one of the pandemics. Welcoming newcomers into our commune. At the altar, pretending to be a man of God. Then the video switched back to clips of the victims. A sweeping shot of some of the wounded lying on the floor in the garage. Holli and Mick tending to them. A shot of the covered corpses.

Then, at the end, a black screen that read.

God will forgive our ignorance, for we did not know the sins we committed. What matters is what we do once the truth has been revealed. For your safety, for the fate of your soul, please let us fight the evil we now understand. We are not against you. We aim only to unveil the horrors we ourselves just discovered. Peter Coutts is no Prophet. He is the Devil Incarnate. And we must no longer allow his influence to shape our world.

I sat down. My body hummed with new energy. If anything was going to convince the commune to see my father for who he truly was, this was it. Silas gave me a knowing look — he saw it too. A smile crossed his features before he went over to one of the desks, retrieved a blank pad of paper and a pencil, and handed it to me.

I got to work.

25

MAURA

By the time I'd finished recording my speech, I was exhausted. And maybe that was a good thing. My words had come from a place of burnout and rage. It was late, and it had been ages since I'd gotten a decent rest. Some of the rebels had made a makeshift sleeping area in the corner of the control room, and I lay there beside Zeke, tossing and turning as he snored.

Nadia and Silas went back and forth on the radio, their voices lulling me in and out of sleep. Information came in pieces. She had eyes on Avi's whereabouts. After an attack on one of the farms, a fire had gotten out of control and was still spreading. Avi had retreated, taken over a home lower on the mountain, and was quiet there. Nadia had tried to approach him twice with no success.

Later, the radios went off again. They had managed to get the contraptions out of everyone's chests. Sid had gone with Holli to the office complex. Eli was in triage, being tended to as well as they could manage. Only one of the patients died during transport.

My sleep was restless. Every time I drifted off, I saw the

patients in the garage. The covered bodies. The moans of pain. The thin legs of the machine someone had stuck into the prisoner's chests. Chaos and death. Father had caused this pain. Hot anger brewed in my body, but I was too tired to bring it to the surface. So I let sleep fade in and out, and when I woke again, the sky outside had lightened.

Dawn approached.

All around me, rebels slept in different positions — against the wall, curled up in the corners, or stretched out across chairs. Slow, heavy breathing and light snores filled the air. Elijah sat in front of the laptop, his head in his hands, eyes closed. James had fallen asleep under the desk, his head nestled in the crook of his elbow.

The only other person awake in the room was Silas. He stood in front of the large window, his hands clasped behind his back. Had he slept? Eaten? Or had he been worried and awake all night?

With effort, I lifted myself from the ground, stretched my muscles, and approached him.

"Morning," he said, without looking at me.

"Morning," I answered. "Did you sleep?"

He looked at me, his blue eyes bloodshot. "Tried." He shrugged. "Our team finally finished sweeping the base-ment floors thirty minutes ago."

"You should get some rest, Silas." I frowned. "You look exhausted."

"I just…" He shook his head.

"Yeah," I said, thinking of how out of control my thoughts had been before I'd fallen asleep. "I get it."

We stood side by side in silence, looking out over the Waste Center. Silas sighed.

"Things are not going to plan," he said. "We need to clear out of here." His voice was stilted, quiet. "Peter will target this place before long. There's too much value here.

Too much risk. More than I realized before we took it over."

I glanced back at the control panel, where James and Elijah slept. "What about the video?"

Silas followed my gaze. "We'll have to go to Abraham's team," Silas said. "We can't wait for Peter to deliver another video. It's taking too long. We don't have the manpower here to stand up to a fight against Hunters. We need to get back together with Avi. Convince him to fight without violence." He shook his head. "I feel so *foolish* that I fell for what he said to us at the Centre."

"You're not foolish. Avi convinced a lot of us that he wasn't going to use force."

"I still don't understand it. We could've taken the commune by now if we'd kept to the plan." He sighed. "I just hope we can talk some sense into him today. We can get the video out, convince who we can from the commune. Most of the loyal Hunters are up at the Peak. If we can band together and get up there, maybe we can figure out a solution."

I nodded. "It can still work, Silas," I said. "I know it can."

He gave me a tired smile. "Thanks for having faith," he said. "I know we're trying to be righteous and go about things the way God intended, but I still worry. I want the best for *all* people. I'm just afraid I can't keep everyone safe if both Peter and Avi are using violence. They won't pause to question who they're hurting."

"All we can do is our best, Silas. This fight was inevitable. I just wish Avi hadn't made things so hard."

He hummed his agreement. I swallowed, studying his profile. His jaw tightened, but his gaze remained on the window.

"Once we clear out, the rebels and I will link up with Nadia to reconvene with Avi. Then we can work on compromising with Peter." He turned to me. "You should stay with the others at the office complex. Be with Eli."

"No," I said sternly. "I have to face my father."

Silas frowned. "You don't have to *do* anything."

"Fine. I *want* to face him, then," I said. "I don't want to sit on the sidelines."

"Helping with medical is barely sitting on the sidelines."

"You know what I mean."

He smiled. "I do. But Morgan would *kill* me if I didn't at least try to keep you out of harm's way."

I laughed because he was right.

"Morning," said a new, deeper voice. Gabriel. Sleep clung to his heavy eyelids, which he rubbed with his fists. His golden hair stuck up in different directions.

"Hey," said Silas. "You alright?"

Gabriel shrugged. "So we're moving out this morning?" he asked sleepily.

"Yes," Silas said. "We should get everyone moving."

"Did I hear we're leaving?" Zeke got to his feet with a grunt.

"You did," said Silas.

I glanced around the room at the waking rebels. Our voices and Silas's plans had stirred them all from sleep.

"Great. We'll clear out," Zeke said. "Head to Abraham, then to Avi."

Silas nodded his confirmation. "After that, we'll need to head to the Peak."

Anxiety swirled in my belly at the thought.

"Everyone up," Silas said, strengthening his voice so it carried around the room to wake the rest of the snoozing rebels as he reiterated the plan to his men.

"We'll head out in ten. We should all be able to fit in the trucks. We can drive along the perimeter of the commune and cut through the farmlands. Whoever needs to go to medical, we can drive. We'll—"

A succession of shots rang out.

Too close.

The garage door beneath us gave an almighty lurch.

The room stilled; chatter ceased. Silas's mouth hung open mid-sentence. I felt my eyes widen, my heart slow, the world around me brighten.

Everyone moved at once. Orders were shouted over orders, so fast and loud they felt like static. Magazines slipped into guns with heavy clicks. Frantic voices crackled over radios and across the room. Zippers, buckles and the sharp sound of velcro as Gabriel forced a bulletproof vest over my head. Panicked boots raced past us, toward the door.

I couldn't catch my breath.

Fingers squeezed my forearm. "Stay close to me," Gabriel ordered.

Silas hovered by the door to the stairs, with the rebels crowded at his back. He looked over his shoulder before he opened the door, his straightened stance ready for battle.

Shouting echoed up the stairwell. More shots rang out.

"Look alive, men!" Silas shouted. "Get to the trucks and get out of here safely. Now!" He moved through the door-frame, footsteps pounding down the stairs.

We all followed, Gabriel on my left, rebels on my right, tightly packed and heavily armed.

I felt outside of myself, disoriented. Everything was too loud. My feet moved against my will. We reached the bottom of the stairs and stumbled out into the garage.

Gunpowder and smoke filled the air. Shots and shouts rang out, the sounds ricocheting off the high ceiling of the garage, and I covered my ears with my hands.

Shots came again, louder this time, whizzing past my

ear. Smoke erupted somewhere to our right, clouding the air in a gray haze. I lost sight of the rebels. Gabriel left my side. Someone was screaming.

"Get DOWN!" Someone gripped my arm, pulled me to the floor, behind a parked truck. Pain shot through my knee and ankle as they collided with the concrete. Instinctively, I covered my head. I could barely tell where we were until the smoke began to clear. The figure beside me — Gabriel, I assumed — stood. His body convulsed as he shot his weapon, bullet after bullet leaving the chamber, the shells clattering to the floor around me like lethal confetti. I stuck my fingers deep into my ear canals. Closed my eyes. And when I opened them, I couldn't breathe.

Because a pile of bodies lay a few feet away from me, visible between the truck tires. And though there were some I did not recognize, there were two that I did. They lay still, blood stark red against the concrete.

The first was Elijah, his camera cases tangled in his long arms.

The second was Silas.

26

———

MAURA

THE REBELLION WAS OVER. Not just over, but lost. I was sure of it. My thudding heart filled my ears, drowning out the shouts and screams and shots. I felt the concrete beneath me, cold and unforgiving. Gabriel's hand on my back went slack. Did he see? Did he know?

All I saw was Silas's face. It was splattered — *splattered* — in blood. His sky blue eyes, once glinting with love and dreams of a life with my sister, were still. Unblinking. Unseeing.

Instantly, gone.

A cry worked its way up my throat, falling out in a devastated moan I could barely hear. We needed to move, I knew. But I couldn't stop staring at Silas. Silas, who had led us here, who had carved the way, who had led us this far into battle. Who had loved my sister so selflessly, he was ready and willing to do anything to make a better world. For her and their baby. For everyone else inside and outside this commune.

He was a pure soul. A good man. A *true* man of God. And now he was gone. For what? So Father could hold on to power he was quickly losing? People were dying for one man. A man who had cruelly decided the fate of so many without remorse. A man who used God as his shield for power.

How many more had to lay down their lives for him? How many more did he have to kill until he could no longer justify it? It was not just blasphemous, not just evil — it was senseless. Stupid actions of a broken man destroying the world because it was easier than admitting he was wrong.

Bullets pierced the air. Someone moaned, yelled, and a heavy weight fell to the ground. I looked up. Gabriel kneeled beside me, fist in his mouth, fighting emotion and grief. James lay next to him on his stomach, hands threaded together over his head, behind the truck's tire. Another rattle of bullets came, and then, silence.

"GET UP." Zeke's voice carried across our row. He slid around the back of the truck, gun still smoking in his hands. "Follow me," he ordered.

Bouncing on his toes, he peered around the side of the truck at the threat that had somehow ambushed us, then sprinted to the next one parked a few feet away. A bullet followed his feet seconds later, shredding across the concrete as it threw up dust.

The room went silent again.

Two rebels followed Zeke's movements. More bullets followed them, one after the other.

Crack.

Crack.

Crack.

James went next. Ahead, a door opened, letting in early morning sunlight. An exit. Zeke's broad form appeared in silhouette. A bullet pierced him through the shoulder. Blood splattered outward, toward the sun.

No!

He crumbled forward, curling toward the side, ducking down and out of sight. I thought of Silas, lying behind me. Dead.

Dead.

Gabriel darted across to the next truck, then turned to me, his face pallid and terrified.

"Come on!" he yelled.

I willed my feet to move as fast and as precisely as they could and somehow I launched myself across the wide open space littered with bullets. Gabriel and I scrambled side by side to the open door, flinging ourselves through it and out onto the dirty ground. Ahead, Zeke, James, and a handful of our rebels hid behind mounds of trash.

The sunlight was too bright, filtering through the gates, exposing us all.

"The office complex," Gabriel gasped.

In the distance, the dilapidated buildings offered the only hope we had left. Rebels hung out of windows facing the Waste Center and shot at the intruders over our heads.

I didn't want to, but I looked anyway. The loyalist Hunters had arrived in a single black truck, indistinguishable from the ones we'd been using. A small team, it seemed, yet horrifyingly lethal. Somehow, they'd gained access to the garage. Shot their way in. I was sure there were more of our dead lying at their feet.

In the distance, at the far corner of one of the mounds, stood a tall, imposing figure, his green helmet turning left to right as he shouted something I couldn't hear.

We were far, but not far enough away that I couldn't see the number on his breast pocket.

11.

It was Luke who had broken into the garage. Luke had

not only destroyed our rebellion. He had killed his own son.

ON FOOT, the Waste Center was much further from the office complex. Driving with Andrew had taken minutes. Through my binoculars, it had seemed only feet away. But trying to stay hidden, walking with the wounded while the majority of us were working on only a few hours of interrupted sleep and a lifetime of defeat, it took us what felt like ages to get on the other side of the fence.

The loyalists did not come after us, but still, fear that rippled across the group of the twenty or so of us left. But more than fear, I felt the weight of defeat settle over us, and that scared me more than being shot at by the Hunters. The Hunters were a threat I knew and generally understood. But giving up had *never* been a choice when we'd started this fight.

Now, it felt like our only option.

Gabriel cried quietly beside me, and the only comfort I could offer him was a hand at his back as we skirted the side of the buildings. Without Silas to direct us, everything felt futile. We walked toward the triage building Mick and Holli had set up, but then what? We needed to reassess. We needed to...

I didn't know anymore. We'd lost the upper hand. We were so tired and so burnt out that even a small group had forced our larger one out. We had saved barely half the prisoners. The footage James and Elijah had taken, the impactful video we'd put together, all of it was on the laptop on Elijah's back, who lay dead in the garage beside Silas.

Now we had *nothing* to show for our efforts.

We walked along the sidewalks, and I wondered if I was dreaming. Imagining Eli gone had been one thing. But seeing Silas dead…I couldn't comprehend it. I couldn't believe it, even though there was no question that it was true.

Ahead, Zeke led our charge, holding his shoulder with one bloody hand. He leaned to the side, as if compensating for the pain. I wanted to throw up. Was this really it? The end of our fight?

We passed the office building where I'd hidden out, approaching a group of guards that clustered around the next building. They jumped to attention, not asking questions, simply helping Zeke inside and up the stairs. I had a strange urge to yell at them, to ask where they had been. Why hadn't they helped us — helped Silas, after everything he'd done?

But exhaustion and grief prevented me from doing so, and I only wanted to get under cover. To not worry about being shot at. To stop thinking about Silas and Mother and Morgan and the hospital being blown apart. To not think about how everything I'd done since the minute I stepped into the creek had been a waste of time.

My mistakes had caused this chaos. I had brought death upon my friends and family, and I would forever carry blood on my hands because of it.

The building we entered had a narrow set of stairs running through the middle. On either side of the small lobby were two doors. One was opened wide, leading into a poorly lit room. The other door was closed.

I recognized Shelly, one of Mick's nurses, as she came through the door, sleep lining her pretty face, her brown hair tied in a low ponytail at the nape of her neck. She smiled at me in recognition as she peeled off a pair of gloves before crossing to enter the other room. I could just make out a brightly lit surface and the back of Mick's coat before the door closed behind her.

Holli bounded down the stairs, her face solemn.

"What happened?"

I found her eyes, but wished I hadn't because everything threatened to come through as tears. But it was Gabriel who succumbed first, his knees buckling beneath him as he fell to the floor. He rested his head in his hands, touching his forehead to the ground, rocking back and forth. His sobs carried out into the street.

Zeke stepped forward, shielding us from Holli, to give her the gritty details of what had happened. I couldn't listen to them. I couldn't relive them. Not again.

I sat on the floor beside Gabriel and held him as best I could.

27

MAURA

I FOUND Eli and Sid in the back corner of what had once been a small room in an old apartment. A lantern hung near the door, providing a dim glow at the entrance. Inside, the boarded-up windows allowed only slivers of light into the room. Three mattresses were spread out evenly on the floor. The middle one was empty. One figure took up a bed on the left — another, more familiar one, lay in the bed to my right.

Sid sat at the end of the mattress, his back up against the wall. His eyes found mine as I approached, settling on the floor beside him.

"Hi," he breathed. He tilted his head, his brow wrinkling. I wasn't supposed to be here yet.

I didn't answer. I laid my head against his arm and breathed. I smelled Sid's sweat, mingled with my own. The sharp scent of blood. It brought me out of my stupor, my numbness dissipating as I was forced to confront my shock.

"What happened?" he asked. His arm found mine and steadied it. I was shivering. "Maura?"

"Silas," I whispered, thinking of his face. *Blood splattered.* "Elijah. A bunch more."

"Hurt?"

My throat felt like it was closing.

"Maura," he tried again, his voice more urgent. "Hurt?"

I rolled my neck, shook my head.

"No. They're..." The word was there, on the tip of my tongue.

Sid straightened, his grip tightening. "What? They're *what?*"

"Sid..." His name came out as a desperate moan. I didn't want to say it. *Couldn't* say it out loud. "The video is gone. I don't..." My voice broke. I swallowed. "I don't know what we're going to do."

"Maura," Sid said. "Where is Silas?" His shoulders tensed. He leaned forward, got to his knees, his eyes begging me for the truth. "Is he alive?"

The question filled the room like a roar, clouding around me so I couldn't avoid it.

"No."

"Oh, no. No, no, no." Rage and grief simmered in his voice. He got to his feet. Put his hand on the top of my head. "Stay here," he said.

I didn't ask where he was going.

Instead, I found Eli. He slept, his eyes lost in a sea of bruises. They had patched him up as best they could. Bandages covered his ear. A splint straightened his nose. His arm and shoulder were wrapped in a tight cast. His leg was slightly elevated on several pillows, a bandage wrapped around his thigh. A blanket covered the rest of him up to his neck.

I crawled from the floor onto the mattress, keeping my back against the wall as I settled beside him. Doing so felt selfish. I could offer him no comfort. I just wanted to be near him. To know he was okay, to memorize his breathing, to touch him. Make sure he was really alive.

My hand settled on his whiskered cheek, and gently I traced the pads of my fingers down to his jaw. His eyes moved behind his eyelids, and he blinked them open. Dark, nearly black irises found me in the shadowed room.

"I'm sorry," I whispered. I felt tears on my nose. "I didn't mean to wake you."

It took a moment for him to recognize me. But a soft, sleepy smile crossed his mouth when he did.

"Hi," he said, his voice like gravel. "It's a good reason to wake up."

I brushed my thumb against his scratchy cheek, and he nuzzled into it, his dark hair falling over his eyes.

"I messed everything up," I said, my chest tightening as the words rolled from my tongue. I felt the tears, the grief, the anger, the frustration all bundled together in the middle of my throat. "I caused all of this pain. All this death and destruction. You're here because of me. Silas is…Silas is…gone…because of me, and now there's nothing left. The fight is over. We lost."

Everything exploded at once, and I devolved into tears, shuddering against the wall, my sobs uncontrollable. And I felt shame at it all, unloading my emotions onto someone who'd been so near death, for my guilt and my bad choices and what I had done to people who had protected me. People I loved. People who deserved better.

I felt warm fingers on my chin, and I wanted to look, but I couldn't. I couldn't stop crying. I would never stop crying. I would lie here forever and force them to leave me here to rot, like I deserved. The Hunters could come and kill me. Father could hang me from the church rafters; an example to those who disobey.

"It's not your fault," Eli whispered. "Hey. Alright,

Maura? It's not your fault." He repeated himself, and I let his words cover and comfort me, cradling me in an embrace I hadn't earned, but sorely needed.

***

RAISED VOICES WOKE ME. Shouts and shushes, the pounding of feet on stairs. I stirred my aching body, moving every muscle gently. Eli lay across from me, his eyes closed, chest rising and falling slowly with his sleeping breaths. For a moment, it was just the two of us, side by side in the quiet room. I could imagine him this way, without his injuries, sunlight streaming in across us in our bed, where we were safe and carefree.

It was a wish I hadn't known I'd had until that moment.

But reality crept in insidiously, reminding me where we were and that we were not safe. That people were hurt. Dead. And that still, somehow, wasn't enough to call this war over.

My face still felt wet and swollen, but the initial shock of what had happened at the Waste Center had fallen away while I'd slept. Gently, I pushed myself up on the mattress, careful not to disturb Eli.

Light filtered in through the hallway, which led past two more rooms and into a shared kitchen and living room. I moved to the door, but it opened before I got there. Sid stopped in his tracks when he saw me.

"Oh," he said. "There you are. You should, uh..." He looked over his shoulder, then back at me. "You should come with me."

"Everything alright?" I asked.

Sid's face darkened. "We have a visitor." He turned, leading me through the door and across the hallway to the other apartment.

The door was already open. People filled the room, leaning against the walls, sitting on the couches, chairs, and the floor. Zeke sat on the counter, a fresh bandage peeking out beneath his black shirt. Gabriel, James, Joseph — no Jonah.

But near the middle of the room sat a man dressed in Hunter gear I hadn't expected to see again.

Andrew.

Breath caught in my throat as I entered the room, studying him. The handcuffs had been removed. His greasy, overgrown hair was slicked back, tucked behind his ears. Deep circles lined both eyes. A tremor plagued his right hand.

Sid crossed his arms as he leaned against the doorframe. He jutted his chin forward at him. "He says he wants to help," he said, eyes narrowed. "Brought us Elijah's camera." He pointed, and I followed his finger to the large camera beside Zeke.

I raised my brows. Looked back at Andrew.

"I want to help," Andrew said. "Maura, please."

"Why?" Suspicion hovered thick in the air. Andrew was as loyal as they came, and everyone in this room knew it. He'd had a single moment of truthfulness when he told me about The Pit. But that didn't mean much.

He sighed, looked at the ceiling, then hung his head. "The Hunters...Peter...they see me as a traitor. They believe I am as much at fault for this rebellion as you. They have blamed me for things I had no part in and expect me to come back to the Peak to repent." He looked up. "But I know what that means. I watched a man step over his son's dead body today and call himself a man of God, all to protect something...that shouldn't exist. And I knew...this was a path I could no longer follow."

"So now that you're facing punishment...the same

punishment given to Maura, mind you, you want to join us?" Sid asked before I could answer, his voice icy. "Now that you have nowhere else to go, you come to us?"

Andrew met his eyes, but didn't speak.

Heat rose in my chest and cheeks. I felt my nostrils flare.

"Is that why you told me about the Pit?"

Andrew's gaze met mine. "I told you about the Pit because I knew you and your friends could do something about it. And I'm here now because it is the only way I can make up for the unforgivable things I have done. I have come to realize that though I thought I was doing God's work, the work was something far more sinister—"

"For sure, the marrying children part didn't tip you off? Marrying your niece, not once, but twice?" Sid asked sarcastically. "The rape? Murder? None of that?"

"You must understand—"

"I don't," Sid said shortly, dropping his arms. He straightened and approached Andrew, towering over him. Andrew's eyes followed him, a glint of fear evident in his twitching eyelid. "I don't understand it at all. You see, I think you're a fucking coward." He bent over at the waist, hovering inches from his face. "You deserve whatever comes to you. You're here for all the wrong reasons."

"Maybe that doesn't matter," Gabriel said.

Sid straightened and turned, his shoulders softening.

"I don't care if Andrew is here for his own self-interest. What I do care about is retrieving the footage."

I eyed the camera.

"Is that still possible?" I asked.

We all shifted our eyes to James. The young man lifted his head. "We can't — the footage isn't stored on the camera," he said. "It's on the laptop. Everything's on that laptop."

"So the camera's useless," Sid said flatly.

"I can still help," Andrew insisted. "I can go back and get the laptop—"

"It still wouldn't matter," James said. "Nadia reported Abraham's hub is compromised. We'd need the control room back. And then we'd need to intercept one of Peter's broadcasts."

"I can distract Luke's men," Andrew said. "Give you enough time to go in and do what you need to do."

It was the first time I'd seen him so desperate. So willing to give up parts of himself to be accepted. It was easy for him. He was frightened when faced with the same consequences I'd had. It disgusted me.

Sid held up his hands. "How do we know this isn't a trap?"

"We don't." Gabriel hopped down from the counter. "But I'm not sure what else our options are here, Sid. We need that video. It's our last lifeline to get through to the rest of the commune. It's the only way we'll be able to reduce casualties *and* limit our reliance on violence." He looked at his feet. "It's what Silas would do. It's what he would want."

Sid bit his lip, clearly conflicted. "Fine. We give him a walkie, then," he said. "Send him in first. He clears the way. We go, get the laptop, and bring it to the control room. And hope to God Peter makes another announcement."

"Every hour on the hour," Andrew said.

"What?" asked Sid, clearly annoyed.

"Peter. You said the comms hub was compromised, yes? That's because he's giving announcements every hour on the hour. He's calling for prayers, and those are going live in everyone's homes."

Sid rubbed his hand against his stubbled chin, his eyes distant. "Good," he said, turning to Gabriel. "We gather up a team, then. As few as possible. Me, you, James, Joseph. Zeke?" He looked up at the large man, who nodded.

I stilled, glancing around the room. I wanted Andrew to be telling the truth. I wanted him to have a spark of good in him and to use it when it mattered.

But I didn't trust him.

"And me," I said.

Sid turned to me. "No," he said. "You stay here."

I narrowed my eyes at him. "No," I countered. "If this is a trap, you need me."

He raised his eyebrows. I looked back at Andrew.

"Andrew has committed many sins. But even at his angriest, he never laid a violent hand on me. He made a promise to God to protect me. And in his own way, he's stayed true to that promise." I turned back to Sid. "So I'm coming. As insurance."

28

MAURA

SID and I argued for the next ten minutes before Gabriel took my side and shut down the conversation. Sid was no longer speaking to him, except to coordinate logistics. I knew he was trying to keep me safe, but he didn't understand the commune like I did. He didn't understand how deep loyalties lay within these borders. I despised Andrew. Perhaps he despised me. But my presence ensured greater safety for the rebels. It wasn't foolproof. But it was something.

We stood on the ground floor of the building, peering out into the afternoon sun.

"There's only four of them left," Gabriel reminded us. "Andrew will subdue who he can, then call back to confirm it's safe. Once it's clear, we'll head to the control room. Sid and Joseph stand guard. Zeke follows in the truck once the mission is complete. I'll be in the stairwell. Maura and James will stay in the control room. Top of the hour is in approximately forty-five minutes."

Zeke waved us off as we exited the building and traveled down the weathered road in a cluster. Sid remained glued to my side, grinding his teeth. Every so often, he looked down at me, shook his head, and kept on walking.

Seeing Andrew walking together with Gabriel, Joseph, and James made everything feel like a fever dream. I had intended to leave Andrew behind forever. The day I'd ended up in the hospital I thought had been our last. I assumed he would be beside my father in this fight.

But penance was a demanding, unforgiving pillar to being a good follower of God. A good follower of the Prophet. I could appreciate how conflicted Andrew was about all of this. But none of it gave me pause for remorse. He had woken up, like I had. He had seen the truth, like we were about to show so many. It was encouraging. But it didn't take away from the person he was, or the choices he'd made.

There would be more penance for those things. There had to be. But I didn't want to be around to see it. After this was over, I wanted a new life.

I was tired of this landscape, of smelling the piles of decay so strong it made my eyes water. There was no getting used to a smell like this, but I accepted it for now. There were more important things to confront. We skirted the buildings and came around the side, hugging the structures to stay in the shadows. The sun faced us, warming my cold cheeks.

There was no security at the front of the Waste Center, and none as we came inside the gates. Andrew had likely been telling the truth about how many Hunters had ambushed us. Eight of them had come. Four were dead.

The video was our last hope. There was a chance Luke and his men had found the backpack, the laptop, and the video, and destroyed it. But we had to believe it was still there. Everything hinged on it.

We walked in silence down the dirt path that led

around the trash mounds. The place was a maze, I assumed by design. And it worked. I could imagine getting lost in here if you didn't know where you were going.

Road indents appeared around the next corner, leading to the entryway of the garage. Ahead, Gabriel skidded to a stop, putting his arm out to block the rest of us. He turned, put his finger to his lips. Sid brushed past me and came to his side.

"Look," Gabriel said.

I followed his gaze, glimpsing a lone guard outside the massive door. He held a gun and wore a helmet, pacing from one side to the other in an even line.

"You're up," Sid said viciously over his shoulder to Andrew.

My husband straightened. Ran a hand through his gray hair and took a deep breath. He stepped out from behind the trash pile and walked forward as if he had been here all along. It took a minute for the guard to notice him.

"Afternoon," said Andrew.

The guard nodded at him. "Thought you were headed to the Peak?"

"I will be shortly. I need to speak with Luke."

The guard tilted his head. "Why?"

"Important business," Andrew said. I wrinkled my nose. It was too vague. The Hunter would never believe it. And I was right. I watched his stature change, the twitch in his arm as he considered reaching for the gun slung across his back. But as disorienting as it had been for me to see Andrew within our ranks, it must've felt the same to this guard. He hesitated. And Andrew took his opportunity.

Like Silas, I had forgotten that Andrew was a trained soldier. He attacked so suddenly, I might've missed it if I had blinked. His hands wrapped around the Hunter's throat, and he wrestled him back into one of the mounds, pressing him deep into the debris. After a moment, the guard's arms went limp, hands drooping at his sides. Andrew snatched something from the front of his uniform, turned his red face around, and waved us over.

I swallowed. Gabriel, James, and Joseph stepped forward, Sid and I behind. I eyed the glass front of the control room warily, expecting to see Luke or another loyalist pacing. But it was dark and seemingly empty. They must've been down in the Pit.

Or they're waiting for you in the garage.

We followed the tire tracks to the door. Sid and Joseph tied up the unconscious guard, leaving him around the side and out of view. Andrew ran the guard's keys over a scanner, and we pressed ourselves flat against the concrete pillar as the light turned from red to green. The door lurched upward.

The dimly lit garage released a smell of gunpowder and blood. I gagged. Held my breath. It was the smell of death, a scent I would never forget. Andrew craned his neck, peering into the garage, and I watched his gaze travel over the space. My pulse quickened, waiting for more gunfire. More blood. More screams.

None came.

Andrew took a cautious step forward. Gabriel, James, and I followed with Sid and Joseph on our heels. If guards were up here, they would've heard the garage open and rushed us by now.

We paused at the Hunter's truck, which our attackers had arrived in, and I held back a gasp as we assessed the space. Maybe it *had* been a bad idea to come.

The truck was riddled with bullet holes. To our left, the ambulance's back doors hung open. Beside it, the pile of covered corpses. More trucks were parked near the door to the stairs leading to the control room, and it was this part of the room I had told myself to look away from.

I found it impossible.

My stomach lurched. I pressed my hands against the truck to steady myself, closing my eyes as I focused on my breathing. I couldn't unsee it.

Large brown stains covered the floor, some so thick they reflected the overhead lights. Broken glass covered the ground near the trucks. Dirty sheets, the discarded stretcher, and useless guns scattered across the rest of the floor like some child's lethal art project.

"Hey!" A voice echoed into the ceiling.

Adrenaline flooded my body. Beside me, my companions froze. Movement came from the corner of my eye, and my heartbeat clogged my throat. I grasped James by the arm and yanked him down behind the truck. Sid and Gabriel ducked too, and we stared at each other, wide-eyed.

"Who's there?" the voice asked.

"It's me!" Andrew answered immediately, coming around the wreckage. James, Sid, Gabriel, and I ducked behind the loyalist's truck at the front of the garage, pressing ourselves against it. I held my breath. Let it out slowly.

"Brother Andrew. Did Luke not send you to the Peak to be with the others?"

"He did," Andrew answered. "But the truck is useless. I need another way to get there."

"Luke does not have the resources for this currently. You should—"

The guard's breath caught in his throat, and I could *hear* the depression of his vocal cords as Andrew's thumbs pressed into his neck.

Yes, Andrew had seen the truth. He was angry. I felt a

sick satisfaction in knowing this hurt him and disappointment in knowing he would *never* hurt as much as so many others.

These thoughts were sins. They were feelings. They were unfair judgments. They were fleeting moments. Whatever they were, there was no man on Earth who could tell me if they made me good or bad. I was in control of that. I now felt confident that my relationship with God did not depend on them.

A gurgled moan echoed through the space. Sid, Joseph, and Gabriel rose to their full height, peering out over the truck. James clutched my arm in a fierce grip. His face had whitened considerably. I felt him tremble.

"Hey," I whispered. His nervous eyes flickered to me. "It's alright. Two down, yeah? Two more to go?"

He shook his head. Closed his eyes. "I don't think I can do this," he said.

I studied his young face, his round, red cheeks. Acne covered his nose. Uneven whiskers peeked out from his upper lip and chin. James was no soldier. He had not known violence before today. The Hunters were used to it. They saw it everywhere they went and used it to control others. But most in the commune had never experienced true violence.

The truth was, we were sheltered. We had been protected by our walls and Father's rules to live a life ignorant of the ugly parts of the world. And now that it was crumbling, there was no option. We were all exposed.

My heart ached for him.

"I'm so sorry about Elijah," I said.

His thin lips trembled. He began to cry. "I should've helped him," he said softly. "I should've pushed him out of the way; I should've shouted. I knew something was wrong the minute we opened that door, and I didn't say anything."

I placed a hand on his arm and rubbed circles. "You didn't do anything wrong," I told him. "What happened, happened quickly. There was little time for any of us to react. You can't blame yourself. You didn't bring those guns in. You didn't shoot."

He squeezed his eyes closed and wiped his nose with the back of his palm. "Elijah was like a father to me," he told me, resting his head on his knees. "He taught me everything I know. He was a good man."

"I know he was," I said.

He nodded, burying his face in his knees, and sobbed.

"But we have to finish what we started," I continued. "What we're all fighting for. What Elijah lost his life for. If we don't show the rest of the commune this footage, we could lose this war," I said simply. "We need to show everyone what the Hunters and my father were doing down there. We need to broadcast the truth. That's your job, isn't it? In Media and Communications? To communicate the most important messages to our community?"

His cries quieted, but his shoulders still shook. Gently, he turned his head against his knees and looked at me. He didn't answer right away, but I could see the wheels turning. I was reminded of myself back when Eli had found me. The massive weight of the truth I'd uncovered had felt so overwhelming that it had been hard to breathe.

"James," I said. "Please. We need you. *I* need you. You're the only one who can do this."

He took a breath and looked up over his arm at me with weary eyes. Endless grief, pain, and fear swam in his tears. But as he raised his head, I saw determination in his tightened jaw. He knew this was the only way, the same as I did.

"We'll move the bodies," Sid said, leaning back from where he stood at the side of the truck. "So you don't have to see."

James looked up at him and wiped his eyes. He nodded. "Thanks."

Andrew's footsteps and heavy breathing grew louder as he walked back across the garage to us. "Here," he said. "He's tied up. I'm heading down to the Pit now."

I stood. His eyes found mine. He gave me a small smile, then turned, crossed the room, and disappeared into the stairwell.

"C'mon," Gabriel said. "Sid. Joseph. Help, please?"

"No," Sid said, eyeing Gabriel. "You stay here too. We'll do it."

Gabriel didn't argue. I wrapped my arms around both boys.

While we waited, James told us about Elijah, how he'd mentored him as a child, taught him how to use cameras and video-editing software, seeing something in him that James hadn't even seen in himself. Gabriel smiled at the shared memories, perhaps not yet ready to speak about Silas's death. But I could tell by the tears he blinked back that he was working as hard as I was not to focus on the grunts and noises of effort Sid and Joseph made as they moved the bodies.

I was glad to hear Sid whistle for us a few minutes later.

"Over here," he said, waving us over, the laptop in his hands. "Joseph and I will stand guard down here. Gabriel will be in the stairwell." He glanced at his watch. "We're five minutes out from the hour. You'd better get up there."

I looked at James. Though his eyes were red, determination shone brighter. I gave him an encouraging nod and together, we moved to the stairwell door. James took the laptop in his hands, hugging it protectively to his chest.

"Be safe," I told Sid and Joseph.

"We will," Sid promised.

29

———

MAURA

GABRIEL, James, and I climbed the stairs to the top floor. The world felt surreal, almost like the ambush had never happened, and I half expected the control room to be full of our rebels. If I watched from the corner of my eye, Gabriel could be Silas — his blonde hair mussed, his grip tight around a large weapon. He worked quickly but thoroughly, guiding us up the two flights and into the control room. But the subtle differences — the lightness of his feet, the way his shoulders rounded forward, the sprinkle of freckles at the back of his neck — reminded me that he wasn't.

After a quick sweep, Gabriel left the room, instructing me to lock the door behind him. James went to work on the laptop and its wires.

The large, black screen mocked us with its size. Electricity buzzed behind it, a constant hum doing concealed work. The ever-present watcher. A perfect metaphor for the commune.

Laptop keys clacked as James worked in silence, blinking his weary eyes as he struggled to focus. It was hard to tell exactly what he was doing, and I didn't dare ask. He had minutes to access the video and tap into the overall communications system. And even though Andrew had taken out two of the Hunters, there was still Luke and another to worry about.

Through the quiet, the hum stopped. The black screen flickered; a momentary rainbow of colors, before it went black again. And then...

Father's face came into view. I recoiled without thinking, hugging my arms to my chest as I studied him. He looked like he had aged decades. Perhaps he had. War in itself was stressful, but maintaining a lie took a toll on even the best of liars. What had he told his Hunters? Had he watched his own followers die for him?

For a normal man, these things would eat away at them. But knowing Father now for who he truly was, I doubted it did. The stress came from something else. It prompted a spark of hope in my chest. Maybe he was feeling the loss of power. The shock of losing so many Hunters to the rebels. Who in his ranks had turned on him? Many, I assumed. Some of his own brothers, even.

It was probably the first time he had felt loss in his life.

Father sat in his office, his folded hands resting on top of his desk. He wore a simple button-down shirt and a pair of black-rimmed glasses. With him were his brother, Isaac Coutts, and...

My chest tightened.

Abigail.

She had retired as the Matriarch, or the head teacher for all young girls in the commune, when she'd had her children. But she *had* taught most of the girls in this commune, me included. Her presence was like a slap to the face — a threat to stay obedient. I didn't like it.

My father's piercing blue eyes stared directly into the camera. Vaguely, I wondered who was filming him.

"Good evening," he said, his voice strained with use. He had been yelling. I narrowed my gaze at him, even though he couldn't see me. "This afternoon we mourn significant loss across our community. The Devil has reached our doorsteps. We have lost families, friends, and leaders in our commune. Our farms have been decimated. The hospital has been destroyed by Outsiders who hate us for what we believe. I applaud those who have risen up to face this challenge, who have gone out to fight this battle. Unfortunately, it is not enough." He shook his head.

I glanced at James, whose flushed face remained fixed on his laptop screen. His fingers worked so fast it seemed impossible he was doing anything.

"For those of you still loyal to me and our God, I ask you to meet me at the Peak. For we must pray. We must be together if God should choose to take us today, and welcome us into His Kingdom of Heaven. Take comfort in knowing—"

"There!" James exclaimed, and suddenly Father's face flickered. His lips continued moving soundlessly, and then we lost him completely.

My face came into view.

It was strange seeing myself this way, so large up on the screen. I stood against the backdrop of the control room. My brown eyes were tired, but fierce. Black curls looped around my jawline, the rest tied up behind my head. My fists had been clenched, and I could see the definition of my tense shoulders beneath the jumpsuit.

I looked angry.

"Hello," I said. "As you know by now, there is an active rebellion going on in our commune. There is a small group of rebels promoting violence, but they do not represent our cause. I urge you to listen to what I have to say and watch what I am about to show you.

"I have been silenced, chased, and marked for death because I know the truth. A truth I wish to expose to all of you devout followers, though I know it will come as a shock. I know the church. I grew up in it. Loved it. I still do, though my relationship with faith and God is now complicated. Many months ago, I made a mistake during my scavenging duty. I went beyond the borders and got swept up in a creek. I was saved out there by an Outsider. A man, whom my father convinced me did not — *could not* — exist.

"Outside these borders, I found a new world. A world the Prophet did not want us to see. He told us there were no survivors. But that was a lie. There were plenty of survivors. Outsiders lived in a world filled with suffering and pain. Not because they deserved it. But because my father coordinated it. He kept them sick, hungry, and struggling to survive. He kept them afraid. Too afraid to confront us.

"For too long, we have only been shown what the Prophet wants us to see. He has hidden things from us. Terrible things. And despite his insistence that we were the only survivors, my father knew there were others out there. Some of his Hunters, too. They exploited the survivors to serve their own interests. Sometimes, for benefits we unknowingly received. Sometimes for their own gain."

The video cut away now, showing Elijah's recording. Rolling into the garage. The rebels' insistence on not using violence. Going down into the Pit, where they first encountered the rooms with the doors. The video revealed the first victim.

My voiceover continued.

"My father kept these prisoners from the outside world to create the vaccines he used to barter with other countries. Vaccines he used to keep us, his loyal followers, alive. Cures he used to keep order, to convince Outsiders to join our ranks unwillingly. But these came at a cost. They came with a life, sometimes multiple lives, of innocent people who did not give their consent.

"The Prophet was only interested in keeping people who agreed with him alive. Not just now, but for many years before the Great Plague. His ownership over medication meant he could pick and choose who stayed healthy. Who got life-saving medical care. Who was deserving. But this is not what God teaches us. God teaches us to love all. To care for all. To heal all. What the Prophet does is not holy or righteous. He is not God. But he chose to play one anyway."

Beside me, James stood and slipped his arm around my neck. I leaned into him, comforted, as we watched the video play on.

One by one, the camera panned inside each room, showing the state of each prisoner, how their bodies had succumbed to the medical procedures, and that awful thing on each of their chests. It cut to the medical rooms, offices, where papers detailed the different virus strains being fed into each patient to create Father's monstrous cures. Then, video of the remaining survivors as they struggled on the floor of the garage. The pile of corpses beside the ambulance. Holli and Mick tending to who they thought they could save.

"The Prophet wants to protect a legacy drenched in blood. He wants to keep us all in the dark. He wants us to submit and not ask any questions. Don't let him convince you to follow him blindly. I know sometimes it is easier not to see the truth. Not to accept it. It's more comfortable to lie in familiarity. But what the Prophet has done is *wrong*. This is not God's will. It is not our purpose. It is not how we treat people who have different beliefs from us. God asks us to welcome strangers with open arms. Not persecute them because of our differences. And certainly not to justify harming them."

The camera cut back to me talking. I looked larger somehow, like my presence on the video had doubled. My cheeks were flushed pink, eyes narrowed beneath my furrowed brow. My nostrils flared as I spoke my next words — words I had chosen carefully, with purpose. With the intent of helping the people in my community understand.

"So even though I know it's hard, I am asking you to look. Open your eyes. See the damage my father has done to people just like you and me. And ask yourself if that's what you want to be a part of. Do you want to follow a man who lies? Who shows us no proof and asks us to follow blindly? A man who can hurt innocent people without blinking an eye? A man who could just as easily turn around and condemn you? Can you look past the things they've told us and see what he's done? Can you admit it's inexcusable?

"If you're like me, then I know you can. If anyone else had done something like this, we would be crying out to God. So why should he be any different? My father may claim to be a Prophet, but he is just a man. A living, breathing human being who is no different from you and me. I believe in God's teachings. And I know, after a lifetime of studying God's word, that He would not approve of this.

"We *all* deserve a world where we live harmoniously. One where we're all free to choose our own paths. Where we come together to help others, even if they look or believe differently than we do. Please," I watched myself say, my features tight with worry, "do not put yourself in harm's way for my father or his men. Let the rebels take the lead on this. Let us fight for what's right. We can offer you protection, but only if you do not follow the Prophet's orders. Stay in your homes. Stay out of sight. Do not come out to meet this fight. The rogue arm of our rebellion is on a warpath, and my father and his Hunters will meet them with violence. I urge you to stay out of their way and let our soldiers, rebels, and negotiators handle things.

"It is my wish to end this peacefully. But we need your help to do so."

The screen went black. I couldn't breathe. The room felt like it might cave in, and I couldn't pass air through my lungs fast enough. Would they believe me? Would they take my words and understand them? Would they be able to see past Father for what he truly was? The video evidence was damning, but was it enough?

There would be plenty of people who'd excuse this. Who'd come up with their own justification for why these things were necessary. But if this many people were willing to join a rebellion, there had to be plenty of people who just needed some proof to be swayed.

The door to the stairs slammed open. Gabriel held the gun tight in his grip. Sid and Joseph hovered behind him. Urgency coated their features, and I straightened, on alert again.

"We need to go," Sid said.

30

MAURA

JAMES SLAMMED the laptop shut and stuffed it into the backpack that he hoisted on his shoulders. I gathered myself, trying to breathe through the sudden urgency. I didn't want to run again. My body ached at the thought.

We crowded around the stairwell door. Fear clutched my heart, urging it to race yet again. This area was a bottleneck. It had been a prime target to gun us all down. It was also the only way out.

"What's going on?" James whispered, his voice high with nerves.

"Andrew's down," Sid said. "He's holding two Hunters, but I don't know for how long. He's wounded. But he—"

"Come in?" Andrew's voice came through static on the radio. Sid looked at Joseph, then Gabriel, then brought his radio up to his mouth.

"We're here," he said.

"Get everyone out of the building," he said calmly. "I have a plan."

Sid closed his eyes and inhaled. "We don't have time for this."

"Please." The radio crackled. "Please listen."

"Where are you?" Sid demanded.

"I'm on the fifth floor. I can hold them off, but I need someone on the fourth floor."

Sid raised his eyebrows.

"On the fourth floor, there are bunkers. There is an emergency button. It shuts the entire place down in preparation for a doomsday event. The entire bunker is sealed within five minutes." He paused. "Did you look at those blueprints I gave you?"

Sid shook his head and touched the radio to his temple. "Yeah, why?"

"Then you'll know on the fifth floor, there are rooms of weapons. Explosives."

Sid's face went blank before his eyes widened. Realization slid over his features. His jaw dropped.

"Wait, what? You can't possibly be thinking what I think you're thinking."

"The bunkers are equipped to handle a nuclear event. It'll be no different from the inside. This way, we can ensure the lab goes. And that they don't come after you."

The radio crackled in Sid's hands.

Horror settled in my gut. I braced myself against James.

"We can't—" My voice cracked. Everyone's head turned to me. We couldn't *what*? I had no answer. Andrew was planning to sacrifice himself to blow this place up, and I desperately did not want to let him. But what choice did we have? Luke and his men would follow us to the ends of the earth to enact what they thought was justice. Leaving the lab intact meant there was always the possibility someone would take up Father's ruthless experiments in the future. And Andrew was willingly giving himself up.

This was the only plan we had.

"It's our only shot," Gabriel said, his face steeled in determination. "This place deserves to burn."

"Maura?" Sid looked at me, over the top of the radio.

I shook my head. Then, slowly, I nodded.

"Okay," Sid said to all of us. He pressed the radio's button. "Okay," he said. "Plan is a go. Tell me what to do."

WANING sunlight spilled through the open garage door, where Gabriel and Joseph hovered near the scanner. Zeke, James, and I leaned up against the truck, watching. I crossed my arms. Uncrossed them. Clasped my hands together. Paced in front of the vehicle, restless.

I was angry. Sid had volunteered to go down to the fourth floor.

There had been little time to protest. He'd been so willing to sacrifice himself, too. But Sid's insistence I understood more than Andrew's. Like Eli, Sid was a hardened survivor. Our Hunters were vicious, but Sid had stared death down multiple times and lived to tell the tale. He *was* the man for the job.

It didn't make the waiting any easier.

Nothing but static came from the radio's speaker, but Gabriel clutched it with a white-knuckled grip. An alarm went off, loud and unsettling; the noise like a dying animal's wail that echoed from the concrete garage's deep interior and out into the dimming sky. The lights clicked and changed from a dim yellow to a dark blood red.

I froze.

Sid had done what he needed to do.

I found my breath. Beside me, James opened up the truck's rear door, but my eyes remained glued to the concrete area, waiting for any sign of movement. Gabriel checked his watch, counting down from five minutes. Once we were sure the door was sealed, we would alert Andrew and go. Once closed, the doors would not reopen for another half hour.

The world felt still and silent. Eerily calm. I could hear the others' breathing.

Come on, Sid.

A minute slid by. Gabriel checked his watch again. His free fingers flexed at his side. In and out. In and out.

Finally, the door opened.

Out of breath, Sid's tall figure appeared at the corner of the garage and gradually grew larger as he approached. I smiled, relieved.

But the door behind him didn't slam closed.

I gasped when I looked, because another figure — one dressed in green — stumbled out behind him. From the way the person shambled forward, it was clear they were injured.

Sid did not seem to realize he was being followed.

"You're kidding me." It was Gabriel who spoke, and Gabriel who moved next.

Sid's wide eyes tracked his movement as Gabriel entered the garage, his watch, the time limit, and us forgotten. His shoulders drew up. His hand reached for his gun. He was so like Silas in that moment it took my breath away. He hoisted his weapon into his arms and pointed it at the figure in the distance.

Sid jogged out of the garage, his forehead drenched in sweat. He looked over his shoulder.

"Gabriel!" Sid hissed. "Come on!"

But Gabriel didn't listen. He kept on marching forward. The injured man moved slowly, battling against gravity as he paused, hunched over in pain, before struggling forward again. The red lighting distorted his face and movements, but I saw the wild grin that filled his features. Dark fluid trailed from his broken leg.

"Father!" Gabriel shouted, his voice deeply pained, loud and demanding. Luke looked up, his gaze landing on his youngest son, and narrowed his eyes.

"Gabriel," Luke said, his lip curling. "This was you? You came back for more?"

"We came back to finish this fight."

Luke gave a mocking laugh. "Have you now? You haven't realized how foolish your brother was to start this crusade? You thought it wise to come back to see how well that ended for him?"

"He wasn't foolish!" Gabriel yelled, his voice trembling. "He was a good man! Better than you! He raised me. He was my best friend. He was brave. Heroic. He wanted better for us all."

Luke threw his head back and laughed. Gabriel pulled the gun higher and tighter in his grip.

"What are you going to do with that?" Luke asked, still laughing. "Shoot your own father? According to you rebels, violence is bad. Unnecessary. You won't pull that trigger."

"I don't want to," Gabriel said. "I don't want to hurt you. You shouldn't want to hurt us, either. Silas didn't deserve to die. He was your *son*. And you stand here and mock him?"

"He deserved what came to him!" Luke bellowed, shifting his weight on his good leg. He winced, adjusting himself. "He betrayed his own family. He thought it wise to go up against the most powerful men still left alive. His disobedience cost him his life. And it will cost you yours, too."

Gabriel scoffed. "Look at you," he said. "You're at our mercy, and yet you still think you're superior? Have you no shame?"

"I have no time for your silly games, boy. There are decades of important research in this building. It is my responsibility to save it. These are things you don't understand. So many of us are alive only because of this research. Because of the procedures we performed, because of the secrets we kept. You should be *grateful*—"

"I am *horrified*," Gabriel spat. "It is an embarrassment to call you my father."

"You don't know what you're saying," Luke answered.

"You killed Silas, and you would do the same to me. Your judgment is flawed."

"My judgment is superior. After Peter is done with the rebels, there will be no place for people like you. Put down your loyalty to rebels. Come back to the side you know is right. Despite what you might think, I would welcome you with open arms."

Gabriel was frozen, the gun trembling in his arms. Luke's balance wobbled. He teetered. Tried to balance himself, but grasped nothing but air.

I saw Gabriel flinch, fighting his instinct to run forward and help his father — the man who had killed his brother, the man who would let the world burn if it meant my father could stay in power. There was no understanding the deep love and connection a child has with their parent, even when their parent would throw them to the wolves.

But he remained steadfast as we watched Luke fall to the floor, crying out in pain as his wounded leg met solid concrete.

"You'll see!" he yelled, his voice echoing shrilly into the high ceiling. "You'll see I'm right!"

"Gabriel," Sid said. "Let's go."

Time was up. The garage door groaned, mechanical gears squealing to life differently than we'd heard before. Something new was happening.

Gabriel walked backward, keeping his gun trained on his father as he backed through the shrinking gap.

"Get back here!" Luke cried. "Hey! Get back here!"

The door launched downward at dizzying speed, and Gabriel ran toward us, kicking up dirt. We scrambled into the truck, crashing into one another, squashed so tight I sat on top of James's legs. Gabriel slammed the door behind himself, sealing us in the truck.

"The door's closed," Sid called into the radio. He released the button. Static crackled, and I heard Andrew's voice for the last time.

"Go now. Be with God." A pause. And then, "Maura," he said, "I hope you can forgive me."

My stomach dropped. Zeke didn't hesitate. His foot found the gas, and the truck catapulted forward. I cried out as I looked back at the sealed garage, pressing a hand to my aching chest. Andrew had never been a hero. I wasn't sure he'd had a selfless bone in his body until today. But he'd fought against his instinct and helped us. If nothing else, I had to admire the bravery.

We drove through the maze of trash, setting our sights on the office and apartment buildings.

I felt the first rumble as we sped through the Waste Center's gate.

Somehow, Zeke kept the car steady as we rolled onward, a deafening boom cracking through the air so loud I could feel it in my bones. It was the sound of thunder, an impossible, terrifying quake that seemed to crack the Earth in two.

In the car's rear window, I watched the Waste Center's building tremble in its frame, uncertain if it was my vision or the actual structure doing the shaking. Another crack, another deafening rumble shook the truck's tires. We swayed. Zeke tugged at the steering wheel. We skidded around the side of the buildings and onto the street.

Through the buildings came another quick succession of booms. Still loud, but the ground beneath us no longer shook. Zeke pulled the truck into park in front of the triage building. Faces peered out at us through the windows, curious and afraid.

We got out of the car. My muddled hearing made the voices around me thick and difficult to understand. Through the narrow alleyways, above the mounds of trash, I saw the Waste Center shake violently.

An almighty screech cracked through the air. The glass windows shattered outward, flying shards soaring into the garbage heaps and beyond. From here, I could see the explosion's heat waves ripple out into the air. The structure began to crumble. A smoke plume erupted somewhere near the middle. Debris flew, hitting nearby piles, causing them to tumble, revealing old decay beneath, and spreading the waste across the dirt paths we had navigated between.

A final, low, groaning explosion rumbled deep beneath the Earth. The building's metal supports bowed inward, and the roof tilted, slipping into the middle like a sinkhole. The remaining structure buckled and collapsed, erupting in a large cloud of gray dust that shot upward until it mingled with the clouds.

I stood, steadying myself on the side of the truck, watching the explosions' aftermath drift up into the sky. It floated there, lingering; a final reminder of Andrew, Luke, and of my father's horrors. In minutes, the wind had picked it up, spreading into a thick, hovering cloud.

My ears began to clear, and conversation slowly trickled in. I glanced around at my team. We had destroyed the lab. We had gotten word out to the people as best we could. We had survived.

Luke would never hurt anyone again. His loyalties lay with him until the very end, and it was up to God what happened next. But I knew one thing for sure. Following laws and rules blindly for the sake of their existence didn't make you *good*. It made you indifferent. It made you complicit in wrongdoing. It allowed atrocities to happen while you turned a blind eye.

We still had so much to do.

31

———

ELI

ANOTHER RUMBLE SHOOK THE BUILDING, and I braced myself against the wall, wincing at the pain. Most of my injuries seemed manageable except for my leg. No matter my pain medication dosage, no matter the way I situated it beneath the blankets, every twinge felt like fire in my nerves.

The pain had prompted memories of the past few days. The cell. The guards. Number 11, and what he had said about Avi.

I needed to get that information to the right people.

Holli appeared in my doorway, looking pale-faced and frazzled.

"You alright?" she asked, a little out of breath.

"What the hell is it?"

She sighed. Tapped the doorframe. "Well, they, uh… blew up the Waste Center."

"They—?" My mouth dropped. "Blew up the—?" I propped myself up on my elbow. Grit my teeth against the pain in my shoulder. "Sid? Maura?"

"They're all on their way back now," she answered. "You need to—"

"Do not tell me to rest, Hol." I groaned, lifting myself from the mattress to sit. "I've got to—"

"Don't tell me how to do my job," she countered, crossing the room. She raised her brows, hands firm on her hips. She looked like Mom. "Let me at least make sure your lungs are clear before this place turns into even more of a nuthouse," she said as she lowered herself beside me, holding up a stethoscope.

Defeated, I took a deep breath before I dropped the blanket covering my chest. Holli put the stethoscope in her ears and lifted the cool metal to my sternum, instructing me to breathe. She worked her way around the sore area where they'd removed the device — a hairless square of irritated skin, surrounded by small clotted wounds.

"Heartbeat's a little fast," she said, curling the stethoscope around her neck. "But you sound a lot better." She checked her watch. "You've got about an hour until I can give you another dose for that leg."

"Fine," I said, distracted. "When they get here, can you ask..."

Shadows moved in the doorway. Hurried feet. Hands tracing the walls. I'd know her gait anywhere.

Maura.

She appeared in the doorway, a flush high on her cheekbones. Her hair hung loose around her face, and when she saw me, she smiled, her dimples deep and adorable, her brown eyes filled with exhaustion and relief. She swallowed. Glanced at Holli.

Holli looked between us. "I...have to go check on someone," she said matter-of-factly. She got up from the mattress, hugging Maura before she left the room.

"Hi," Maura said, lingering in the doorway. My throat

tightened. I couldn't help the smile that spread across my lips.

"C'mere." I pat the space beside me.

She crossed the room and sat, the mattress sagging with her weight.

"You look…" Her eyes traveled over my face, bare chest, and wounded leg. My stomach somersaulted.

"Handsome?" I gave her my best shit-eating grin.

She smiled and shook her head. "I was going to say, *better*."

"So…not handsome?" I frowned.

"Always handsome."

I reached my hand out, and she took it, threading our fingers together. Her palm was pleasantly cool, her body buzzing with heightened energy. She placed her free hand gently against my cheek, brushing her thumb against my beard. I nuzzled into her softness before she leaned in, surprising me, and closed the space between us.

Her lips were cold from the winter wind as they pressed against mine, urgent and desperate. She tasted like fresh air and salty sweat, of fear, relief, and rage. I slipped my hand behind her ear and into her hair, ignoring the ache in my shoulder. My pulse thundered as I kept her in my grasp, letting her mouth explore mine. I never wanted to stop kissing her. Tasting her. I wanted her closeness. To feed her need. To hold her and never let her out of my sight again.

But when she sat back, her lips bruised pink, her hand gripping mine as she caught her breath and wiped her mouth, I knew she wasn't here to stay. My heart ached even more than my injured body at the idea of her leaving.

"Sorry," she said, her face flushing.

"Why?" I smiled. "We could keep doing that."

"Eli." Her voice had a tone of warning. "We're going to

the Peak," she said. "Gabriel and Sid — they want to link back up with Avi. Talk some sense into my father. End this once and for all."

I tightened my grip on her hand.

"No. You can't trust him," I said.

Her eyes widened. "What? Who?"

I shook my head. "Avi. They told me, when they had me in that holding cell…they showed me photographs. Proof. Avi worked for Peter. He was a spy for the U.S. government. He got medical care from the Coutts Non-Profit and fed them secrets about what the government was doing, how to combat them. He helped Peter. They had a falling out because he wanted what Peter wanted." I frowned at her, hating the anger unfurling in my chest. "He wanted power. And when he didn't get it, he went off to build the Centre. He built an army. To accomplish what he'd initially set out to do."

She froze. I saw the information work its way into the plans she'd made in her head. The beliefs she held about Avi. Watching disappointment cross her face hurt me more deeply than I realized it would. It was the same disappointment I'd watched her carry after she saw Andrew kill that man. The same disappointment she shouldered after Coal Creek, after uncovering her father's lies, after realizing the world was so much more brutal than she'd ever thought it was.

I wanted to hold her. To fix it. To tell her it would all be alright. But that wasn't what she needed. And it also wasn't true. The world often disappointed us. It was built that way. The answer wasn't to try to convince ourselves it wouldn't. The answer was to combat the disappointment, evil, and injustice with love. To thrive in the face of it. To offer an alternative that wasn't death, destruction, and bigotry.

And if anyone was going to deliver that message to the world, it was Maura Coutts.

She reached into her shirt and pulled out a folded piece of paper. It was well creased, the edges worn with dirt. She cradled it in her hands before she handed it to me.

I took it, smiling at the memory — the Polaroid photograph of us.

"I'll be back," she promised, squeezing my arm as she got up from the mattress. "I'm going to end this."

Time slowed. I considered what life might be like if this were the last time I saw Maura. Touched her. Kissed her. The fear threatened to unravel me, destroy the glimmers of hope I'd dared to dream for a future in this world.

Our future.

"Maura?" I called. She stopped at the door, her chin to her shoulder as she brought her eyes back up to me. "I love you. Okay? So…you have to come back." My heart swelled at my declaration, and even though it terrified me, even though I didn't know how this would end, I meant it with all my being, and I needed her to know.

She laughed. Darted back across the room to kiss me once more; soft, eager, and filled with burning promise.

"I love you, too," she answered. "Thank you for showing me what it means."

32

MAURA

I FOUND Sid in the room across the hall, scarfing down a sleeve of crackers. Gabriel lay beside him on a moth-eaten couch, his arm over his eyes. The room hummed with quiet conversation, none of it distinct enough to eavesdrop on.

"Hey," I said.

Sid looked up, crumbs clinging to his beard.

"How is he?"

"Better," I said, unable to help the flush that crept up my neck.

Sid's smile widened. He swallowed.

"I *bet he is*." He wiggled his brows.

"Stop that."

"Nurse Maura," he joked, leaning back. Beside him, Gabriel's chest fluttered with a giggle.

"Yes, very funny. Listen. He told me something." I leaned in close to his ear. "We can't trust Avi." I explained what Eli had revealed to me. Sid's jaw dropped. Gabriel uncovered his eyes and straightened.

"So, he worked *with* Peter?" Sid asked.

I nodded, trying to ignore the dread in my stomach.

"Our goals have to change then," Gabriel said. "If Avi is on a warpath for another reason…for control." He shook his head.

Heavy footsteps raced up the stairs. A rebel burst through the door, a radio clutched in her hand.

"Gabriel?" She scanned the room. He looked up. "It's Nadia," she said, holding out the device.

Gabriel drew his eyebrows together, confused, before bringing the radio to his mouth. "Nadia?" he asked. "Come in?"

Silence. Static. Then, "Gabe?" She whispered his name. Her voice was too low, too quiet. I didn't like it.

"You okay?"

"It's Avi." Her voice cracked. My heart dropped. "That video from Peter — it was a trap. They're ambushing all the loyalists coming to the Peak. He's…" The pause was endless. "He's holding them all hostage." The radio crackled. She cut out. "—threatening to kill them one by one until Peter surrenders the commune."

My blood ran cold. *Hostages?*

"I can't take him myself, Gabriel," she continued. "I don't know what the hell's gotten into him. We need you. Zeke, Sid. Whoever you've got."

Gabriel looked up and met my eyes, the color drained from his face. I inhaled. Exhaled. Shook my head. Once again, I was helpless.

Too late.

"Are you safe?" Gabriel asked into the radio.

"We're okay," she confirmed. "Just hiding. I'm sorry. I tried to get close to him, but he wouldn't even speak to me. Just shoved a bunch of armed guards at me and told me to fuck off." More static. She hiccuped. "I'm sorry. I really thought I could reason with him."

"Don't be sorry, Nadia," Gabriel said. "Send us your exact location. We'll head out now."

It was like all the air had left my lungs, and it was impossible to try to reclaim it. Every inhale came in a sharp burst. A pain appeared in my side. The world began to spin.

Avi had promised. He had been so steadfast and reassuring when Silas and Gabriel came to the Centre. He reassured us he was fighting the same war we were. I had tried to write off the hospital as a mistake. An act of passion. Violence from an angry man who didn't know how to tackle something so big.

But *this*? This was different. Tricking people, holding them captive, and using them for his benefit was exactly what my father had done.

WE CLEARED out the triage safe house; rebels piled into trucks, as many as we could fit. I sat squashed between Joseph, Zeke, and another female rebel. More filled the trunk. Sid drove while Gabriel navigated, and we left the decimated Waste Center behind.

Smoke still lifted from its remains, as if screaming out to the heavens for help. Its last cry to the universe. I tried not to think about Andrew or Luke, and certainly not about Silas or Elijah. I couldn't reflect on the horrors Father's men had committed down there. What they'd done to those poor people, and God knew how many more.

Everything in the vicinity smelled like rot, worse now because of rogue fires that had erupted near the blast area. But the smell drifted away as we rode on, through the farmlands, and back into the mountains.

The disappearing sun left little light for us to see. Sid kept the headlights low, and they bounced along the uneven landscape until we found the road that would lead us back toward the Peak.

Empty fields spread wide into the distance on either side. Bare trees dotted the sides of the road. The truck came around a curve.

I gasped.

The scenery had changed so much since I'd seen it last, only days ago. To the far right stood the Sciences and Innovations area. Or what was left of it. The hospital had mostly crumbled, the aftermath a heap of burning metal and brick scattered out across the once pristine roads. Damaged buildings; shattered windows, singed brick, and gaping structural holes. Fires still burned, scenting the air with burnt rubber.

To the left, where the farmlands had once flourished around the nuclear cooling towers, were hundreds of acres of dead grass lit aflame. The closest land was black, sprinkled with ash. Two of the greenhouses burned in the distance, the fire consuming the massive structure and all the crops within. It would be a devastating loss of resources.

Lights spotted the mountain in the distance — people still in their homes, or fighting Father's war? People following my father's orders to come to the Peak, or people waiting for us to help them run from Father and Avi's madness? The sheer magnitude of the number of people still on the Peak overwhelmed me. How could we save them all? How could we help them?

Silas would know. But Silas was dead.

I reached for Zeke. He let me dig my nails into his arm.

The landscape arched upward, and we climbed an incline. Through the window, I glimpsed a field full of panicked animals, running from their impending doom. People ran up and down the sides of the dirt road we traveled. I wanted to tell them to go home. To hide. To get out of here. But even I didn't know what advice would keep them safe anymore.

We passed the greenhouses. A large group stood on the outskirts, desperately trying to put the fire out. I gasped, then turned back into the dark car, feeling ashamed of myself for not being able to look.

My fault. My fault. My fault.

No.

I thought of Eli.

This wasn't my fault.

I didn't do this.

This was the work of two men. My father and Avi.

The thought made me furious. This was no way to live. In fact, it was possibly the *worst* way to live. Not everything needed to end in blood and fire.

We reached the base of the mountain and started climbing. Sid took the roads quickly, whipping us around corners, gripping the steering wheel tightly. His jaw worked from side to side.

Sid was angry, and he had every right to be. Like so many others, he had lost so much. He was a soldier, a *marksman*, Eli had once called him. Yet he hadn't resorted to violence. He still wanted to work things out peacefully. To me, that meant anything was possible. We could still come to a reasonable solution.

It felt like hours and no time at all getting to level ground at the top of the Peak. The truck came around the last few bends. Beneath the tires, I felt the pavement disappear, giving way to coarse gravel and rocky terrain. My heart beat in my throat. I glanced at Zeke apologetically, realizing how tight a grip I'd kept on his arm, but he was lost to the outside, his gaze steady on the building in the distance.

We entered the large parking lot that preceded the massive church. The structure loomed above us, an enormous architectural tribute built to honor God. Now, it felt like it only honored my father. I peered up at the large circular window, thinking of Father's office and the hallway attached to the room where Luke had brutally murdered my mother.

If this were a tribute to God, its walls wouldn't be covered in blood. And it wasn't just hers. Thousands, maybe millions of victims lined these halls. Because of the decisions Father had made. Because of his selfishness, greed, and lust for power. He had disgraced the temple we had worshiped in.

That ended here.

Stairs led up to the massive wooden door, and Sid parked our truck beside a cluster of Jeeps. Avi's trucks. I had expected a rebel guard or perhaps a Hunter, but these stairs and the surrounding area were empty. Darkness had finally settled over the commune. The only light shone from the church windows.

A knock. I jumped. Zeke grabbed for his weapon. Sid swore.

At the window stood Nadia, her blue eyes wide in fear. Sid exhaled, then opened his door to get out, sweeping the tall woman up in his arms. The two Hunters who had come with her stood behind, their weapons strapped tightly across their backs.

"God, it's good to see you," Sid said, his breath carrying away in the cold night air.

On the Peak, the temperature had dropped considerably. I shivered without a jacket.

"You have no idea," Nadia said. "You all alright?"

Sid nodded.

"Maura," Nadia said, reaching for me. She pulled me into her body, and I hugged her in return.

"Nadia," I said, gripping her arms. "I need you to listen. Avi's been lying to us." I told her what Eli had told me, what I'd told Sid and Gabriel. The others craned their heads, listening. Nadia's eyes bulged in shock as she took in the new information.

"No," she said, shaking her head. "*No*."

"Yes," I assured her. "We need to see what he's doing, figure out what his plan is. There's still time to stop this, okay?"

She nodded.

"Where is everyone?" I asked.

Dazed, she glanced up the stairs, toward the door. "They went in once it got dark." Her lip quivered. "Maura. Neither of them deserves to control us. *You* can reason with them. It has to be you. Avi is banking on your anger. Your father is banking on your obedience." She narrowed her gaze. "You don't owe them either."

Her words rang true, prompting a surprising spark of yearning. I *wanted* to confront them. I had so much to say, so much I wanted them to know and understand.

Longing unfurled in my stomach as the last of our trucks made their way into the parking lot, headlights washing across the pavement, reflecting off the other trucks. They parked haphazardly around us, and rebels spilled out to join us at the base of the stairs.

Our team at the Waste Center had seemed alarmingly small, but seeing us all together gave me more hope than I'd had in months. I no longer tasted my fear. I swallowed. Breathed in the cold air. Avi couldn't fight all of us, and neither could Father. It was still possible to get them both to see reason.

"Maura," Gabriel said from beside me as the last of our ranks joined us. "Are you ready?"

I glanced around at the people surrounding me. Sid, the fighter. Gabriel, the wounded brother. Nadia, the soldier. Zeke, my protector. I thought of Eli and Holli at the triage unit, with Shelly, Kendra, and Mick. I thought of Neil and Mia back at the Centre. Of Morgan. Of Silas. Of Mother and all of my siblings. These people — the people who had taken me in and showered me in a warmth I had never known from strangers, my family who had loved me in ways we had never been taught inside the commune — they were my strength. They were the fire feeding me as I nodded and started up the stairs, with the heart of our rebellion behind me.

33

MAURA

INSIDE, the church was well lit. Light spilled out into the entryway, illuminating the shiny stone floors. All my life, I had come through these doors for an afternoon of worship, one of Father's sermons, or a lesson from Abigail. For so long, this had been a place of refuge — a place of hope. Somewhere I felt safe.

My identity was born here. I had learned about God and the Prophet here. I had been told about the wicked Outsiders and how to live a good, devout life. But over the past few months, all of these things had been challenged or destroyed.

Guards rushed us the minute we entered the pew-lined church, guns aimed and ready to shoot. I faltered at their presence, but once they recognized us as fellow rebels, they backed off.

"Maura." Gloria, the woman who had helped us to the Centre after we'd left Coal Creek, pushed through the crowd of rebels. Her long hair hung in a braid down her shoulder, her one good eye studying our group. "Sid,

Nadia, Gabriel." She looked beyond and nodded her approval. "Avi will be glad to see you."

She waved us forward, into the belly of the church.

The room was half-filled. Rebel guards stood among the pews between commune members, some of whom I recognized, others of whom I didn't. Most were men. Here because they had promised to protect their families. Farmers, blacksmiths, and soldiers. They had given up their bodies to Father before, and had come here, willing to do it again. But there were women too, and even children. Families convinced today was the Day of Reckoning.

At the altar, someone had torn down every embellishment — the crucifixes, the photos of Father, the blessed linens. The chairs had been rearranged against the far wall, where loyalist Hunters sat tied up, their mouths sealed shut with duct tape. Some had black fabric bags over their heads. A few muffled moans came from them.

All the way on the left, I saw Abigail, arms and legs secured to a chair, the side of her face purple and yellow; one eye swollen shut. The children clustered at her feet, limbs tangled together as they struggled to comfort each other through fear. Beside Abigail sat a row of other women – Father's youngest wives — restrained to their own chairs, their children at their feet.

The man guarding them had dark skin and a familiar face. Darius. The man who had worked closely with Sid and Eli in Security at the Centre. When we'd met, he had been immediately distrustful of me, but we'd worked through it. Come to an understanding. Would that hold true here? Or did his loyalties to Avi run deeper than I'd realized?

In the middle of the altar, Avi sat in a velvet-lined chair, his legs crossed and elevated on…

Horror clutched my heart. Gripped my throat. There was no air. Nothing to breathe.

I found Zeke's arm again.

Avi rested his heels on the back of a dead man. A dead Hunter, to be more precise. The corpse lay face down, body rigid, neck turned at an unnatural angle.

Avi peered down the aisle, and I followed his gaze to a kneeling, restrained figure at the bottom of the short set of stairs.

My Father.

I wasn't sure I had ever seen my father kneel. If I had, it was at an altar, where he was positioned above us. His bowed head showed the bald spot at his crown. His hands were tied behind his back. He wore the same outfit he'd worn in the video we'd interrupted — a white button-down shirt and a pair of dress pants, with a brown belt threaded through its loops.

If he hadn't been in such a vulnerable position, I might have thought his down turned head meant he was praying. But there was blood splatter on the side of his face, and his nose was bleeding. My breath caught in my throat when I realized the blood wasn't just on his face. It was on the floor, at the head of the pews. Vaguely, I made out a shoe.

More Hunters.

Someone — or multiple someones — lay in front of the altar.

Stomach acid burned my throat. I struggled to swallow it.

"Ah," Avi said, raising his head as the rest of the rebels filtered inside. "You made it. Welcome. I hear you took the entire Waste Center down. And Maura. That video?" He smiled. "Incredible work."

His voice echoed into the rafters, a sickly sweet compliment meant to test my loyalty.

"What are you doing?" I asked. My voice sounded too high, unnatural to my ears. I started down the aisle of pews. "Avi, you promised."

Avi narrowed his eyes at me, then pulled his feet off the dead guard. With a groan, he got to his feet. "Why, we're removing the cancer, Maura. We're ripping out the rot at the root. Your father is an evil man."

"I'm not debating that," I said, moving cautiously down the aisle. I kept my eyes steady on Avi, careful not to look at my father. But in my peripheral vision, I felt eyes on me. "Why include everyone else in this?"

Avi's eyebrows drew together, then apart. He seemed conflicted. "The people around him, who look at him like a God? They're just as bad, if not worse," he said. "They came here willingly. Tried to protect him. If they choose to die for him, that's on them. You, of all people, should know that." He frowned. Crossed his arms over his chest. "I thought you'd be pleased," he said simply, as if I had disappointed him.

"We talked about not meeting violence with violence," I answered.

Avi chortled. "This man uses violence for everything," he said, tilting his head toward my father. "And you ask me not to meet him with the same?"

"I'm asking you not to meet the rest of the commune with violence, Avi."

"We *needed to*," he said. "Wiping out the hospital meant they could not tend to their wounded. Wounded who, if the roles were reversed, would leave you for dead."

"And wounded people who are innocent," I retorted. "Children. People who had no say in what happened outside these walls. People who had no idea what was going on. Who have no part in this rebellion. People we promised to keep safe."

Avi waved his hand as if this were just a nuisance. "They took no care trampling through our neighborhoods and cities," he said. "Why should I do the same?"

"Because," I said, softening my voice, "you are a good man, Avi. You took my group in. You took *me* in, even though you knew there were risks."

"Because you had been so hurt by this man who called himself a God!" he shouted, his voice suddenly filled with a fury I struggled to understand. "Because you had grown up in the shadow of evil. And you escaped. And you *thrived*." His eyes were wide and wild, spittle flying from his mouth. He stepped forward, then took the stairs, standing beside my father. "I dragged him down here, Maura. I took him down off his pedestal for you."

"I didn't…I don't…" I shook my head as I continued forward, still searching for words that wouldn't come. Because on some level, I *did* want this. I wanted Father to suffer. I wanted him to see the heinous things he had done to us. I wanted him to admit his wrongs.

As I came closer, I heard my father's mumbled prayers. And now I could see the guards on the floor next to him, soaked in their own blood. It stank of iron and guts, making my stomach roil. And through all of this, at my presence, at the declaration of his evil, when faced with what he had done, at the mercy of rebels who had once served his ranks, at the daughter who had once obeyed his rules, he did not even have the decency to look up to meet my eyes.

"It's as I thought, isn't it, Maura?" Avi taunted. I opened my mouth to try and explain. To tell him how I felt. That nobody deserved this kind of treatment, that he was perpetuating Father's goals. And that I did want Father to pay for his sins. But not like this.

"All I had ever wanted was what was best for this

community," Father said, finally speaking. "The world was broken. I fixed it."

"*You* broke it!" Avi screamed at him, his face flushing red. "You condemned us all to death!" He swiveled wildly on his heel and looked at me. "Don't you see?" he asked. "He doesn't even *see* the error of his ways! He doesn't care! He still thinks that what he did was right! The only way to finish this once and for all is..."

The world slowed. Avi's pupils shrank, freeing his fury. A flash of rage. Crazed, unbridled hatred.

Avi put his hand on his hip and unsheathed his gun from its holster. He pointed the gun at my father's head and pulled the trigger.

His skull exploded in a mess of blood, brain, and bone.

THE CHURCH SCREAMED. A collective horror filled the space between these walls, bouncing from window to floor to pew to ceiling. Avi's arm, neck, and face were covered in blood, his arm shaking from the force of the bullet. Smoke rose from the gun's barrel.

Father's body hit the floor with a thud. What was left of his face made a squelching kind of sound, and I tasted acid in my mouth. Felt it in my nose. My ears rang. The lit church blurred at the edges, fading out, then in again.

Abigail wailed from her chair, head thrown back, like a woman possessed. People, frantic now, began to move. The guards stiffened, hands tightening around weapons, fingers hovering over triggers. Guttural, terrified screams weaved together with shouted prayers.

Avi finally looked up, his eyes red-rimmed and full of wrath. He dropped the gun on the altar, where it lay like a blemish beside the guard. He shook with adrenaline or rage, I couldn't be sure, and hit the blood-slicked floor with heavy feet. He picked up my father's corpse by his collar and dragged him up the aisle, as though he were nothing more than a sack of flour. People in the pews covered their faces. I heard dry heaves. Cries for mercy. Pleas for help.

Avi would not hear them.

"Here!" Avi yelled. "Here is your Almighty Prophet!" With force, he dropped his body onto the stairs. "He is just a man. Not a God, like he claimed. God did not *save* him. He is not all-knowing. He is a failed leader who helped run our country into ruin! He was a cancer! Eliminating him was our only choice. Don't you see that?"

He looked around the room, at his guards, at us. A few of the guards nodded, and my stomach dropped. This was not right. I knew in my heart of hearts that things did not need to end this way. They *couldn't* end this way. Avi was no better than Father. Violence against a group of people different from him was just perpetuating the same strategies my father had used.

"Avi, for fuck's sake." It was Darius who stepped forward. His dark eyes darted back and forth between my father's body, the people in the pews, and Avi. "This isn't—"

"Isn't what, Darius?" Avi asked, spinning on his heel to face his man. His nostrils flared, upper lip sneered as he challenged him with tension. "Is this not the goal we came to accomplish? Did the Coutts not deny your mother insulin? Did she not die as a result of their medical negligence, all in the name of God? You came to me many nights to share your pain and grief over her death. Is this not justice? For you? For her?"

Darius looked at his shoes.

Avi turned away from us, settling behind the chair he'd been sitting in, his hands gripped on the back. "A new age has come to this commune. The Coutts have hoarded resources for long enough. It's time for a new leader. Call *this* your Day of Reckoning."

"What the fuck do you think you're doing?" Nadia stood at my side. Her gaze was soft. Disappointed. "Avi," she said. "This isn't you."

"Is it not?" he asked. "I promised us a world where we were all equal. Where we would gain access to the Coutts resources, so we didn't have to struggle and *suffer* while all the people here still enjoyed life's luxuries. Isn't that what we always wanted? What we always talked about?"

"We talked about *equality*. This isn't that."

"Equality means they reap the consequences they have sown. Equality means they now have to suffer because of the choices they made."

"These people didn't choose this, Avi. These people—"

"Are still cancerous!" he interrupted. "They're danger-ous! They believed a man was God and listened to his every demand without thinking. They left us to *rot* out there. They took everything from us. Forced us to comply, or die." He sighed, then bent down and picked up the gun he'd discarded. "They deserve the same, Nadia. You know it deep within your soul."

"Do I?" Anger rose in her tone, her upper lip curled in a sneer. The information I'd given her rested on her tongue. I reached out and grabbed her arm. She looked down at me.

"Wait," I said.

She pressed her lips closed.

We knew Avi was a liar. We knew what he was here to do. But we needed to tell *everyone*.

Outside, the sound of approaching trucks stilled me. New headlights washed through the windows. I looked back at Avi, who was smiling.

"Ah, yes," he said, ignoring us. "The rest of our guests have arrived." He pocketed the gun. "I asked rebels to gather up who they could off the mountain. I'd like everyone still within these borders to listen to what I have to say. It's too bad we couldn't get this on the television like you, clever girl," he said, directed at me. I sneered at him. "But this will have to do."

Avi's guards seemed uncertain, but moved as a collective group despite the strange tension in the air. The doors to the church opened, and new rebel guards marched in.

"Welcome, welcome!" Avi said, greeting the newcomers. He came back down off the altar and stood beside my father's body proudly. I couldn't look. I couldn't even think about it, or I'd vomit.

Instead, I looked between Gabriel and Sid. They knew about Avi. They knew this wasn't about saving the world any more than it had been when my father had taken power. But Avi was on a rampage. Confronting him now would be dangerous. We needed to be sure others would be on our side.

"Is it done?" One of the rebels asked as he came down the aisle.

"Holy shit," someone else said behind him. "Peter's dead! Look!"

"Are you sure—?"

"Dead, dead?"

"Avi!"

Avi's face broke into a wide grin as the newly arrived rebels rejoiced. But they hadn't been here. They hadn't seen what Avi had done or heard what he had said. They didn't know he was a liar.

But I could see it now. I understood. Avi was going to try and step into my father's role. He was going to condemn all Coutts, like my father had condemned all Outsiders.

I couldn't let that happen.

I *wouldn't* let that happen.

Even though it was subtle, I noticed the distinction between the new arrivals and the rebel guards that had been stationed in this church. There was still a sense of unease. Apprehension. They eyed each other anxiously. They could see Avi's hysteria. And even though worry stirred in my belly, I still had a spark of hope. It wasn't much, but it was something.

All I needed was that spark.

34

MAURA

REBELS MARCHED commune members in through the doors until the church was bursting, forcing us back against the walls. Even though they followed Avi's orders, the rebels seemed reluctant. Even the ones who were vocal about how much they'd despised Father.

On the altar, Avi proudly showed off Father's corpse to the few rebels who appeared pleased with his actions. It was horrifying — a public display of how normalized violence had become in this world. Others around us averted their eyes, focused on their guns or their shoes, or the people in the pews. They could see, as I did, that despite our collective hatred for my father, what Avi was doing was deeply disturbing.

I took the opportunity to pull Sid, Nadia, Zeke, and Gabriel aside.

"He's going to try and claim power," I whispered. "People are going to lose themselves in grief, look to a new leader, and defer to obedience, even if it harms them. We *need* to draw a parallel between Avi and my father. Show his hypocrisy. We fight for equality, and we do not stand for lies or violence."

I turned to each of them. "Can you stand with me?" I asked. They nodded in turn, and I felt gratitude work its way through my chest. "We must appeal to the rebels and Hunters alike. To their humanity. Nobody wants to revisit the past. We need a new way forward, one that doesn't bring us all to a bloody end. We have good people here around us," I said. "There are more of us than there are of them."

Nadia's face hardened. Sid worked his jaw. Gabriel put his arm around me and squeezed. Zeke sighed heavily. If any group of people could do this, it was us. Our team had been blown apart and tested to its limits. We had lost important people. We had been chewed up and spit out, trampled over, shot at. We had healed injuries and worked through pain, endured sleepless nights, starving stomachs, and nightmare-filled dreams. All for the hope of a better world.

We had already faced men like Avi, who would stop at nothing for power and revenge. Giving up now honored nothing — none of our sacrifices, our battles, or scars. We were too bloodied and enraged to allow him to step into power. We'd been fighting for something different. Something better. Not more of the same.

In a strange sort of primal way, this evening could have been a regular mass. On Holy Days, we would often pack in here together as a full congregation, the church bursting at the seams as Father gave a sermon. Well, today there would be a sermon, all right. Just not from Father. And not from Avi.

Tonight, it would come from me.

On the broad mahogany stage, Avi chortled, slapping the back of some rebel who stood with him. Behind them, the Hunters, wives, and children wailed, their cries mingling together with the rest of the congregation. The sound was so loud, it permeated the entire space in a constant hum, settling deep in my ears and seeping into my skin. These were grieving cries. Cries of fear.

Commune members spilled into the pews, terrified and confused. Guards stood in the aisle, glancing over their shoulders, uncertain. Even if they were uncomfortable, they didn't seem to have the courage to leave their posts. Which was most fascinating of all.

The Coutts had been painted as the people who blindly followed orders. But since I'd explored the Outside, I'd come to find it wasn't just the Coutts. It was *humans*. Perhaps it was in our nature to follow the crowd. Even when we knew it was wrong. Even when it didn't feel right.

All it took was one person to change the direction.

A cold wind swept through from the back of the church. Someone pulled the wooden doors shut and sealed us in with a muted boom. I looked up at the altar. Avi held a microphone.

"Good evening!" bellowed Avi, his deep voice reverberating across the large crowd. "To those of us who are left."

The room stilled.

A smile crossed Avi's weathered face, making him look manic. "This," he said, pointing to my father's body, "is Peter Coutts. Your Almighty Prophet. I killed him."

Cries and gasps came, but Avi shouted over them.

"You might wonder why I'm here. Let me introduce myself to those of you who do not know me. My name is Avi. And I myself have been running a community since what you call the Great Plague came to our shores. We have been successful because we all contribute in our own ways. We are kind to one another. We treat each other with respect. And much of this works because we have never harmed each other the way the Coutts have harmed us."

I froze at his hypocritical words. These words came easily to him. Like Father, Avi really thought he was doing something right.

"I'd like to take a minute to thank our rebel forces. The Hunters who helped us infiltrate. Our own Maura Coutts for getting us through the door. But now that all the theatrics are over, we must rebuild from the inside." He paused, tapping the microphone against his chin. "I am a big believer that to have a healthy, functioning society, we must eliminate the rot. Those of you who have followed Peter for your entire lives are a danger to us all, whether you understand this or not.

"Right here, right now, I'd like you all to come up the aisle and pledge allegiance to me. Put your loyalty to Peter Coutts aside. Recognize that what he did to you was a tragedy and admit you're ready to pay for the terrible choices he made."

Gabriel stilled beside me. I reached over and gripped his hand, tuning Avi out. He squeezed back and met my eyes. I looked across our small group, at Sid, Nadia, and Zeke. We nodded to each other.

Now was as good a time as any.

Together, we edged our way through the crowd to the center aisle. My body trembled. Armed men surrounded the church, and although I no longer believed in leaving things completely in God's hands, I felt protected. I under-stood the people in this room better than most — certainly better than Avi and my father.

We wouldn't stand for this.

Not again.

Father's body was barely cold, and Avi was already

guiding us down the same dark path. Once he had obedience, what then? Men like Father, like Avi, they would never be satiated by power.

I reached the altar. Here, I could smell the blood, like I was swimming in it. I gagged. Swallowed vomit. Narrowed my eyes at the man commanding the stage.

Avi looked down at me warningly, then flashed a wide grin. "Maura, Gabriel, Sid, Zeke, and Nadia," he said. "Some of my most loyal soldiers in this war for justice."

I faked a smile, the last I would ever give him, and reached my hand out for the microphone.

He paused. But he was predictable, just like Father. A room full of his loyal rebels watched him. A room full of people he wanted to control. He would not deny me the chance to speak. I had been an essential piece of this puzzle. Ignoring me now would hurt him.

He handed me the microphone, and I gripped it, warm in my hands. I inhaled, trying to hold the contents of my stomach as I turned to face the crowd.

I paused, listening to soft cries, muttered pleas, and prayers. Abigail sniffled beside me, but to her credit, did not cry out for help. The children whimpered. Someone recited the Hail Mary.

"I am not up here to pledge allegiance," I said, my voice booming against the walls. "I am not pledging allegiance to anyone. And neither should any of you."

I felt Avi's presence stiffen beside me, but ignored him.

"Now wait just a minute—" he tried to interject. But his voice was quiet. Without the microphone, you could barely hear it.

"Over the past few months, I have been on a long journey," I said. "One I never dreamed of making. Alone, I learned of the horrors my father had committed. And it took me a long time, but I felt it was important to make everyone in the commune aware of it. Because we have been lied to. We have been sheltered. We've been taught to fear something that maybe didn't need to be so scary. We were taught to believe in something that maybe wasn't so righteous.

"But the beauty of God is that he forgives. Unlike the Prophet, who punished everything that went against what he said was his word. God celebrates our differences. God loves us all; he created us in his image. He gave us different personalities, the ability to believe different things, and the ability to make our own choices.

"Believing in God doesn't make you a good person. Not believing doesn't make you bad. What I've learned is that the world is nuanced. And if we believe in God, that he is almighty, then he created the world that way on purpose. He doesn't expect one man to hand down commands and have his people blindly follow it. If that were the case, we wouldn't need to have these borders. Father wouldn't have needed to lock people outside. Men would not resort to violence for respect or power. I believe no man should be the leader of everyone. Look at where it got us."

I watched people in the crowd turn inward toward each other, whispering. I watched a woman's eyes light up at the thought of something new. Others nodded their heads. Some I watched bless themselves, close their eyes, and pray. They might not believe yet. But they would, I hoped, someday.

"Now, for the rest of you," I said, directly addressing the rebels. "Those from the Centre. Those who have put their trust into Avi. You should know he is a *liar*."

I turned to face Avi directly now. His face was screwed up in a scowl, eyes narrowed, arms crossed over his chest. A blotchy red hue appeared on his skin, beneath his beard and into his unruly hair.

"Avi worked for the Coutts. He was a spy. He fed information from the U.S. government directly back to my father and his men. You have every right to be angry with my father. I know what he stole from you. I know what he did. But you should know the truth about the man standing in front of you, too."

Muttering came from the crowd. But I did not take my eyes off the man standing in front of me. His nostrils flared, fingers digging deep into his fleshy biceps.

"So, no, Avi. You are not fit to lead us. You have no right to ask for allegiance. You lied to us. You used violence and fear to get us all here in this room just to listen to you. With that kind of leadership, we will head down the same path as my father's. You don't get to call the shots. You can help. You can participate. You can contribute your great knowledge to create something even better than before. But I refuse to watch this place fall under the shadow of another power-hungry man."

I turned back to the crowd. "Avi promised to kill anyone who still swore allegiance to Father. He wants violence in this commune. He broke promises with the rebels and made us split in two. We had wanted to come in without bombs, hoping not to shoot a single bullet. Silas made him swear it. But he betrayed us."

Tears came, and I let them.

"Please," I said. "I beg of you. Come together with me. Demand a better future. There are more of us than there are of people like him. We deserve more. All of us. Together."

Silence hung in the church, making my stomach heavy with anxiety. Gabriel stood beside me, put his arm around my shoulders, and squeezed. If nothing else, I had spoken for us.

And then, the room erupted. At first, I thought it was applause.

No.

Shuffling feet, moving bodies, shouts of rage. A sea of people rose from the pews, leaned forward, their faces tight with anger. Hands gripped seats. Rebels straightened, bewildered and furious. Men grimaced with strained necks, shooting hateful gazes toward me.

I hadn't done enough. I hadn't said enough. My words did not resonate. I swallowed against my dry throat, waiting for them all to condemn me.

A woman in the front row pointed her finger at me.

"You!" she bellowed. "You do not order allegiance from us!"

People bled out from the pews, rushing down the aisle, the sides of the church, cries shifting to angry growls. Narrowed eyes, flared nostrils, and flushed faces darted forward.

They were coming for me.

Then I realized.

They were coming for Avi.

35

MAURA

PAINED STARES, bared teeth, and curled lips rushed the altar in a hungry mob, their wild rage unleashed. They scrambled around pews, down the aisle, boots slipping in blood as they rain through the corpses littering the ground. Not just commune members. Rebels, too. Emotion rose like a wave, making the large room feel claustrophobic and full of heat.

Instinctively, I moved to the side, forcing my way through the crowd and toward the stairwell to my father's office. I thanked God these people did not have eyes for me as I paused on the split landing and clutched the banister, struggling to catch my breath.

I turned to face the church.

Avi, who had neither the agility nor the foresight to anticipate what was happening, had moved to the back of the altar, pressing himself against the wall behind the tied up Hunters, who thrashed against their restraints.

"Now wait a minute!" I heard Avi yell over the baying crowd. But they were relentless.

Avi shrank back, eyes darting from side to side as he

looked for an escape route. The crowd persisted, pressing forward, hands over heads, reaching, yanking, and grabbing.

"Liar!"

"How dare you—"

"Coward!"

"You *killed* him—"

"Fuck you!"

"—rebuke you in the name of Christ!"

The mass swallowed him, and I lost sight of his dark hair as they pushed forward still, wailing and screaming, clawing their way through each other.

Sid, Nadia, and Zeke climbed through the empty pews toward me, eyes wide and worried.

Where was Gabriel?

I scanned heads, finding him at the opposite end of the church, untying the women. Beside him, Abigail tried moving in her chair, toppling over and disappearing from view. Gabriel straightened and shouted something to the women. Then, with a small, red-faced toddler wailing on his hip, he led them all to the church's front door.

"Maura." Sid stood, breathless, at the bottom of the stairs. "We can't let them…" He looked over his shoulder.

He was right. This chaos was a symptom of our suppressed anger and fear. For most, it probably felt good to fight. To take it out on someone. People might consider it justice, and maybe, in a way, it was.

But it wasn't the solution.

Movement came from the corner of my eye, and I peered down at the opening to the stairwell. Avi crawled toward us on his hands and knees, his face bright red with open wounds, patches of hair and beard missing from his head.

He looked up at us with bleary eyes.

"Help me," he whispered.

The crowd shifted at his words, finding him. Avi looked over his shoulder fearfully, scrambled to his knees, and jogged forward, a limp in his right leg. "Please!" he shouted.

He pushed past Sid, Nadia, and Zeke, tripping on the stairs as he climbed toward me. I could smell his fear. His sweat. The blood of from open wounds. Such a thirst for power, but a coward when it turned against him.

The crowd raged forward, at the foot of the stairs now, where Sid, Nadia, and Zeke held them back from climbing further.

"Get out of our church!"

"Fool!"

"You filthy piece of—"

"—let me at him—"

"God condemns you!"

He stood at his full height before me, chest heaving with heavy breaths, his round eyes begging me to *do something*.

But I had. I had told them the truth. And these people — rebels and commune members alike — were showing him how they felt about it. This was their choice.

There would always be men like Avi. Men like Father, those men down in Coal Creek. It was an inevitable way of life. What mattered was making sure they didn't hold the power. Not bowing down to the bully. Because nothing good would come of it. Men who held no empathy or care for their fellow humans would cling to power forever. By any means necessary.

We had the power to stop it.

I faced the crowd. Held up my hand.

The shouting quieted, but anger still weighted the air. I could feel it in my bones. I felt my nostrils flare as I brought my gaze back to Avi and studied him. He looked so small, so weathered and worn. Just like my father. Like every man who had ever held power in this commune and beyond.

Just a man.

"This is not the way forward," I said. "I hear your anger. I hear your frustration. I understand it." I turned back to Avi. "Do you?"

His face crumbled, his mouth opening and closing like a fish out of water.

"Your thirst for power mimics the man you condemn," I said. "You and your violence are not welcome here." His face paled. Sweat trickled down the side of his face. I raised my brows. "Did you hear me?"

"I—"

"I said, you are NOT WELCOME HERE." The words bled from my chest. All my rage, loss, and grief spilled out, and I was pleased to see him take a step back. "Go back to the Centre with whoever still chooses to follow you. You may be able to convince them, but you will not spread this hatred here." My chest felt light for the first time in years. I could see the world so clearly. Somewhere beyond this there was hope.

Avi cowered, bumping up against the stairs' banister. And then, like a spooked house cat, he darted off, scurrying through the crowd. Hands pushed him as he went, urging him toward the door until he reached it.

The door opened, and he was gone.

I watched in silence, finding Sid, who smiled up at me, giving his nod of approval. The crowd dispersed, holding hands, rubbing shoulders, releasing Hunters from their restraints. Some found linens to place over the bodies. Others remained on the kneeling benches to pray. Anger settled into exhaustion and reflection.

For nineteen years, I believed God walked with the

faithful, helping them overcome fear so long as their obedience never wavered. A beautiful thought, but also a lie. Obedience was nothing more than a tool those in power used to keep us in check. Obedience relied on fear. Fear I no longer had.

Healing would not happen overnight. It would take generations. We would pass down our knowledge and experience to those who came after us. We would warn them of what happens when the wrong people get into power and how hard we had to fight to overcome it.

And hope to God they would not be as ignorant as us.

EPILOGUE

THE LATE SPRING sun washed the Peak's side with warmth, coupled with a gentle breeze. The air smelled of earth and fresh flowers. Nature had finally recovered from winter's frost, blooming, growing, and thriving, just as we had in these last few months.

So much had changed since my father's death.

We no longer considered ourselves a commune. People were free to come and go as they pleased. People who had never left our borders now crossed rivers, hunted prey in unexplored forests, and traveled together with Outsiders who showed them safe routes. The bustling Saturday markets still caught me off guard, seeing Coutts and Outsiders together, trading, talking, and laughing. The world was healing itself, people and environment alike.

The late spring harvest had brought an abundance of lettuce, carrots, and radishes, and I carried them in a heavy basket up the paved road that led into a cluster of houses.

Our small cul-de-sac bustled with life.

Leo and Holli sat outside on their porch in a pair of rocking chairs. Her front yard blossomed with fresh flowers and herbs, waiting to be collected and transformed into something new. After the fight was over, they had redistributed resources across the commune. We had lost nearly all of our crops in the war, but with more hands from the Centre and Holli's excellent survival knowledge, we had made it through to spring. They'd become something of the impromptu leaders of our community.

I waved at them from the street, pausing at the end of their driveway.

"Take some flowers for Morgan," Holli called. "She's been asking for those peonies."

"Thanks!" I answered. I clipped a handful of pink and yellow flowers and tucked them into my full basket.

At the end of the road, children yelled, their pink faces full of laughter as they chased each other around Gabriel. He covered his eyes playfully, counting backward from ten. He lived together with Sid, Zeke, and Nadia in the last large house on our street. They'd taken in some of Zeke and Gabriel's young siblings.

Gabriel had taken up a job in education, where he taught school-aged children how to properly care for farm animals. Nadia joined the new Medical Center, where she was training to become a nurse. Zeke and Sid were part of a commune-wide cleanup crew that worked diligently at bringing our land back to its former state.

I paused at the end of our driveway, peering up at the two-story rustic home I'd grown up in. It had only felt right to come back here after everything was over. I couldn't go back to the Peak. It held too many painful memories of Andrew, Abigail, and Joanna for me to even consider it.

Abigail and the wives still loyal to my father's cause had retreated to the Island of Repentance. My father's loyal Hunters had joined them in the surrounding areas and traded their fish and lumber for our meat, produce, and labor. They still adhered to Father's ways, but kept to themselves. They knew any move to try and gain any semblance of power on this land would be quickly extinguished.

It felt like a fitting place for Abigail and those like her. They wanted so badly to be devout and righteous, and so they would be among their own. Those beliefs were isolating and restrictive. They belonged with Abigail and others like her on the Island of Repentance.

I carried the basket up to the porch, entering the house through our screen door. The fresh breeze swept through the interior, making the home smell clean and fresh. Mother was everywhere in these walls — in the hand-printed wallpaper she'd hung in the hallways, her stitching in the dated couch that pulled apart from use, in her knitted quilts that we kept in every bedroom.

I walked the long hall toward the kitchen, glancing into the living room. The photograph of Father had long been removed, replaced by photographs we'd found and framed, including the wrinkled Polaroid of Eli and me back at the Centre. Back then I could've never dreamed of the life we lived together now.

A loud shriek came from the kitchen, and I heard my sister's throaty laugh.

Morgan often worried about a repeat attack from Avi and his loyalists. But she hadn't seen how fearful Avi had looked in that church. How vicious that mob was. How ready they'd been to tear him limb from limb. Avi and his men returned to the Centre after we'd chased them off. Their small team produced and scavenged items we'd trade them for every few weeks, like scrap metal and tallow. Plus, with their diminished numbers and resources, they were reliant on our trade agreement, which included Avi staying *far* away from the mountains.

I entered the large kitchen. My sister stood at the stove, making faces at Silas Jr., who sat in his bouncer on top of the dining room table. He had Silas's bright blue eyes, but Morgan's dark, curly hair.

"Hi," she said, stirring a steaming pot. "Put it here." She pointed to the kitchen island. I did as I was told.

"Here." I gathered the flowers into a bundle. "From Holli."

"Oooh!" she squealed.

I deposited myself in one of the dining chairs beside my nephew, massaging my sore arms. Silas gurgled at me, and I kissed the side of his head.

"How's he been this morning?"

"Oh, it's been a party," she said, arranging the peonies in a spare vase from the cupboard. "We've been sleeping, pooping, eating, and burping. You really missed out."

"Whoa, whoa, whoa. Only one of us has been doing that," came a deep voice from the hall.

Eli ducked beneath the archway and entered the kitchen. He had developed a limp on his left side from nerve damage. Mick had said he'd been lucky to keep his leg. His nose still had a kink in it, and his shoulder hadn't quite healed right, but he was here, and he was alive.

Every morning I got to wake up next to him and feel his warm skin beneath my fingers. Sometimes, I just watched him. The rhythm of his breathing. His scars and freckles. The rogue whiskers on his chin. Once, a reality together had felt impossible. Now, I couldn't imagine anything different.

He came around the table, wrapped his arms around me, and kissed my neck. I inhaled him, relishing his distinct, familiar smell as I ruffled my fingers through his dark hair.

"Market was good?" he asked, sitting beside me.

"Busy," I said.

"That's good!" Morgan exclaimed, and I nodded. It meant things were getting better. We were beginning to rebuild our lives.

It hadn't been easy, but slowly, things had begun to take shape. Outsiders and Coutts families had taken up space in empty houses; our living arrangements no longer determined by our ranking in the commune. People were eager to help clean up the commune, to take up jobs that meant something, and try new skills. Commune and Centre members alike partnered up to bring back our agriculture, education, and medical systems.

It was far from perfect. But it was ours.

I prayed every night. We said grace over dinner and went to church on Sundays. Mass was led by different members of the congregation, always alternating people from the commune and the Centre. Nobody was forced to attend.

Kids went back to school, where boys and girls had equal learning opportunities and chances to explore the world. Farmers went back to planting their crops and rebuilding greenhouses. Scavengers traveled far and wide to explore more of the world and discover resources we hadn't yet uncovered.

We were still figuring out how to blend our worlds together. We had a long way to go. But we would get there in time.

My relationship with God continued to be complicated. I caught myself often wondering if I was deserving enough of the things I had built. Of being here, in this house, safe with the people I loved. Nightmares came frequently. At times, I became angry over what had transpired, and sometimes felt rage bloom in my chest, overwhelming me until I couldn't breathe. I often thought of the people who should still be here. But these were things I could not change. So I prayed for their souls instead.

For the first time in my life, I had people around me who truly understood me and accepted me for who I was. I no longer had to hide parts of myself. I didn't have to pretend to be someone I wasn't. I could do what I liked, be with who I wanted, and choose my own path forward. Every single day.

It was freeing.

It was beautiful.

It was a happy life.

THE END

ACKNOWLEDGMENTS

In 2016, my husband and I started watching a documentary show called **Escaping Polygamy**. It followed three sisters who had escaped a polygamous cult called the Kingston Group and helped others escape from similar situations. Their stories and strength were so moving, it sparked an inkling of an idea. The rest, as they say, is history.

Over the years of telling Maura's story, I did a lot of research. I watched cult documentaries, listened to podcasts, read books, and even interviewed a survivor. I took a lot of time to try to understand what draws people into cults and even more time to understand how difficult it is for someone to get out.

I always aimed to keep this series and story as true to life as I could. It was important to me that I not just write a great story, but that I show how complicated situations like this can be. There are a lot of conflicting feelings, beliefs, and habits that follow people long after they've left an oppressive group or situation. It takes a lot of work to deconstruct from these kinds of environments, and it's rarely ever pretty. But all the survivors I read about or listened to had one thing in common: recognizing the strength and bravery it took for them to leave a damaging environment in search of a better life.

Writing this story has been nearly a decade in the making. I wrote dozens of iterations of my first book, and it went through even more rounds of feedback until I found my groove. Initially, this series was intended to be three books, then five books, until I settled on four. Characters were cut and added, scenes were dropped, revised, and pasted together. But ultimately, I am incredibly proud of Maura's story. If you've read the full series, thank you for sticking with me.

There are people who have been with me since the very beginning and people who came in along the way. I am so unbelievably grateful to you all.

Michelle Scissom, for encouraging me so hard in the early days when I was doubting myself, hating everything I wrote, and wondering if I could ever DO IT. Thank you for pushing me out of my comfort zone and into my first publishing endeavor. Your support and encouragement mean more than words can say.

Jen Hatfield, for painstakingly reading every single iteration of this book through the good, the bad, and the ugly. Thank you for loving my characters, my story, and me through this all.

Debbie Wingate, for telling me all the things I needed to hear and reading each draft with a keen, editorial eye. Thank you for all of your excellent suggestions, your kind words, and warm friendship during this process.

Monica Grier, for legitimately keeping me sane through all of my self-doubt and publishing struggles, for reminding me that I can do this, and talking me down from the ledge just about every other week. Thank you for your friendship, humor, and wit.

Liesl West and Laura Graham, for being the most excellent critique partners in the entire world. Your feedback, support, and encouragement have made these past three books the best they could be. I am so unbelievably lucky to benefit from your wisdom.

My Advanced Reader Team, for being the most fabulous group of cheerleaders. Thank you for being such hungry readers and loving my characters and story as much as I do. I am endlessly grateful for your support throughout this series.

My incredible family — Matt, Liam, and Devin. Thank you for loving me and giving me the support and encouragement to chase this dream of mine. It is a wonderful thing to be so loved. Thank you for showing me what it means.

And of course, to you, dear reader, for reading this series! I hope you love this world and these characters as much as I loved creating them and bringing it to life. Thank you for your support.

ALSO BY CAITLIN MAZUR

<u>The Forgive Me Father Series</u>

Book 1: Forgive Our Ignorance

Book 2: Forgive Our Sins

Book 3: Forgive Our Survival

Book 4: Forgive Our Fight

THANK YOU!

Thank you so much for reading **Forgive Our Fight.** If you enjoyed this book, please consider leaving it a review on your platform of choice. Reviews significantly help indie authors like me increase visibility and boost credibility for future readers.

ABOUT THE AUTHOR

Caitlin Mazur writes thrillers, horror, and dystopian fiction about underdogs who are underestimated, over-looked, or pushed aside, and what happens when they rise and discover their true strength.

A lifelong storyteller, Caitlin began writing on her parents' old computer and never stopped. Her works include a variety of shorts published in multiple anthologies, a horror novella, and a four-part dystopian thriller series. For Caitlin, speculative fiction isn't just about escaping into other worlds. It's about holding a mirror up to ourselves, asking hard questions, and finding hope and power in unexpected places.

When she's not writing, Caitlin lives her best life in Central Maine. She's a freelance writer, a wife, a mom to two amazing kids, and the caretaker of a small menagerie including dogs, cats, a bearded dragon, and chickens. You can join her in sharing the journey of storytelling, strong women, and thrilling adventures on Instagram (@caitwritesstuff) and TikTok (@caitlinwritesstuff).

instagram.com/caitwritesstuff
facebook.com/caitlinwritesstuff
tiktok.com/@caitlinwritesstuff